Lord Appleby's Gorgeous Imposter

Scarlett Affairs
Book 3

Cerise DeLand

ARE YOU SIGNED UP FOR DRAGONBLADE'S BLOG?

You'll get the latest news and information on exclusive giveaways, exclusive excerpts, coming releases, sales, free books, cover reveals and more.

Check out our complete list of authors, too!

No spam, no junk. That's a promise!

Sign Up Here

www.dragonbladepublishing.com

Dearest Reader;

Thank you for your support of a small press. At Dragonblade Publishing, we strive to bring you the highest quality Historical Romance from some of the best authors in the business. Without your support, there is no 'us', so we sincerely hope you adore these stories and find some new favorite authors along the way.

Happy Reading!

CEO, Dragonblade Publishing

Additional Dragonblade books by Author Cerise Deland

Scarlett Affairs Series
Lord Ashley's Beautiful Alibi (Book 1)
Lord Ramsey's Red-Headed Ruin (Book 2)
Lord Appleby's Gorgeous Imposter (Book 3)

Matrimony! Series
If I Loved You (Book 1)
Because of You (Book 2)
You Made Me Love You (Book 3)

Naughty Ladies Series
Lady, Be Wanton (Book 1)
Lady, Behave (Book 2)
Lady, No More (Book 3)
Lady, You're Mine (Book 4, Novella)

The Lyon's Den Series
The Lyon's Share
The Lyon's Perfect Mate

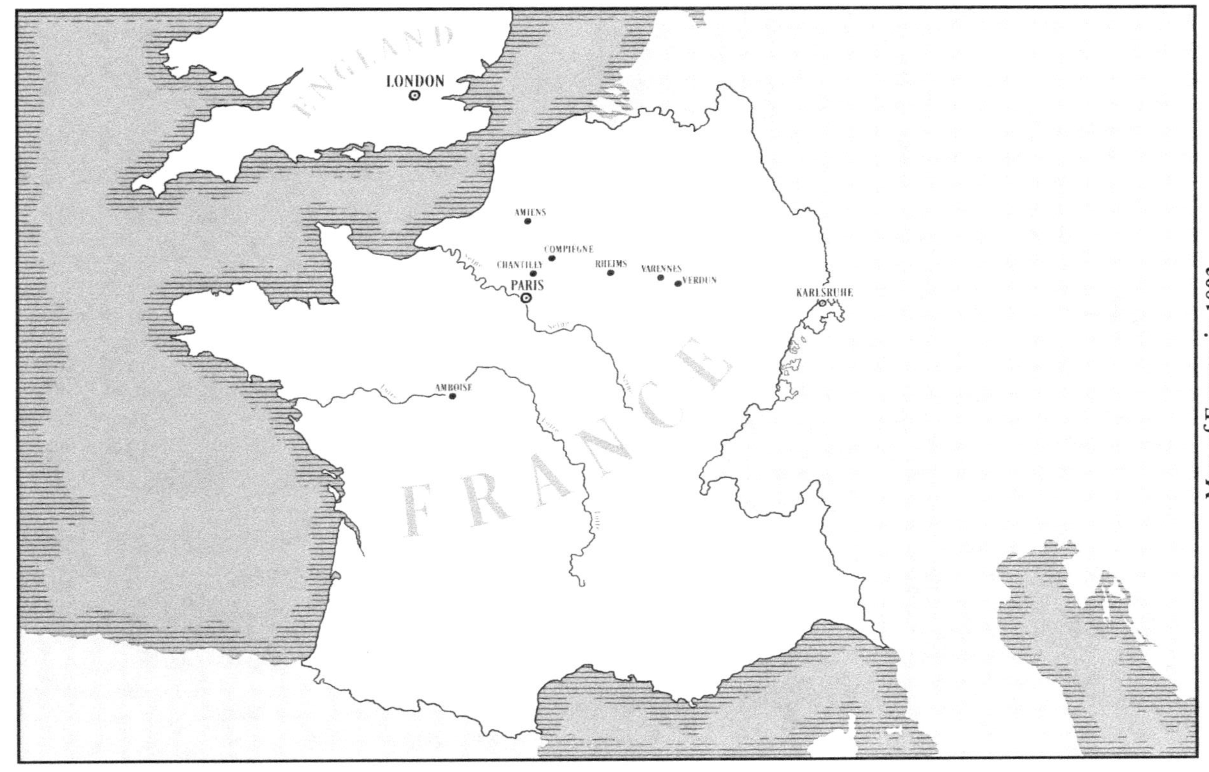

Map of Europe in 1802
Designer, Xenia Sukhareva

Prologue

September 1, 1792
rue du Four
Saint-Germain-des-Prés, Paris

"MADELEINE? MADELEINE!"

Papa was yelling up the stairs, crazed, in a rush.

Vivi's mama put a hand to her forehead. "Oh, he must not scream," she moaned to the three girls. "The servants will hear and run for those brutes in the tribunal!"

But Papa kept shouting for Mama.

Vivi glanced at her older sister, Diane, who shook her head at her. They both knew Vivi's mama was the only person who could ever calm their father.

"Madeleine! *Ma chou chou!*" Papa called her to him. Then, of a sudden, he stood—his arms wide and his hands to the frame—and paused in the doorway.

Mama threw down the gown she was folding and ran toward him. A hand to his cheek, she whispered. "*Monsieur*, be quiet, please. You will awaken all in the house."

Vivi winced. Her mother was right. They had to leave soon and without notice.

"Keep packing," Diane urged Vivi on a whisper. Her next

older half-sister, who was the practical one among the three girls, had already packed her treasured gowns. Di was careful about so much, especially demanding green gowns to enhance her beautiful copper hair and hazel eyes. "We must have all we can carry, and you cannot allow anything to deter you."

"Ba. All this is *froufrou*," said their oldest sister Charmaine with a flourish of her hands at her clothes piling up in her own large valise. "The only things we need are gold and our jewels."

Vivi cringed at Charmaine's impertinence.

Diane scoffed. "Char, this is your role! *Tragedienne!*"

Charmaine gave herself airs as a lady to be saved by a handsome prince. "Better than you, *ma poule!*" she shot back, and spun to their father. "Where *are* the diamonds? Where did you pack them? We must know!"

Their father glared at his oldest child with distaste at her insolence. His stare was not a new expression to bestow on the fifteen-year-old. "You need to know only how to pack, *cherie*. Do it."

Diane raised a brow at Charmaine. "And stop whining."

Charmaine snapped shut the top of her tiny gold *étui* in which she always carried her perfume. "Whine? I am the practical one here. Even Madeleine will not admit—" Charmaine was never respectful to Vivi's mama, always addressing her by her given name.

"Charmaine," seethed their father, "you try me too often."

Diane clamped a hand on Charmaine's wrist. "Fill your valise."

"You brought these fiends on us, Di, with your visits up the street to the neighborhood committee." Charmaine had followed Diane to the Section meetings at the crossroads of rue du Four. The members of the Bonnet-Rouge neighborhood section yesterday threatened many in the local area with arrest. Diane had run home and told her father.

The vicomte was a liberal and had supported much of the government reforms…until the past year. He had brought them all to Paris two days ago from the country to get his money and the family heirlooms, but after Diane had told him about the Section's threat, he had decided immediately to send the family out of Paris.

Charmaine took out her fears on criticizing Diane. "You fancy yourself a *sans-culotte*, silly girl."

"And you?" Diane replied. "You were out in the *ruelle* near the kitchen trying to steal the scullery maid's beau!"

"Stop this, girls!" Vivi's mother scolded them.

"No!" Charmaine threw her fanciest fan into her valise and whirled on Diane again. "You're a princess of the blood. Such a child. You haven't even had your monthly flux yet!"

"I am old enough to listen and learn the right from wrong of politics," Diane shot back. "Whereas you wouldn't know a Jacobin from a Royalist."

"Thank God, I say."

"Girls! Girls!" Their father cut his arms through the air. "Stop! We must go now."

"*Papa*," Charmaine whined. "I have not finished packing."

"Unless you wish to wear that gown to the guillotine, girl, you will shove it in your case and run downstairs now!"

Charmaine stamped one foot on the floor. "You are horrid, Papa."

"I will be a worse tyrant than Robespierre unless you do as you are told!"

Charmaine fumed.

Papa scoffed, then turned on his heel, taking Vivi's mother, his mistress, by the elbow toward the hall. "Now listen to me, Madeleine. Do as I say…"

"He's not coming with us," Charmaine hissed as she sent a glower of hatred toward the door. "I heard him last night. He's scampering off to Brussels."

Diane cursed beneath her breath, a usual sign of her frustration with Charmaine's intolerance for everyone and everything. "He wants us to split up so it is difficult for the committee mobs to track us. Stop being an imbecile, and finish packing!"

"An imbecile?" Charmaine snorted. "Just wait. You will see how right I am!"

"*Mes amis!*" Another person ran up the stairs. The three girls turned to see their young male house guest appear on the threshold.

The tall, lean, dashing Tate Cantrell was everything a girl could want in a suitor. He had the clean, sculpted looks of an artist's finest work. With a square jaw, arched cheekbones, and wide, flaring eyebrows, he was a handsome creature. Even his coloring was superb, all wavy, rich caramel hair and blue-green eyes that shone like Chinese jade in sunlight and mellowed to turquoise in the shadows of evening.

Vivi adored him. Diane did, too. Charmaine had claimed him as her own the first night he appeared at their chateau. Even the maids giggled and preened in his presence. To his credit and his discretion, because he was so very upstanding, he did not flirt with any of the three sisters nor any of the household staff.

"Are you ready?" asked the breathless Tate, leaning one hand to the doorframe. He had arrived at their country home in Neufchateau to visit them last autumn. He had escaped home and his terrible father in England, only to come to France and be caught in a war and a revolution that named him an enemy and blocked him from returning home. Instead, he remained with the family of the Vicomte de Neufchateau in the eastern department and had become, over the months, their friend. To Charmaine, the young Viscount Carrington, with his large blue-green eyes and a wealth of golden-red hair, was the one she intended to seduce and marry.

"Let him carry me away to freedom on his estate," Charmaine often boasted to Diane and Vivi. "He will love me. And soon."

Vivi thought that could be true. Charmaine was lithe, elegant, very beautiful, with hair the color of glistening moonlight and eyes of sapphire blue. Plus, she was older than Vivi by two years and possessed that asset most men talked about. Breasts.

"A second more, Tate!" Diane bounced away to open a bureau drawer and pull out her diary. Then she dropped it into her damask reticule and buttoned the finely crocheted flap. "Now I'm ready!"

He marched to the bed and grabbed Charmaine's and Vivi's bags, then reached for Diane's. "I'll carry those down."

"You will not!" Diane batted his hand away from hers.

Vivi called to her little dog, Beau, and scooped him up in her arms. With a hand to the dog's wicker bed, she took the circular stairs beside Tate. "I'm glad you've come, Tate. You'll calm Mama. She's nervous about leaving Papa to go by himself."

At the bottom of the stairs, Tate and she glanced at each other and the sight of her mother and father embracing in the small salon.

Tate took Vivi's arm and pulled her around to him. "I'll try to calm her. I will go as far with all of you as the *Barrière d'Enfer*. Another coach arrives for all to change into. None of you will be noticed."

"But what do you do?"

"Tomorrow I leave Paris by a different route."

Vivi shook her head. "No! Come with us!"

He flinched. "I cannot. Someone in the Bonnet-Rouge has learned I am related."

"The scullery maid?" she ventured.

"Perhaps. I have it from a friend that the local police want me. I refuse to be caught." He smiled.

Terrified for him, Vivi grabbed his arm. She had often chided him that he was more than their great friend and English nobleman—he was a British spy. Tonight it came back to haunt her as a sad jest—and a deadly idea. "How will you go?"

"Best you do not know, *ma petite*."

She clutched him nearer. "I fear for you!"

"Get in the carriage," he whispered, and dropped a kiss to her hair. "I'll see you all safe to the road south to the Loire."

Then he faced the salon where her mother and father held each other and wept. "I'll get your mother," he said with sorrow.

Vivi swallowed her fears for all of them and followed her sisters to their waiting fiacre. Papa's majordom had hired a carriage to take them away from the city. Their own traveling coach, sumptuous and marked with the family *écusson*, was gone. After King Louis was guillotined in January, Papa had ordered it broken up, the fittings sold to metal workers and the wood burned. He did not want them going about so easily identified.

Charmaine took her time getting inside, hemming and hawing about the narrowness of the cab.

Diane huffed. "Move along, sister."

Her mother climbed inside.

Vivi paused.

Across the street on the corner stood a public carriage, a fiacre of shabby paint and worn fittings. The nag looked ill and tired. At this hour of the night, it stood alone in the alley, save for their own carriage and two stray cats.

But in the window was the face of a man Vivi had seen before. Yes, she had seen him in the *ruelle* with the maid—and once with Charmaine. When she spied him, he sank backward into the shadows of the cab.

But Vivi had seen enough. Remembered more. He was a very young, handsome fellow with glistening black hair and bright eyes. Blue or hazel, she could not tell. He had facial contours so sharp one would say they were cut by glass. His only warm characteristic was his sun-kissed Provençale complexion. He was the same man she and Tate had seen speaking with the family's scullery maid. The one they had overheard early this morning at the kitchen door talking to the maid about when they might meet for a rendezvous. Odd, too, it was, because the maid was far from pretty and the fellow was a delicious-looking devil.

Vivi's little dog, Beau, yipped at the carriage. He always picked up her distress. She ran a hand over his furry little head.

"Come now, Vivi." Tate came up to her and followed her line

of vision. "Is that—?"

"*Oui*, the one with our maid."

Tate cursed beneath his breath. A hand to her elbow, he said, "Ignore him. Get in. Now. We must leave."

With a challenging lift of her chin, she gave their observer one last hard look—and got in.

Tate took a moment to speak to their driver. She heard his deep bass giving instructions to stop at the customs *barrière* south of the Faubourg Saint-Germain. "I will disembark there. You will drive on through the night to Chartres but only on the back roads, just as you were instructed before. *D'accord?*"

Vivi heard the driver agree, and in a moment, Tate climbed in and sat down beside her. Across from them, Diane swallowed tears. Vivi's mother appeared like a statue of marble. Charmaine sat atop her reticule filled with whatever she thought to keep from anyone.

Vivi sniffed. If Charmaine were not her half-sister—and the oldest legitimate one, at that—Vivi would tell her exactly what she thought of her ill-mannered ways. Charmaine was fifteen and should by now know better than to treat all as if she were a princess royal. Their blood might have some Bourbon in it, but it was drops. Charmaine acted as if it flowed pure and blue. And none of it, in any quantity, could save them from the wrath of Robespierre and the bloodthirsty heathens in the local Bonnet-Rouge. It was what condemned them.

Their coachman lashed the horses to a trot and headed past the ruined Saint-Germain-des-Prés Abbaye where so many had been brought to trial lately. Even in the country in Neufchateau, many had warned Papa not to come to Paris. *They don't like aristocrats in the city,* many of his friends remarked. The guillotine was employed far too often. Men and women were sent to death within minutes of appearing before twelve judges. Gossip said the accused were given little time to defend themselves. But Papa had not listened. He needed to go to Paris, he said, for those things he had hidden there.

Vivi wondered if those items were as valuable as all their lives. But she could not be so bold as to ask, and Papa would not be so willing as to tell her or anyone what those items were.

The coach picked up speed.

All grew quiet inside.

But the driver had challenges. The mobs were out in force tonight. Darkness gave them courage. Becoming ghouls of the night, they were poor folk who ran amok. They yelled about bread and salt, brandishing their fists and their knives. A few even had pistols.

Their coachman shifted down alleys and went on with dizzying speeds. He reined his horses to a stop with speed far too often, then turned away from barricades, roadblocks piled high with old furniture, crates, and barrels.

Their driver had slowed, turning once, then twice down different, narrower roads.

"He goes north again," Vivi's mother rasped. "He should not."

Tate spoke up. "He's expert, *madame.*"

"Is anyone able," asked Charmaine with disgust, "to outrun a mob?"

Tate had opened his mouth to answer when a roar of shouts rose to their ears.

The five of them stared out their windows.

"Dear God." Vivi's mother caught her throat.

A crush of peasants thronged toward them. The driver slowed. Vivi watched, horror stricken. Their man had to stop. He could not simply run them to ground. But she heard him shouting to back off, back off as he lashed his whip at them.

But a few men grabbed at the door, threw bottles at the frame. One cracked a window, then another. Glass splintered into the cab in a shower of sparkling drops.

"Oh, oh!" Mama yelled. "I...I am cut!"

Shards of glass stood straight up out of the backs of her hands.

"Cover yourselves!" Tate shouted as he wrenched off his

frock coat and hung it over one window.

Vivi tucked Beau to one side and worked off her shawl. Like Tate, she tried to hang it over the window near her.

Then the door was flung open. All inside gasped.

A man reached inside, his grubby hands big as dinner plates, grabbing and snatching. Catching Mama's gown.

She yanked it away and hit him with her leather portfolio. But he kept snatching. "The green gown. I want the green girl!"

Vivi caught Diane's eye. Her sister blinked. Tonight, she had worn her best green gown.

Tate hauled himself up and kicked the fellow in the chest. The man fell backward.

The coach started and stopped in fits. The mob kept up the pace. Yelling and screaming, they rocked the carriage—and it idled.

The door flayed wide, banging against the side of the coach, open and closed. Open and closed.

The same man Tate had kicked reached in again. This time he went straight for Diane.

"Get the door," Charmaine shouted at Tate as she shrank away from the man who wanted only their sister.

"Fool," Diane spat at her, and stood to help Tate capture the swinging door.

But two women reached in, pushed him with a great yell, and he fell backward. Splayed on the floor, arms and legs flailing, he tried to turn to get up.

Diane cursed at the women, then reached out to grab the door handle—

But they each grabbed an arm and took her!

"Noooo!" Vivi yelled.

Her mother screamed. Tate scrambled to his knees. To his feet. Braced on the frame, he stuck out his head—and leapt from the cab.

Door wide open, Beau barked and, in one huge jump for so tiny a dog, followed Tate.

Vivi gaped at the loss of all three.

Their driver lashed the horses. But it took a second, or perhaps it was an eternity, to get the animals to move once more.

The sounds of the mob retreated, yelling in whoops of delight.

The coach picked up speed. The carriage door banged closed.

"No, no," Vivi complained, clutching the hand pull above. She pushed at the door with her feet, jamming them against the wood. She had to get out, help Tate get Diane and Beau.

Her mother curled into a ball and wailed. Charmaine sat, her eyes big as wheels, staring at Vivi.

The coach careened around one corner and down a dark street. Inside the three slid on the benches and careened into each other.

"Help me, help me, help me," Vivi kept calling to them, working the handle of the door. But the other two women were crying, stunned. And try as Vivi might, the carriage door was locked. Stuck.

Tears scalded her cheeks.

Minutes or centuries later, the coach slowed. All three women braced themselves on the seat.

"Where are we?" Mama whispered.

But staring at the street marked by half-timbered old houses, Vivi knew they must be in the outskirts.

The carriage rattled back and forth to a stop. Vivi banged on the box. Sticking her head near the broken window, she shouted up to their man, "Where are we?"

"*Barrière d'Enfer, mademoiselle.*"

The post road to the south. "You wait?" she asked him, fearing this answer, fearing others might come for those who remained in the carriage.

"*Oui.* The rendezvous, mademoiselle. *Monsieur le Comte* arranged for the change of carriages. I am to wait."

Her father had told the man to stop here. Yes, but now... Would Tate come? Would he be able to rescue Diane and Beau?

Vivi checked her mother's gaze. The woman rocked back and forth, moaning. She knew only her fright.

Charmaine's expression was blank.

They could give no advice. No help. No admonishment to their coachman to drive on or return.

Was it simply best to wait, as her father had planned? Vivi did trust him. She did.

But was the driver telling the truth?

A new fright sent arrows of agony through her.

Was Tate strong enough, wily enough to escape the throngs? Did he have coins on him to hire a carriage to come here? Could he find Diane? Wrest her free? And bring Beau too?

Vivi huddled into her cloak. She would not cry. Would not!

The night grew longer, colder. The wind picked up and buffeted their carriage. Mama sat rigid as stone. Charmaine sneered and complained.

Would Tate find them here? Could he? If he was even still alive. What could one man do against a heinous mob?

Vivi clutched herself more closely. She was cold and hungry. She had to pee.

Had they brought a bourdalou?

She winced. Along with so much else, a porcelain pot to pee in had seemed unimportant, even irrelevant when one's life was in danger from a mad mob.

She reached inside her pelisse and checked the time. Most precious to her was the large watch pinned to her bodice. Her grandfather's watch was a sacred piece because he had given it to her days before he died. He pinned it on her dress himself, his palsied hands shaking. "To be noted on days you are happy."

And note the hour I am terrified, too. She shook it all away. *Think. Think!*

She leaned out the broken window, careful not to be caught or cut on the glass. "How long did the vicomte say to wait?"

"Until I can no longer, mademoiselle."

Vivi swallowed her need to scream at him to whip the horses

to a trot. To return the way they'd come and find Tate with Diane and Beau in tow.

But she heard no screaming mobs. Saw no one around the corners. Ahead of them were the two white stone buildings of the *Barrière d'Enfer*. No one was about, which meant the tax collectors had abandoned it, perhaps because they anticipated the mob's arrival. Maybe Papa knew they would run if there was trouble, and he had chosen this site for their driver to wait for the change of carriage because it was not only identifiable but safe.

"We should go," Charmaine said.

Vivi's mother slowly turned to peer at the girl. In Mama's deadly regard was her answer to Charmaine's statement.

"He's not coming, Madeleine!" Charmaine was so irreverent. "They've got Papa, I bet. Tate and Diane, too."

And Beau.

Charmaine fumed now, crossing her arms. "I do not want to go to prison!"

Vivi's mother narrowed her gaze on the girl. "Be quiet."

"I don't—"

"Shut up!"

Charmaine blanched, but soon recovered. "You are fools to think you'll survive this if we wait."

Madeleine de Massé, the woman who had been wed to one man and, when a widow, was taken by that man's older brother as his mistress, clamped one hand over her niece's and dug her fingernails into the girl's flesh.

Charmaine flinched.

But Mama did not let go. "If you wish to leave us, Charmaine, do."

Charmaine opened her mouth.

But Mama flung her hand away toward the door. "Go," she said through gritted teeth, "and be done."

Charmaine settled into the squabs. For the first time since they were very small, Vivi watched Charmaine slowly shed tears. Not many. Not for long. And as she came to the end of her little show of despair, their coachman shouted.

Alarmed, Vivi saw another hired coach approach, and it came at dizzying speed. The coachman lashed the reins and the horses scrambled to a stop. The carriage moved forward, parallel to their own.

Commotion inside the cab sounded like someone disembarking.

Suddenly, Tate appeared at their door, peering in their broken window.

With a shout of triumph, he pulled and yanked and finally opened the door and climbed in. Winded, his clothes ripped and filthy, his cheek bloody, he fell onto the bench beside Vivi and handed her the little dog. Beau whimpered and snuggled into Vivi's cloak.

She leaned over to Tate, her hand to his brow. "Diane?"

"No." He gulped. The tracks of his tears on his bruised cheeks told her of his own despair. "No. I...I could not. They had her. Gendarmes. Too many of them. And they took her to the tribunal."

"At this hour?" In the eerie moonlight, Charmaine went pale.

He only stared back at her, his eyes glazed. Then he turned his head toward the squabs and swiped at his face with his knuckles. Presently, he calmed.

Vivi took his hand. She knew how honorable he was, and believed he had done all he could to recapture her sister. If he said he could not take back Diane, then it was so.

At length, she drew away and noticed the cuts on his temple and cheeks. "I have ointment," she told him. "In my trunk. What else hurts?"

His left hand lay limp and swollen in his lap. He glanced down. "This."

Vivi gasped. He should have told her before this. *What to do? What to do?* She unwrapped the scarf around her neck. "Your hand. Is it broken?"

"I don't know. Hurts like hell," he murmured, his grimace

full of pain.

"Charmaine has laudanum in her reticule in one of her étui. Charmaine?"

The girl pulled away. "It is a small dose. I will need it for my headaches."

Vivi glared at her. Was there anything in this world more heinous Charmaine could do than to deprive a friend of succor? In disgust, Vivi said, "Very well. I have my medicines in the boot. We can stop."

"No, we cannot!" Tate shook his head. "We drive on lest they follow. We do not stop, Vivi. We never stop."

$$\text{Chapter One}$$

February 18, 1803
Théâtre de la Gaîté
Paris

TATE CANTRELL CLIMBED the steps of the Paris theater on the left bank, weaving through the jostling, exuberant crowd. Good God, how many were here tonight to see the performance of the French star of Drury Lane? The wily one who had eluded him for five months?

The theater was jammed with eager patrons. He could not fault them. He himself was smiling that after those long months he had finally found the woman for whom he'd searched—and discovered her in Paris, of all places. Why she'd disappeared was a mystery, for the woman loved every bit of attention anyone paid her. Where she'd absconded to and why she had secluded herself, he had no idea. But he'd learn, by God. He wring it out of her.

He scoffed. He was an experienced British envoy. A seasoned spy for Scarlett Hawthorne, the heiress merchant, in London. He knew dozens who deceived easily and often.

Charmaine de Massé could easily be one of them. She had led a remarkable existence full of wealth, prominence, loss, deception, and cruelty. She was the oldest daughter of a well-intentioned minor Bourbon vicomte who worked for reform but who fell nonetheless to the guillotine courtesy of Robespierre. Her major characteristics, however, were her pride, her selfishness, and her artfulness. She'd had years of practice, lying to her family and cheating them out of a share of the family treasures she hocked. Charmaine de Massé was a clever charlatan who could easily pose as someone else. She'd often pretended to be sweet, innocent, and kind. Duping far too many.

He paused, seizing his anger at Charmaine's disappearance and molding it to his purpose. His focus must be on the greater goal of finding—and keeping—her half-sister, Vivienne.

Dozens surged around him, talking of their excitement as they rushed through the foyer. Many buzzed, hoping Bonaparte and his wife would appear to honor the French émigré who had escaped Robespierre with her family. First Consul Bonaparte, who had reestablished order and sanity after the Terror, loved the theater and attended often and without prior notice. He also liked blonde actresses. Too much, too quickly, it was said, tongue in cheek.

"Pardonnez-moi, monsieur." Tate stepped to one side, the crush of theatergoers on the stairs enough to send one tripping down them.

He nodded to a few to whom he'd been introduced last night in Madame Récamier's salon. That occasion had been acclaimed in the gossip sheets this morning as the notable Earl of Appleby's third—if more louche—*entrée* to Parisian Society. His second had been at Bonaparte's court in the Tuileries three nights ago. His first, at Lord Ashley's home last week, had been his formal entrance. He was this time, after decades of secretive journeys throughout Europe, an official in Ashley's entourage of British informal envoys responsible for aiding in the peaceful ties between France and her longtime adversary.

Of course, being in charge of balancing currency values for products imported and exported between the two former belligerents was a dry task to which he publicly applied himself.

But wringing the neck of that acclaimed London actress Charmaine de Massé was his only goal. Shocked to learn this morning from his friend and spymaster, Kane, Lord Ashley, that Charmaine was in Paris, Tate readily accepted the invitation to attend. Backstage afterward, he would corner her and squeeze the truth from her lovely, deceitful lips.

He had searched for her last spring in England and found no traces. Wherever the wily lady had gone, she had influenced her youngest sister Vivienne to disappear as well. His tenants told him so. Whatever had induced Viv to leave her little cottage, her garden, and her beloved flocks of chickens and ducks, even her darling donkey Fred, had to have been momentous. To his eternal dismay, Tate had no clue what fable Charmaine could have woven to enchant Vivienne to follow. Viv brooked no nonsense from her oldest sister and had created a life without her.

"Bon soir," he greeted one of Bonaparte's generals upon the stairs up to the private boxes. Tate bowed to the lady on the officer's arm. The military man came tonight with a ravishing brunette creature who was definitely not the plain-faced little wife Tate had met last night at Madame Recamier's. Using his excellent French and anything else he'd learned in years abroad, he intended to make many friends.

"How are you this evening?" He met one and then another. "Well? Very good. Very good. As am I. Enjoy the play. I do love a fine comedy. Please, after you."

He followed the crowd up, made the landing on the second tier, and turned to begin his hunt for box four. He was late. Had planned to be. He had little appetite for the conversations required in such situations when he had a precise mission. Or he should say, he did not care to indulge in such frivolous talk when he had so much anticipation of tonight's long-awaited success.

He had searched for Charmaine Massey for too long. Tonight was his triumph. The end of his search for the woman who stole from so many for so many years.

Ah. Box four. He opened the door.

He was greeted by a chorus of welcome from Kane, the Earl of Ashley, whom he'd known since he was a lad of thirteen, and three of his friends, whom he'd met last week at Ashley's reception. Aside from Kane and Tate, none in the box were agents. Or at least as far as Tate knew, they were not. The Chilterns and Lord Manning declared that they had come to Paris to enjoy the winter's entertainments. They were not alone. Ever since Lord Cornwallis had signed the Treaty of Amiens last spring, hundreds of British had flocked to the French capital. Lord Elgin and his wife, the Cholmondeleys, and even Charles James Fox had come to drink the wine, stand for lavish new *a la mode* wardrobes—and hope to dine with the little Corsican and his oh-so-charming wife, Josephine, who ruled over the new *beau monde*.

Tate had no tolerance for politics. Not tonight. He had run to ground the woman who had disappeared last spring along with her younger sister. He would get from Charmaine where his darling Vivienne was. Then he would go find her and do what he had intended last spring. He would propose marriage.

Kane did his duties as host and introduced Tate all around as his newest colleague.

Lord Chiltern put down his monocle as they all took their chairs. "You're to improve the rate of currency exchange for goods, Appleby?"

"I am." Tate tucked his program inside his frock coat pocket. "My usual job." *Not my only one. With Scarlett, one tracks whatever mystery will lead to excellent intelligence.*

"I understand you've practice," said Chiltern with an arched brow, "with Italian funds and Ottoman."

"Just so," Tate said, his attention on the red velvet curtain.

"For the Levant Company out of Jaffa?" Chiltern persisted. "I understand they are very corrupt. Isn't that difficult?"

"But interesting," Tate demurred. It was not in his remit to discuss how well an official British company like the Levant managed its trade. Jerusalem's prices rose and fell with the local sultan's delight in his newest wife.

Meanwhile, Chiltern's little wife lifted her chin, but she fluttered her fan. Her attitude denoted that she really could not care less about the specifics of money. "I simply do not understand exchange of coin. Though I do wonder how anyone makes a profit."

"Confusing, I admit, Lady Chiltern," Tate said blithely, "even to me." Grateful for her interruption, he smiled. He wished no discussion of his expertise, and he was very happy that the orchestra offered up a round of ditties, a sign for the audience to quieten.

He wanted only to see Charmaine. The little cheat.

Just as everyone settled in for the curtain to rise, two more people entered the box. Lord Ramsey arrived with a lady on his arm. Ram, Kane, and Tate had been friends since they were children. With quick introductions by Kane, Tate learned Ram's friend was Madame St. Antoine.

The name flitted through Tate's memory. He'd read her dossier in Scarlett Hawthorne's offices. Madame St. Antoine had been school friends with Scarlett, the young lady who ran their network from the offices of her merchant company in London. Madame St. Antoine was a fiery redhead of exquisite beauty whom no man worth his salt could ever ignore or forget. But Tate's and Kane's boyhood friend Ramsey appeared stiff, formal, as if he could not bear to notice that the ravishing widow on his arm was his most glorious asset this evening.

"I am delighted to meet you, madame," Tate offered, raising her hand to his lips.

"*Merci beaucoup, Monsieur le Comte.* As am I to meet you," she said as she settled in the chair beside Tate. "Are you here for an extended stay in Paris?"

"*Oui,* madame. I am to talk with a few financiers about the exchange of currency."

"A difficult task, monsieur. Our first consul has not yet brought all the provincial currencies into line. And we have many who counterfeit with great abandon."

Tate frowned. "I hear the government hunts for them diligently."

"Indeed, sir. And quickly sentences them to death. By guillotine, no less."

Tate winced. "Harsh. But it is right the government detains them. Destroys their presses. Nothing hurts commerce so badly as poor means to buy and sell goods."

The lady arched her lovely red brows. "The primary reason the Bourbons no longer rule is the abuse of finances. Bonaparte must get it under control or he will follow the *ancien regime* to the grave."

Tate agreed with her. But he was grateful they were in a theater box full of British. Even she was by blood an Englishwoman. Adopted informally by a lady she called her aunt, Amber St. Antoine, née Gaynor, had lived since age nine in Paris. She had married a Frenchman, a vintner from the Champagne, who had died a few years ago. But it was clear by madame's rhetoric that she sympathized with republicans.

Tate suspected she did more than sympathize. That was why Scarlett had allowed him to read madame's biography in the merchant company's records room. St. Antoine worked against the hegemony Bonaparte commanded over France and much of Italy. Scarlett would not have given him such information of St. Antoine's activities unless it were vitally important he understand the lady's sympathies.

The orchestra, small as it was, raised its decibel level. Tate set his jaw, anticipation mixing with satisfaction as he settled more into his chair.

The play would start soon. Tate folded his hands together, his attention on the floor, where most of the audience was composed of men. Dandies. Out for an evening to look over the newest actress to seduce.

Tate snorted. Charmaine was no *jeune fille*, not like Madame George, the girl of sixteen who had opened in Racine's *Phèdre* the night before last at a theater across town. Charmaine refused to compete with the more famous French girl who was turning heads with her talent—and had demanded she debut after the girl. Returning to her country, according to the Paris gossip sheets, she had insisted that she would honor the occasion by performing only comedy.

Charmaine was crafty, wishing to grab the city's attentions soon after the other girl debuted. Charmaine was older, twenty-five or -six. But she looked younger. Always had. Short, small boned, with a glorious mane of platinum hair, and perfectly formed doe eyes, aquiline nose, and exquisitely arched cheeks, Charmaine looked timeless.

And always she used it to her advantage. She was polite and exuberantly charming. Well read, too. But she possessed another quality, which few living men or women could match. She was that rare commodity, descended from Henry Bourbon in some obscure way, and an émigré of the noble lineage whose father had been ruthlessly hunted, tried ingloriously, and quickly guillotined.

With a bit of Bourbon blood from the Orleans branch, Charmaine claimed to be a minor princess. Josephine Bonaparte, said the gossips, had heard of Charmaine's fame in London and the lady's plight. With compassion for the actress, Josephine had personally persuaded the Minister of Foreign Affairs, Talleyrand, to invite Charmaine back to her homeland. After all, the talented woman did not ask for her lands returned. What, asked the first consul's wife, could be the harm in having her on stage here in her home?

Charmaine's denial of interest in claiming the estate was a prudent decision. In fact, it was a concession to those who had bought up pieces of her father's estate since his death. But all of that was moot: Bonaparte had decreed that none of the properties confiscated by any government entity since the fall of the monarchy would be returned to any aristocrat who claimed previous ownership. Certainly no woman could make a claim.

As for how Charmaine's reputation appealed to Parisians, it

was rumored that she said she had long ago forgiven the terrorists who had run her and her family from her home. That she had not said she forgave those who'd abducted and killed her younger sister Diane, however, was a mark against her. Few remained alive or in power from the era of Robespierre, but it was not wise to speak against anything that had occurred then. Here in the country of her birth, Charmaine proclaimed she was now simply a humble actress who had earned her living in the theaters of Drury Lane for the past six years. She would be delighted to claim Paris now, too.

Tate shifted in his chair. The men below jostled about, laughing, joking, eager to view the French lady and raise her reputation…or lower it. Gossip sheets this past week proclaimed that the ethereal Charmaine de Massé (not that English bastardization of her family name, Massey) was a paragon. Even the stories of how her hired coach had been attacked by two highwaymen just outside Rouen on the journey here did nothing more than endear her to her countrymen. Word was that she had climbed from the carriage and faced the point of two pistols by the cutthroats, then offered up her money.

Tate scoffed. He bet she'd slipped her pistol from her reticule and threatened any idiot to come closer and steal her money. Too bad for them too if they tried to take her little dose of laudanum. The lady killed to get it—and would, Tate had always believed, to keep it.

If that story of her glorious heroism was not enough, he knew she most likely encouraged the stories of her youth to be broadcast by every rag in town. He had watched her share it often.

She loved to tell it with sighs and wringing hands, and it always contained the same bleeding-heart prose. For many years of her youth, she had endured poverty and exile with her family. The story served to burnish Charmaine's triumphal return to her native land. She'd been a young girl who fled Paris in a rickety carriage, sitting on a valise in which she'd stuffed the family's diminished fortune. Then, hiding beneath her cloak her two little sisters and her mother from the mobs, she had encouraged them all as they endured three weeks' sojourn through hail and rain and flood to the coast of Brittany. There they departed on an English smuggler's sloop for the rocky coast of Southern England. In that country where most could not bear the look or sound of a French man or woman, Charmaine had helped her family rise above the suffering and shame of their impoverished immigration to a land where no one loved them.

Tate swallowed bile at the tale.

Too bad it's all lies.

He grumbled to himself about lies people told themselves...and embellished for others. No wonder Charmaine became an actress. She lied with practiced ease.

The orchestra's serenade drifted to an end. The crowd hushed. The red velvet drapes swished open, the golden tassels swaying in the candlelight.

Tate sat, unmoving, triumph rushing through him that he had found the woman who'd had the gall to steal from him. After all he had done for her, her Aunt Madeleine, and her young half-sister, his darling Vivienne, Charmaine's theft gutted him. He'd shepherded them from Paris to Norfolk. Protected them from cutthroats, aided them, offered home and peace, and, after his father's death, even given them a small income. Yes, Tate had done what he could. But while some would call his actions kind, he called them atonement. He could never make amends for how he'd failed all three women. That night, he had failed to recapture Diane. It was one act he could never relive. Never change. The defeat for which he'd never find forgiveness.

Still, he had devoted much of his life to making up for it. He'd even used his associations with people, his language skills, and his understanding of French agriculture and products to allow him to stay in France and spy for Britain. Scarlett Hawthorne knew his talents and his desires. Over the years, he had brought to justice, and even with some finality, a few French agents who operated *carte blanche* in Paris and in London. But now to learn that Charmaine had suddenly reappeared in Paris alerted him to some new web she wove. It infuriated him. It alarmed him.

Perhaps she had her own reasoning for her actions. Charmaine always did. She'd taken jewels from her Aunt Madeleine. Published Diane's diary as her own. She'd even stolen beaus from Vivi. Charmaine suffered no remorse. Madeleine had forgiven her. Vivi had not. Diane could not. *He* would never forgive her for her pride and her duplicity.

The audience laughed. The rafters shook with it. Tate was not amused.

He winced. *The play, old man, the play!*

The first act proceeded apace. It was an old play by Molière. Charmaine was known in England for her tragic heroines, Juliet and her Desdemona. But for her return to Paris, she had insisted that she would honor the occasion by performing only comedy, preferably Molière. Tate knew the works of the famous French playwright well. He had seen them performed in Paris and villages all over the country. To see a play full of *bon mots*, a story of people who once loved and married, might have been a huge draw to Tate tonight, had the circumstances been different.

All at once, there she was. Graceful, artless, beautiful Charmaine de Massé, the oldest legitimate daughter of the Bourbon martyr Charles Gilbert Moreau, Vicomte de Neufchateau. Charmaine waltzed through her role like a woman in command. Tate commended her presence, her elegance of hand and body, her timing. But what a change she was from the girl who had acted in shame that night she and her family had fled Paris. She'd been perhaps fifteen, a girl, really. Yet he'd watched her lure a suave young man and take him from the likes of the family's scullery maid. Charmaine was at that young age already a practiced coquette. For years, Tate had tried not to criticize her too much because a decade ago she had the naïveté of youth. Yet his view of her was always shaded by what had happened that night when the mobs came for them and tore at their clothes and ripped Diane from their carriage.

Tate scowled. He sat forward. He should be enjoying Charmaine's performance. He hoped *she* did. After all, once he got hold of her, he was not letting her go until she told him where Viv was. He'd arranged a carriage to spirit her away with him. He'd even rented a small room behind a café on the quay of the Seine. He'd frighten her. Yes, he would. But he would not relent until she told him what he needed to know.

It shouldn't take long. Charmaine was many things—stubborn, stingy, and mean. But she was also a coward. Once she gave him what he needed, he'd let her go. He'd find Viv, bare his soul to her, and persuade her to make him her own. Then he would return here to finish his work for Scarlett and the Crown.

He inhaled. Satisfaction like red wine flowed through him. Warmed him with…

She glided across the floorboards. A lovely bit of fluff in purple and red satin, an elaborate wig of powdered white swaying on her head as she walked…and spoke.

What was wrong with her? She sounded as if she had frogs in her throat. Was she ill? Her voice was much too raspy. Too deep.

And the way she lifted her shoulder to give her male lead the cut direct was…not possible for Charmaine. She'd been injured in their flight from Paris when the coach lurched into a rut near Chartres. She'd broken her collarbone. Never to be mended as it should be because of delay, the bone had created for Charmaine what her detractors in London called her "stiff comedown" to male romantic leads.

"Do you know her?" Amber St. Antoine leaned toward him of a sudden to ask.

"Very well." He could not drag his gaze away from Charmaine. She was…enchanting. Her voice too low, too much of a contralto, husky and bold. Her sounds were mellow seduction. Her glide across the stage was an angel's. This was *not* Charmaine. By God, this one had never been anything like Charmaine. *No.* No, he knew this woman. This daring creature whose every word brought fire to his blood and yearning to his heart. "Too well."

His mind reeled backward to the first time he'd met the three daughters of the Vicomte de Neufchateau. The oldest girl, Charmaine, was small, delicate, with rivers of angelic white-blonde hair. The second girl, Diane, was bigger boned than her older sister, with golden-red hair like the copper of her father's. But the youngest girl, their half-sister Vivienne, was different. She was the child of the vicomte. The man proclaimed it often, for he loved her dearly. Vivi was illegitimate. Her mother was the vicomte's mistress and the widow of his younger brother. When Tate first met Vivi, he thought he'd seen double and lost his mind. She was the exact mirror image of Charmaine. Her twin, but not. Not in temperament, not in wit, but in every little curve of her lip and arch of her elegant brows. In the classic oval of her face and the sparkling sapphire of her eyes, Vivi was Charmaine.

Their voices were different, Viv's darker, deeper, rich with the sultry essence of earth. But more than that, what marked them as unique was their character. Gay to staid, spontaneous to calculating, the two could not be more different. And so this woman on the stage was definitely not Charmaine Massey of Drury Lane. This was his sweet Vivi of Cantrell Farm, who adored her dog, her donkey, her chickens, and her herb garden. This was Vivi masquerading, substituting as her older sister.

He sat back, mesmerized. He could not absorb her form, her stance, her sound fast enough to sate his madness. What was this? Some poor joke on Paris? Did Vivi and Charmaine work on this together? *Why?*

Oh, he would have Vivi spouting answers. Was she covering for her sister's newest attempt at…what? But Vivi would never do such a thing for Charmaine. Vivi loathed her sister's duplicity. Was Charmaine ill? Perhaps there was a simple explanation, a more innocent one. Was Charmaine ill and Vivi here to collect her sister's wages?

He blew out a breath.

Beside him, Tate heard Amber St. Antoine lean over toward Ramsey and say, "Lord Appleby knows the actress. Have you heard of her before tonight?"

Ram did not even deign to look at the lady beside him, and only nodded. He would never divulge information that was not necessary. But he knew full well that Tate was very familiar with the Massé family. Ram knew all the details of how, when, and why, too.

Yet all Ram said to Amber was, "I have seen her in a few comedies in London, yes. She is accomplished."

Amber sat back, widening her eyes, perplexed by Ram's seeming indifference, but trying to make conversation. "Word is that she supported her father's mistress and her sister with her earnings in the theater."

Charmaine sent a pittance. This one on stage raised animals and worked a garden so that her mother and she could eat.

"So I have heard," Ram responded, his gaze never leaving the stage.

Did he see the differences in the Charmaine of London and this one?

Tate would ask Ram about it. Kane, too. *Tomorrow.*

Not tonight.

Because tonight, I am going to the dressing room of that French imposter down there and getting the truth straight from her lovely, lying lips.

Chapter Two

"MADEMOISELLE DE MASSÉ!"

She made haste to her dressing room, a crowd of men on her heels. As she strode, she tore off her gloves and her cape, dropping them in her maid's outstretched hands.

"Mademoiselle de Massé!"

"My wig," she said like a curse, and worked the ugly thing off and into Alice's care. Her own hair fell free, locks of it falling around her shoulders and freeing her of the ruse she had agreed to and hated.

"Mademoiselle!" The chorus of men clamoring at her dressing room door was gratifying but frightening.

She skirted around them. "Let me by. Let me by."

A few were gentlemen. They stepped aside. But crowds meant chaos. Terror. She'd had enough of that in her life. *Enough. Enough!*

She stepped into her dressing room, and they followed.

She spun to her maid. "Close the door, Alice. Admit one gentleman at a time." The woman was tall and sturdy, able to fight off hordes of men. *Even those three who attacked us along the road near Rouen were discouraged by her.*

And I was useless. Brandishing a pistol that shook in my grip.

She put a hand to her throat. The memory of the robbery

outside Rouen made her angry. Her blood ran cold when anyone ran after her or called for her. But these men were praising her.

She swallowed. *Do not be a ninny.* The play had gone well. The applause was thunderous. The bouquets were so numerous that she could not leave the stage. The manager had to come help her walk away.

Now she had to react. Smile. Greet her public.

Mon Dieu, *I hate crowds.*

Alice had trouble closing the door. She kept telling those assembled to take their feet from the threshold, but they did not do it. They pushed and insisted. A few shouted.

"Miss! Miss, I cannot—!" Alice appealed to her.

"Mademoiselle!"

She stilled at the sound of one rich male voice.

No, no. I am dreaming.

But he called again—and his was a deep bass unlike any other man's. Dark as fine Cabernet wine. Hard as iron. Unforgettable.

"Mademoiselle Charmaine de Massé?"

Insistent. A question with a touch of English accent on her family name. It should be pronounced "Massey."

"Mademoiselle! Vivienne!"

No. Who would call for Viv? Not here. Not tonight.

"Vivienne!"

No, surely…

She craned her neck.

Tate!

She whirled away from the throng, a hand to her forehead, her smile dead on her lips.

It could not be Tate Cantrell! Why would he be here? Was he not in some tiny German town?

"Vivi."

Tate. He's come to the play. Here in Paris.

She turned slowly back. She always faced the inevitable, didn't she?

Her eyes flitted over the crowd that filled her dressing room doorway.

It *was* Tate. He stood inches above the fray. Everywhere he went, he'd always brought color, action, relief, and succor. In the profuse candlelight of her drab dressing room, he illuminated the shabby grays of the décor. He moved relentlessly forward through the crowd toward her, determined, focused, so handsome she gulped back the urge to cry. But it was her Tate.

The irrepressible Tate had always brought brilliance to her life. From his wavy whiskey hair to his large blue-green eyes and the sharp arch of his ruddy cheeks, he was a delicious man to look upon. To talk to him, to see him smile, to make him grin was the ambition of many a girl. All tried. Few succeeded. *I was one of them.* But his gaze implied only friendship. Never more.

This was Tate. Her friend. Her best friend. *Tate.* Her tension dissolved. He was near, and that always meant that she was saved from…

No! I am not saved. Not redeemed.

She snapped aside. Focused on the man right before her. Forced a smile to him. A tall, dark fellow in impeccable silks with his knee out, his hand toward her, like a courtier from her father's entourage. A man out of time, yet in this one, he struck a pose that shot her to the past, her childhood. A supplicant to her father. A man bent on seduction of her mother…or her oldest sister, the flirt.

She blinked. This man in front of her now simply wished to make himself known to her. To capture the latest Paris sensation and take her home.

Another man of similar fashion maneuvered the first away. He sought to gain advantage. "Mademoiselle de Massé," he murmured, pronouncing her family name as it should be in this country of her birth, not like the English bastardization of it.

The way we were known after the fall. And ever after. When we were taken in by the English who sought to ease our pain of loss. The English. The Cantrells.

"*Oui, oui,* I am happy to accept your cards," she told each man in turn. All handsome devils. Outfitted in their finest to impress her. But then, hope was eternal—and always perilous.

She knew her callers' expectations, their assumption that they might offer her supper after her performance, wine, the allure of their apartments, a kiss, later a dalliance, perhaps? And in time, a more permanent relationship?

Alice caught her eye from across the room. Yes, it was time.

Alice bent and disappeared to open the little basket that was Louis's wicker cage. The little dog burst out, yipping above the din of the appreciative male audience and nipping at a few ankles of those who did not move as quickly as they should. Louis, smart fellow, claimed what distance she could not as readily.

I like my space. She smiled at the next man who inched his way forward and lifted her hand to his lips. He had a flat face and a funny, tiny nose and nibbled at her hand…like a rabbit.

She snapped to attention. Whoever this man was, she wanted no part of him. She could do much here in Paris. Act. Pretend. Deceive.

Yet she was incapable of some things.

"Know thyself." That was her mother quoting the Greek maxim.

I do. And entertaining men who can never appeal to me physically will not aid me in my goal.

"Mademoiselle de Massé."

Tate.

She surrendered. She had to. He stood right before her and she could not help herself—she stared at him. Her heart sank to her knees. She had not thought that her skills as an actress would be tested so soon in this city. Nor did she imagine that this man, above all others, would be the one to call her to task.

Had he not been in the little German *margravate* of Baden? Before she left London six days ago, that was what she'd read in a gossip sheet. Tate, the charming Earl of Appleby, had always gadded about Europe. She had read the scandal sheets in London that told of so many British abroad. She'd believed what she'd read and thought her way clear of him. For she knew that if Tate Cantrell were in Paris when she was, he'd meddle in her plans. And that, she could not tolerate.

"*Bon soir*, mademoiselle." He took her hand, pressed his warm mouth to her flesh, and made her belly quiver.

"*Bonjour*, Monsieur le Comte." She inclined her head. She knew him—she could let the gossips spread that fact. After all, she'd spent the last decade in his country, on his lands, in a cottage on his manor grounds. One fact she would not now acknowledge publicly was how their relationship had once been more than that of friends. So she lied and said, "How lovely to see you here this evening."

He looked up at her through those thick, caramel-colored lashes of his, and his jade-green gaze warmed and challenged. "How I have missed you."

Of all the compliments he could have given, he chose the one that churned her anger at him. She had missed him all her life. Loving him, wanting him, watching him come and go, accepting finally that he would never be hers. She licked her lips. "I am honored."

"Are you? I am undone. I thought I had buried in my heart how bewitching you are," he said in the mellow voice that could melt her like a candle. "I was wrong. One glimpse, even so far from the stage, and I knew—"

"*Excusez-moi*, monsieur." She put her other hand atop his and squeezed. He spoke French and so did she, but she could not have anyone overhear what he might say. "Do not—"

"Hurt you?" He turned to English. His large eyes turned mellow and reassuring, his soothing expression taking her back to the weeks when they fled the mobs and he had saved them all from disaster. Mama, her sister, even Beau had been the beneficiaries of his courage and his kindness. "Never, mademoiselle. I simply must talk with you in private."

"Not here. Not now." She had to collect her responses. Were there not scripts for occasions when you confronted by surprise the love of your life?

"Then later. Where do you lodge?"

"Please. Do not press me."

"I must. I will. You know I will not rest until—"

"Yes. Yes, that I do know."

"When?"

When had God created a man so beautiful that to look at him blinded a woman to all else in the world? He seemed broader of shoulder, sturdier of muscle than when last she'd beheld him. His hair—that cinnamon blond the English defiled by calling ginger— fell over his broad brow. The lines fanning from his eyes told of the years he bore, the years they had been apart when she had yearned for him—all in vain.

She wanted to ask him truly how he was, where he'd been, why he was here in Paris. But she dared not. Whatever his reason to be in Paris, it was not her business. She was here not to meet him or enjoy his company, but to conduct her own affairs. Conversely, what she did was none of his affair.

"When? When will you see me?" He leaned closer. That cologne that distinguished him all his adult life—that grassy mix of German vervain and orange—washed over her and took her breath. He kissed her wrist, far from the place where the rabbit had put his lips, and with two fingers to her chin, Tate raised her face. In English, he whispered, "It must be soon."

"Monsieur." She gave him her mask of polite refusal. "Please, do nothing rash."

"Never, mademoiselle. Not to you."

She snatched back her hand. "I have an engagement for which I must prepare." That was in French, loud enough for others to hear.

"Skip it."

"Impossible," she told him, and at Tate's heels, her little dog proclaimed loud and long how he needed Tate's affections now.

She bent to pick up the dog. Louis had not nipped Tate's heels. Of course not. Animals never attacked those they loved.

"Bonjour, Louis," Tate whispered, and put his large hand to the head of her hairy little mutt. If Tate were a harsh man or an angry one, he could take her little dog's head and crush it in his fingers like so much paper.

But Louis—remembering the man whom he had loved above all other males—nuzzled into the fond embrace of big, bold, sappy Tate Cantrell, now the Earl of Appleby, the man who had given Louis to her as a pup and who had given her, her mother, and her half-sister Charmaine a cottage, income, beds to sleep in...and hope to live on.

"Surely...mademoiselle," he began, obviously avoiding use of her given name in this crowd, dwindling though it was. "Surely you agree about the need to talk."

She shook back her long, pale curls that flowed over her shoulders. Then she gave him her most impervious stare. She had to convince him to stay away from her. To never reveal, never voice her worst fears and say her name. "Monsieur, I am very busy. As you can see. And I am tired."

He scoffed, his hand still caressing her sweet Louis. The dog was a traitor to cuddle Tate like a long-lost father. "A few minutes tonight."

She needed to prepare what to say to him. So much for being a good actress. "I must ask you to leave."

"Make me go."

She swallowed her anxiety that he would make a scene and ruin her entire plan.

"Alice!"

The maid stepped forward. She was nearly as tall as Tate. He noticed with a smirk.

"Go with this gentleman to the wig closet"—she lowered her voice even though she spoke English to her—"and give him my address."

The first man who had paid her attentions must have overheard and understood, because he raised a hand and stepped forward.

She put up one staying hand. *"Un moment, monsieur, s'il vous plaît.*"

"I won't be put off." Tate bit off the words.

She set her eyes on him with all the power that her older sister would have used on an adversary. But her tone was soft, as she did not wish to be overheard by any of these *flaneurs.* "You are not. Alice will give you my address. Come day after tomorrow."

"Tonight."

"No. I am committed. Sunday, monsieur, or not at all."

He bowed, but his eyes gave no quarter. "What time?"

Persistent cuss. "Alice will send it."

"Tell me now—"

She huffed. "Do not make a scene here, Tate."

His eyes flared wide at mention of his given name.

Her gaze fell to his appealing, full lips. Oui, *I recall too well their luscious feel.* "Please. Leave me. I have an engagement. Alice, take this gentleman out and lead the others as well."

Tate clutched her hand once more. "I am thrilled to have found you."

His delight could never temper the fact that he had discovered her. Now she had to stop him from doing her any more harm.

"You may call upon me day after tomorrow, monsieur. At two o'clock." She smiled perfunctorily at him, then threw an apologetic look to the other men who'd been eager to have their time with her.

Tate set his jaw. "I do not breathe until then."

She caught her own breath. How could he so unravel her fine coil of good intentions in a few stirring words?

"Louis," Tate crooned to the dog, "I will see you again very soon. Take good care of your mistress."

Wiggling in discontent, the dog whimpered as Tate put him back to her arms.

Viv set her jaw and called forth all her determination to complete this plan of hers with speed. Tate could ruin every detail. "*Avoir,* monsieur."

Chapter Three

Rue du Bac
Paris

TATE CANTRELL INVADED her dreams.

He always had.

Viv blew out a breath and rolled over in her bed.

The Earl of Appleby and his easy charm, his blinding good looks, his understanding of all vicissitudes of life, his dislike of dissolute fathers and unethical siblings—she had loved him for that…and more.

She punched her pillows. Why did she even try to sleep?

He had always robbed her of sleep. When she was an impressionable seventeen and he was her morning riding companion, her adviser on raising chickens and on how to ignore Charmaine. When he overwhelmed her with his kindness, so unusual contrasted to other Englishmen's regard of penniless French émigrés. When she had fallen in love with him against her mama's advice. When he had come to her, held her close, and revealed that he must marry another. Ah, *oui*, she had lost many nights to the relentless love she bore the chivalrous Tate Cantrell. Tonight was no exception.

Last night at the theater, his appearance had robbed her of

her reason. She hated herself for it. But Tate Cantrell could steal anything from her. The greatest thing he'd taken from her, she had tried to snatch back years ago. But hearts were difficult to retrieve, she'd learned bitterly. Now she concentrated on flirtations to carry her through any trials of life.

Even this one.

She sat up, angry at herself. To the devil with hearts and Tate Cantrell.

She put her feet to the cold floor, felt around for her slippers, and stood. Alice had closed the drapes, as she was supposed to each night after a performance.

Louis roused from his bed of old sheets and towels. In the reflected moonlight, she could see him lift his noble head, stare at her, and wait for her signal to return to his dreams. She smiled and waved a hand. With a groan, he lay down again.

Viv stepped to the window and flung wide the heavy blue velvet. She needed room-darkening drapes, total blackness, and silence to sleep. Even that did not bring her peace. Not in Paris. Not with what she'd promised to do.

"Give over," she urged herself as she gazed out her bedroom window. She'd demanded the manager of the theater find her a house with bedroom suites facing the rear, away from the street. She did not mind the tinkling sounds of the little men who collected the midnight soil or the kitchen garbage in the *ruelle*. They tried to be unobtrusive. Unlike anyone in the broader boulevard of rue du Bac who bustled about at all hours. What she had minded was that he chose a house in Saint Germain. True, it was close to the theater. But too close to the past.

She'd stop complaining. She'd count her blessings. She liked the dawn, the discovery of a new day and fresh opportunities, preferred it when she was not a woman of this ridiculous occupation with need to stay up half the night, preening and carousing, flirting with men she'd never allow to come to her bed, let alone take her heart.

She padded to her wardrobe and, in the light from the moon,

pulled down from its hanger her old riding habit. Worn navy-blue serge of last year's fashion, the outfit had one bright feature of convex buttons of dead gold. Buttoned at the waist, the lapels opened for a froth of cambric to spill out. The costume declared she was a lady, but an odd one. She might once have had fashion sense, but now had no notable means or endeavor. She was simply some young woman with limited means—and a taste for trousers out for a morning ride.

Eager for her outing and her anonymity to enjoy it, she slipped behind the coral Japan screen, relieved herself, and washed with the basin of cool water Alice always left for her.

In minutes, she slipped out the door, down the stairs, and through the kitchen to the *ruelle*.

Sinking back against the solid oak door, she inhaled the fragrance of this part of town. Swept by the soft breezes of the Seine, this was sweet Saint-Germain. The part of the city from which she'd departed one night with her mother, two sisters, her dog Beau—and nameless crowds chasing after them. This house she rented was many streets away from that house of long ago. That one was in rue du Four. The house her father preferred. The house smaller than his official *hôtel particulier* near the Place Royale across the river. But the smaller house, quaint but as lavish, was the one he'd purchased for his mistress, her mother.

That house was close enough for her to walk to view it, if she wished.

She did. To behold it was one of the functions of her purpose here, wasn't it? To face the past. Conquer it. Settle all hatreds. Then never think on it again.

But that was a process.

She ran a hand over her brow. Of course it was. She'd gather her stamina for it. Save the house for later. Today, she had other views to see.

This morning, she would begin at the stables, where her majordom, on her orders, had contracted to hire a spirited, responsive horse to give her the daily exercise she required. A fine mare who knew the city as she did not. One who allowed her to survey the town she had left as a thirteen-year-old, cringing at the mobs who banged on the door of an old hired carriage, stabbed at their horses, and abducted Diane.

THIS BEAUTIFUL FEBRUARY morning was crisp, the winds off the Seine brisk but refreshing. Viv sat tall in her saddle. This was her element. Her fingers caught the tendrils of her pale blonde hair escaping her tidy jockey's bonnet. If she was to wish Tate Cantrell out of her hair, this was the weather in which to do it.

She grinned.

Only one man will do today. Her hired groom.

The fellow, riding close behind her, his pistol at his hip, was the very type of brusque male specimen she had requested from the stable master. Fortin was his name, Robert Fortin—and he was all she needed this morning to begin to familiarize herself with the city she'd never thought to see again.

From the cloudless skies and the blazing sunlight, she could say this placid place was a city she favored. Unlike her ugly memories, this city of gleaming white stones and glossy rose bricks buzzed with the early morning *vendeurs* who came from the countryside to sell their products. Housemaids strolled around to fill their baskets with eggs, winter turnips, and potatoes. The trinket sellers and pickpockets were not yet awake to irritate the crowds. Instead, the road along the Seine at this seventh hour of the day was filled with horsemen who came out for the air—and not for the company.

She liked her morning jaunt that way, too. Alone. The privacy, the serenity was what she needed, and would need often when she was here in Paris. Her mission was too roiling for her to be congenial to any and all. She would keep her acquaintances dear, but not close. She had little energy for friendships. Her best friend had been Tate, and that relationship gained her few satisfactions. Fewer as years rolled by.

Now she did not have the time or charms of duplicity to hold a friend. She hated her late nights at the theater, but she would simply drag herself out on as many mornings as she could find energy in order to find some balance to her task. No matter her fatigue. This morning, however, she had vowed she would force herself to view only a few places that marked her life here—and doomed her family.

Head high, she crossed the Seine on the famous old Pont Neuf. She surveyed the dark old frontage of the ancient royal palace of the Louvre, looted by the mobs so often during the revolution. But recently, First Consul Bonaparte had reopened a few of the rooms to show off the priceless art he stole from the Italians he had conquered. His belief that war should pay for itself in such booty made her smirk. The penalties that rubbed the noses of his enemies in the dirt of their defeat would come back to haunt him. For excess demanded revenge, didn't it?

She snorted. An unladylike comment on the ways of Renégades, but then, only her groom was witness to her sneer.

She turned away from him so that he could not see her next expression. Because it was ironic—or perhaps diabolical—that her own reason to be here smelled of revenge. That she disliked the odor of her own goal spoke volumes of the dislike she had for the job she'd agreed to do.

Wrong you are even to debate it, Viv!

Angry at her wavering, she spurred her horse to trot onward. The Tuileries palace loomed before her, a gorgeous place that once she recalled she had visited with her family. She remembered only a thousand bright flames, probably candles in cut glass chandeliers. Now it was the abode of Bonaparte, the house given to him by the generosity of the government he so eagerly led. The gardens, rather a shabby gray in the February chill, were still a grand parterre design, once the pride of the Bourbons. Even her father, minor member of that family as he was, had often remarked at their beauty, wishing he had the ability to duplicate it at their chateau so far away in the east.

Poor man. He had tried repeatedly to improve his lands. But he'd failed so often at agriculture that he had no money for the likes of parterres. He would instead bemoan his inadequacies and smother his shame in too many lost card games and too many conniving mistresses. In fact, until he took her own mother, his sister-in-law, as the one woman who could tame his excesses, he had not known any devotion to his crop production, his credit, or his mortal soul. Too bad it was too late to save his finances or his failing estate—or even his reputation as a roué.

Viv turned her eyes away from that part of her past. Her mother had loved the man. Why, only Mama knew best. But that she had done so with her whole heart still had not absolved the hurt that Vivienne—who exactly resembled his oldest daughter— was the one who had no legal right to stand in his light. Instead, Viv had the heritage of Pierre, his younger brother, the man who had died eleven months before she was born and who was her father in name only.

Viv halted her mount. The sight before her brought tears to her eyes. Cringing, she caught her breath at the sight of the huge, vacant plot where, according to witnesses, her father had been marched up a platform, hauled to *Mademoiselle Machine Horrible*, and murdered in the middle of the square.

"Come away, my dear."

She sniffed back her tears, caught and yet not surprised by the sound of the bass voice in her earshot. Tate Cantrell again. Was he her personal Paris plague? She chanced sight of him. So broad-shouldered, muscular, and bold, he presented that vibrant mix of flashing blue-green eyes and sugared cinnamon hair that made her mouth water. As if she weren't in his thrall already, he added to the drama of his presence in a magnificent mahogany-brown riding habit. "I should expect you everywhere I go now, is that right?"

His eyes danced. *But of course*, said his look. "I know you well."

Indeed. "Too well. You cannot annoy me into conducting a conversation with you."

He gave a laugh. "Then I shall annoy you enough to protect you."

Once she would have kissed his cheek for that. Now, congenial as his promise was, that irritated her. She ground her teeth and urged her horse back toward Pont Neuf. "I have enough protection."

He rode beside her, easy as if he'd been invited. "He does look the part. I hope you pay him well."

"Ba! Look at him, monsieur."

She nodded toward her groom. Older, gruff with a day's growth of beard and a bulbous nose long disfigured by too many brawls, Fortin flashed his black eyes at Tate. Then, with suave menace and a hand to the butt of his pistol at his side, he said, "Monsieur, if you please."

"I assure you, sir," Tate cooed in the sweetest French as he raised both gloved hands, "I am a friend and I mean no harm."

She sniffed the air.

Her guard grimaced. "The lady does not want you, monsieur."

Tate checked her eyes. "I believe she does. In fact, she always has."

Viv opened her mouth to object.

"No, monsieur," Fortin cut in, angry now.

Tate shook his head and reassured him with the most benevolent of smiles. "I have only a few sentiments to convey, monsieur."

Fortin cast her a glance and tipped his head at their intruder. "What say you, mademoiselle?"

"Speak your piece, Cantrell." She would not honor him with fine addresses. He tempted her. She could not let him see it. "Be brief and be gone."

"Of course." He kept to English now, making her grumpy

French groom snarl. "Obviously, you are here pretending. But I cannot fathom why."

That Tate would not say—even in English—that she was impersonating Charmaine was prudent, even kind of him. But she could not tolerate his revealing anything more. He had to go. "Stay away, Tate."

"I have thought on this all night. I know what you used to want," he said, cool as a charming friend in some coy conversation of no import.

A dream. Never possible.

"When you were thirteen, my dear, you prayed for a return to Neufchateau. Especially because you never thought you'd have safe means to do it."

"When we are children," she said, staring straight ahead, "we all want things we can never have."

"But now," he argued, "with a peace treaty and émigrés welcomed back to France, all of a sudden you have a passion for being someone you never wished to be? Someone you even disliked?"

Indeed. Charmaine's character was never one I applauded. But opportunity comes rarely. "People change, Tate."

"Not you. Not like this, *ma cherie*," he ventured, his voice full of longing, and her heart pounded at his endearment. "I don't know how you have accomplished this—shall we call it transformation? Or why. But I will."

"Do not meddle, sir, in my business. This is my quest."

"And that of your oldest family member, as well?"

Again, he did not name Charmaine. She was obliged to him for that discretion and that alone. "More, I cannot say."

He snorted. "I bet you can't."

"Sarcasm buys you nothing with me."

"Really?" He pretended affront. "I thought I was being diplomatic."

She set her teeth. "Do go away."

"Why?"

She rode on, ignoring the way her skin heated at the force of his stare.

He was not deterred and rode beside her. When her groom dropped back because of the surging crowd, Tate leaned toward her. "Why, Mademoiselle de Massé? What do you plan?"

The fragrance of his cologne, the nearness of his stalwart body and the memories of how dear he once was to her, roused her heartbeat. But she caught herself. Irritated at his never-ending allure, she shot a fierce glance at him. "I am earning a salary." *Charmaine's.*

He dropped his jaw. Then blinked and nodded. "You are good at it, I grant you. How did you become so accomplished—and rather quickly too, eh?"

"Study," she snapped. *Imitation.*

"Books. You read books. Plays."

"A fine education," she tossed back at him. "You did so yourself."

"To pretend that you are something you are not is dangerous."

She laughed, halted her mare, and glared at him. "And you of all people should know that is true." She had often told him she suspected he was a spy.

"Touché." He had the courtesy to blanch, but recovered quickly. "I work for king and country. But what is your motivation?"

She rode on.

"I do not believe you are here only to earn a salary that should go to another."

"That is your problem, sir."

"Was your coach attacked by highwaymen?"

She did not flinch. Tate often tried to catch someone off guard by a shift in topic. This question, however, did not surprise her. The manager of her theater had shown her a few gossip sheets with news of the attempted robbery. Evidently, Tate had read them too.

"It was." She went onward, showing lack of concern for the incident that riled her still. At least it had until Tate Cantrell became a bigger challenge by appearing in her dressing room and disassembling her life.

"Did you defend yourself?"

She frowned. "It pains me that you have to ask."

"Many reports gave different details."

"Ah. The way of gossip."

He grinned. "However, I do believe that anyone who touched you or yours would find themselves shot to pieces."

"Thank you." She had learned the art of marksmanship from him. Standing in his embrace, balancing, sighting, calculating, and swooning every moment for his regard, his touch. "They took my pistol. But I surprised them with the carriage shotgun and winged one thief in the arm. My maid frightened off one with her screaming."

He gave her a pained look of shock. "Your maid is a harpy, is she?"

"'Every woman should have one defensive skill.'" She quoted him directly.

He chuckled. "So they got nothing?"

"One carried off my reticule, my money, and my lovely little pistol." *And my necessary arsenic in Charmaine's étui.* "But he got not a hair on my head, nor Alice's either."

"Commendable."

"Thank you."

She gave him no more, and they rode in a companionable silence.

"Whatever you plan here," he said with sudden pain in his voice, "it is not wise."

She would not grace him with another refutation. Plus he knew her so well that she was putting up a front.

"Diane is gone. Your mother and father. Any friends the family had are most likely not alive to comfort or help you."

That she knew. Had known all along. She was alone in this.

"And where is your *other* family member, hmm?" He was tight lipped with anger, then reached out and grabbed her reins.

Her horse halted.

She caught back a gulp. "Stop this." To her horror, that was not an order, but almost a plea.

His hand went from the reins to cover her fingers. His were long, strong as iron, and covered in blood-red leather. "This is Paris, my girl."

She bristled at being his *girl*. Once she had yearned for it. Now, she was inured to his charms. Totally. "What of it?"

"This is not Norfolk and the quiet of your cottage."

His words made her ache for the serenity of the land she'd left behind. The rustle of wind through the lindens and oaks. Rain as it pattered on the slates before her little blue door. The sweet lowing of cattle. The brays of Fred her old donkey and the ripe smells of her chickens and ducks. "It certainly is not."

"You know nothing of the dangers here." He spoke rapidly in English. "Nor of the profession you have adopted. In London, an actress might avoid the toffs who would toss a girl for a penny. Here they are tough to tame. This city is filled with different menaces, even after all these years, for one who bears blood so blue."

"You do not frighten me," she said, tipping up her chin. Of course, she lied.

He blew out air and gave up his hold on her. "I will be near."

If he acted the swain, he'd scare off those she needed to attract. "I don't want you near."

"Has that changed?" He sounded…gutted.

"It never was," she blurted, and cursed herself for it. He shocked her with such a statement, and she could not allow him to become more to her than…he'd ever been. A friend. Just a friend.

"A bit of acting? Don't, my darling."

"I am not your—"

"You are. Now that I have found you—"

"You can leave me, Tate. Please, just go." She could not have hm near her. He knew not what she'd agreed to do. She could not have him learn. He'd hate her.

His thick, caramel-colored lashes flickered. His chiseled features, so manly with his added years, at once resembled stone. He was flummoxed because she had never shut him out. Too sad for her sore heart that she'd been so silly. "I will return."

"You'll find nothing," she said, praying her acting skill proved her words.

"You hope," he muttered.

"*Adieu*, monsieur." Clicking her tongue, she urged her mare onward.

This time, he did not follow.

Success rippled through her. But only for a minute.

He would return to her and ask for more. Of course he would. He was incorrigible.

He was the young man who had jumped from their carriage when Diane was snatched by the horde. He was the lad who'd failed to take Diane from the mob, but who had scooped up Viv's little dog Beau and saved him for her. He was the one who'd demanded his father give her family a cottage on the Appleby estate. He was the young man who had held her in his arms and apologized when his father required he marry another girl, an English girl, for her money. He was the man who had offered to marry her...but never declared he loved her.

He was the man who carved for himself a name in the British Parliament for improvements in roads and bridges. He'd published a treatise on crop rotation. He was an earl of the realm. Rich. Dashing. Her friend. Once that. Once more. Now no longer.

The indefatigable Tate Cantrell. He'd demand anything. Of anyone. Even her.

But this knowledge of where Charmaine was, and why, he would not get.

Because this time, unlike all others, Vivienne Marie Annette de Massé was in charge of her own destiny. She had plans he could not change. She had promised—and unlike so very many, she never broke her promises.

Chapter Four

TATE SAT WITH Kane, Lord Ashley, after dinner at Monsieur Jean Lenoir's house in rue Saint Denis. The merchant financier was one Tate had cultivated to put fair prices on a few French goods to go to Britain. But Lenoir's second, less publicized, job was the one Tate found more interesting. That was to aid the French army in supplying itself. Others did the same as Lenoir, but it was vital to cultivate them all.

So Tate was here with Kane tonight because he'd been invited and because it added to his social status. Lenoir kept a fashionable house and his chef was renowned. Guests came for the cuisine—and to meet Lenoir's associates. Few mentioned that the regular entertainment was Lenoir's wife at the piano or their daughter's singing—and with good reason. One did not disparage one's host or his family.

But Tate and Kane had accepted the invitation to dinner, ever happy to pick up nibbles of news about army supplies or troop movements. Tonight, the four military officers in attendance were delightfully inebriated, but as yet, no crumbs of intelligence had fallen from their mouths.

"Too bad," muttered Tate to his old Eton pal as they took chairs in one corner alone. "I could have stayed home and tended to my knitting."

Tate's "knitting" being calculating the value of a recent purchase of surplus French barley to go to Britain. The French crop had been very good this year, and the British needed grain desperately.

"What of your other pursuit?" Kane asked him.

"No word on our famous friend yet," Tate said. Scarlett had suggested a covert objective for Tate when she assigned him to Paris. He was to search for a school chum of his, Kane's, and Ram's who had gone missing a few years ago after visiting Verdun. They all suspected he had been sent to a French prison for counterfeiting, but Scarlett needed to know if he was still alive. "I have begun a plan, but nothing firm yet."

"And the other problem, you noticed three weeks ago at the theater when you were with me and Ram?"

Tate blew an exasperated breath. Kane knew about his past involvement with the Massé family. Tate had shared little of his desire for Vivienne. But every other fact of Viv's impersonation of her older sister Charmaine, Tate had told his friend. Yet about the newest—the ugly rumor that Viv was called to an assignation with Bonaparte—Tate had said nothing. In truth, he was furious when the rumor was confirmed over and over by stories in the morning *libelles*. All of them began with the line that a few nights ago, Bonaparte had summoned the "Divine Massé" to his chambers.

"I follow her each day." *So does another.*

Tate had begun his watch that very day after he'd ridden with her along the Seine. She went few places. To a modiste twice. To a *chapelier*, a hatter, once. She continued her riding three mornings a week to the stables from which she hired the same mare and the same gruff and burly groom. Tate knew it must be a deprivation for her to ride so infrequently. But he concluded the reason was that when she took to the stage five nights a week, she was quite exhausted and preferred to sleep when she could.

"Still not talking to you?" Kane asked.

"I stay well away. But I watch, and I have hired more men to spell me. I hope for news about the other sister. I've done my best." *Done my best* was code among them for having sent an encrypted message to the offices of Hawthorne & Company. "But I have no clarification." Scarlett had not replied to him with any information on the whereabouts of Charmaine de Massé. Tate did not fault Scarlett for tardiness or failure. Kane and Ramsey had warned they expected that Fouché read all their correspondence to and from London. Scarlett would respond to Tate only via private courier when and if she had any useful information.

"Well then." Kane savored a sip of his Armagnac. "Do you know that she was invited to the Tuileries after dark?"

"I do." Tate's jaw twitched with anger.

Kane pursed his lips. "May I suggest a change of scenery?"

"Your house?"

"Much more intriguing than my library." Kane's ice-gray eyes glimmered as he lifted his glass to drain it.

"That's hard to imagine." Tate had a special fondness for his own library. And come to think of it, so did Viv. It was where she'd learned so much Shakespeare by heart and performed so well at Christmastime that Charmaine had taken it up to imitate Viv. Charmaine had left Cantrell Manor in Norfolk and used her knowledge to earn her living on the stage.

"Others begin to leave here," Kane said, bringing him back to their discussion. "We can follow, then we'll discover new horizons…and pretend we've never seen them."

"Ah." Tate laughed, catching a note of the scandalous in his friend's baritone. "As a happily married man whose wife is *enceinte*, should you even admit you know of this scenery?"

"Trust is a necessary commodity of marriage," said Kane with the arch of a black brow. "Besides, this house we must visit."

"Do we have any official reason to accept?"

Kane leaned forward. "I am often invited. The host is related to a banking family, and I have a large purchase from him I'd like to conclude."

"More barley?" Tate asked.

"Lyon silk."

Tate was impressed. He knew one man who handled most of Lyon's Paris stock. "Is it Montagne you speak of?" One of Paris's old guard, returned now in the seemingly liberal atmosphere of the Consulate, and yet, by all accounts, even more licentious than he had been before.

"It is. I think we must go, you and I."

"I hope the music is better."

"More than that, Tate—my majordom Corsini tells me that two nights ago when the *Théâtre de la Gaîté* was dark, the leading lady was invited to Montagne's."

Tate ground his teeth. "Did she go?"

"No, she wrote and told him she would come tonight."

"Hell." Tate shot to his feet. "Time we bid our host here good night."

TATE SAT IN Kane's carriage as it sped toward the infamous man's house. He tapped his fingers on his knee, silently fuming about Viv's recent social activities. The horses could not carry them to Île Saint-Louis in the middle of the Seine quickly enough. It was one thing for her to suddenly become notorious. Invited to Bonaparte's suite in the Tuileries after a performance for an assignation, she insulted the first consul after he kept her waiting so long that she rebelled and left. That was an act that lifted her up as independent and endangered her with those in government. Other men would try to conquer her. She would be invited to more parties, other rendezvous, other bacchanals, so that men could test her mettle. This particular salon that Kane took him to was one of those where a young lady of discreet upbringing should never be found.

Tate cursed silently. Viv would leave that house with him tonight. She must. She would not be mauled by such disreputable rogues. If he had to, he'd haul her out over his shoulder.

Why she went irritated him. He knew only one reason why she should go to this man's house. The fellow was a relation of the banking family who had purchased her family home after they fled and Robespierre lost power. Certainly, buying it back seemed an unimportant goal, given all the years she'd been away. She hadn't even gone to look at the house on her morning rides. So what she did here, other than acquaint herself with more and more of the *beau monde*, was a mystery.

Still being a social butterfly might be a means to some end. What could she want?

God knew that Paris offered every pleasure a man—or woman—of means and imagination could want. Since the Bourbons had settled the religious wars between Catholics and Huguenots, improved the bridges and the streets, and encouraged the strolling vaudevillians and street plays, the capital city was home to every titillation one could imagine. In every corner of the city, one could find any vice on offer.

Gambling, dice, wresting, and racing were the milder entertainments. Gypsy fortune tellers roamed with men who claimed to be magicians. All peddled tobacco and snuff or hallucinogens. Just as ubiquitous were prostitutes catering to all tastes, genders, calibers, and prices. Children, cross dressers, even kidnapped virgins were available for an evening or weeks. Sale of opium or any other toxic substance in all their forms was a street trade. Everything could be had for a price.

With the end of the Terror, Parisians had taken up a natural fear of the extremes of human depravity. Nowadays, most Parisians tempered their appetites and turned to milder pleasures. In place of the lawlessness that had permeated the city, and much of the countryside too, people worked hard for their bread. Grain was expensive. The poor starved just as they had before anyone marched for lower taxes and more salt for their cellars. The fine gentlemen of the Directory had tried to institute some sense of order into society. Alas, when kindly persuasion did not work, and the directors called upon their three strongest leaders to form a new government, it was their new leader, their first consul, who called for even stricter order.

Bonaparte imbued his Minister of Police Fouché with the need for more men on his force. The consul ordered more and more newspapers shut down, street minstrels swept off the corners. Increased patrolling of the streets, especially at night—and more lamp lights to hinder thieves. Those with bigger ambitions to rob homes and businesses were discouraged by the patrols.

Yet for those who could afford it, and those whose reputations were oblivious to it, licentious entertainments *were* available. A man or woman just had to know where it was offered in just the right quantities. Often such diversions came from the those highest in Society.

Kane's carriage idled in front of the blazing sconces set aside the doors of Monsieur Cyprien Montagne's large and gracious house. Commissioned by the Jarre-Montagne family during Louis XIV's childhood, Montagne House was a *hôtel particulier* of great fame. Situated at the tip of the Île Saint-Louis, the manse of creamy Parisian dressed stone commanded a view up and down the Seine. The courtyard and gardens had been designed by Le Nôtre, the famous landscape artist who'd finished Versailles, the Tuileries, and Vaux le Vicomte. Most in Paris revered Montagne House as a national treasure, and no one had broken into it during the troubles. The grand dame stood as she had, glorious and intact, for more than a hundred and fifty years.

"Shall we?" Kane asked, straightening his frock coat, as eager as Tate to go inside.

"Have you been here before?" Tate was surprised Kane had accepted the invitation of the owner. Kane, very careful of his reputation, was head of the British envoys in Paris and acted as if he were the equal to the official British ambassador, Charles Whitworth. Kane's current role as head of Scarlett Hawthorne's agents was his secret one. To come here to Montagne House was off the mark for Kane, but in Paris, it had always been true that a man could go anywhere at any time—and even brag about it. Kane never would discuss coming here, but if good relations came of it, he valued it.

The owner of the house, Cyprien Montagne, was one of the last remaining members of a famous banking family who had dealt with the last king. The current owner had outlived that shame. Now Cyprien, no longer a banker himself, was a returned émigré, invited by Josephine and approved by Fouché. But he was a silver-haired roué of fifty years of age. A confirmed bachelor, he was known in his youth and now for abducting young girls from the countryside and selling them to anyone, male or female, who crossed his palm with the right number of coins, which he demanded be only gold ones.

Kane considered the elaborately molded iron front door with a grimace of distaste. They waited for the groom to open the carriage door. "Before I was married, yes, I was here. Once. Everyone should know of it, especially those in our line of work. Have you heard of the infamous Cyprien?"

Tate's left eye twitched. "I've met him before. In ninety-seven. I was a green boy of twenty-three. The master and his two mistresses did a tableau. One I have not forgotten."

"Word is the man has reformed."

Tate barked in disbelief. "Why? Does he tie only one mistress to his bed these days?"

"You always surprise me at who you know in this town."

"A bigger shock, isn't it, that I know nothing about one of whom I should know everything?" Tate grumbled.

"Let's go in and see if we can change that."

When Kane's coachman swung open the door, Tate was first out.

Chapter Five

MONTAGNE HOUSE TOOK Viv's breath away. The front courtyard resembled her father's at Neufchateau, the family's country estate landscaped with elaborate parterres. February made it gray and crisp. Winter stilled the few tress and sheared shrubbery, robbing them of all rustle and flow. Like Papa's, this garden was dead. Inside, the reception hall of blue-veined marble was as chilly as Papa's, and the walls of robin's-egg-blue plaster could not warm her.

Why had she come?

"Resolve, Vivi." Her sister's brusque contralto flowed through her.

Viv stole courage from her purpose. She'd fought coming for hours. It was now after ten, but she'd bear this as long as she could and hopefully be in her bedroom, undressed, by midnight, Louis at her feet.

Start this, Viv. The sooner begun, sooner done.

Tate's image clouded her vision. He'd stop her from coming here, seeking out men who had hurt her father and her family. She paused, recalling Tate's presence each morning she rode. He was such a stubborn man, and she loved...*no*, she appreciated him for it. But, determined he could not dissuade her, she gathered her gumption and donned the bravado of Charmaine. To the flesh-and-blood man who stood before her, she arched her brows in an imperious smile.

Monsieur Montagne's tall, gaunt majordom batted not a lash at reading her card. But then, the man who ran the household of a libertine had to have a quiet mind and a strong stomach, didn't he? For Viv, he needed only to know her ancient family name and her celebrity. As an actress, she fit into this brand of Society. As the disrespectful chit who'd walked out on the first consul, she would be the most notorious woman here tonight in this house of ne'er-do-well bankers. Montagne's own cousins, the Jarre branch of the family, were never ones to celebrate their ethics or their morals. She smirked as the majordom gave her what was a triumphant smile of welcome and turned his trim back to lead her toward the main salon.

She lifted her ivory fan from its tassel on her wrist and whipped the thing in her anxiety. "*Slowly*," she could hear Charmaine correcting her. "*No windstorms*, ma minette."

The grand salon of marble, gilt, and glass blinded her—and make her run. The dome above, allowing the velvet sky and stars to shine through, inspired her to fly up, far away. Yet stay, stroll, pretend, she must. She would. Could.

The massive room was alive with dozens—perhaps a hundred—of the *nouveau* bejeweled and silk-clad *beau monde*. At her approach, they paused; many murmured, some awed, many not. She could not care. She was here to find a few men, marks who would make her sad heart lighter.

"Mademoiselle de Massé for you, monsieur." The butler presented her to his master and bowed himself away.

Her host was ostentatious in his welcome. A courtier of the last Louis, a sycophant of the Corsican military officer who was so bold as to wish to be as powerful, Cyprien Montagne honored her with a royal flourish.

Her hated fan to her beribboned décolleté, she gave him a trill of her feigned delight. "How charming. I am delighted to be invited."

"I am so thrilled to have you here, mademoiselle." He spoke with that precise Parisian elocution that denoted him an aristocrat of the *ancien regime*. Bold to examine her cheeks and gauge the size of her breasts, he looked far too long to be polite. *Arrogant ass.*

He wore a Prussian-blue jacquard waistcoat, blazing white stock, and a gunmetal frock coat shot with silver. The look was elegant, dramatic, with the deep blue a strong counterpoint to his small gray eyes and mass of slickly pomaded silver hair. Noticing her appraisal of his attire, he grinned because he assumed she approved. Then he took her hand and wrapped it around his arm. "I will introduce you, but you must at least for few precious minutes allow me to bask in your pristine beauty. The stage is so far distant that it does not allow mere mortals the full perfection of your face or form."

She let the damn fan dangle. She had all she could do not to quiver at the way his eerie eyes once more took in the rounds of her breasts above the dangerously low-cut gown. "You are too complimentary, monsieur."

"And I must ask, why use all that makeup on the stage to cover your beauty? Are we not more natural these days in every way? I say that the manager does not know his trade as well as many of us have been led to believe. I will speak with him next week of these things."

"Oh, sir, you know we must use the powders and wigs to make us noticeable for those in the rafters."

He took her hand and lifted it to his lips. "I would recognize such beauty were I a hundred leagues from you."

She had to show some sophistication and play to his game. "Monsieur, you flatter me too much." The bastard must not guess what she really sought in his house.

"Never. Allow me to do so often and I will lay my heart at your feet."

She lifted a finger and playfully wagged it at him. "No need, sir. I am immune to all but those who offer me sincere companionship. Besides, I am very busy and the work is tiring. But to acquire friends here, I will soon begin calling hours. I will make it one of my afternoons when the house is dark. I do hope you will consider yourself invited every day."

She had planned this approach. Ladies in London had hours when others might come to visit. But she had no idea if French ladies did that these days. She should have asked. But what should she worry, though? If she were wrong, so be it. She was an actress. A British actress. Such women did as they wished.

"How good of you." He beamed and led her to the side of the room, where their conversation was more private, yet more noted by many. "I do hope I will be among those who are invited."

"Monsieur, your presence is one I do welcome." *God help me.* "I am new here, and I confess I need a friend. A companion and a confidant."

"You have me, mademoiselle, as your chevalier."

She preened. *Now, what about your cronies? I have a few names I must pin on faces.* "I am honored. Now, please, lest we set tongues to wagging, do introduce me to your guests. I may not be the height of Society, monsieur, but I do remember the particular nature of Parisian etiquette. I am from a well-regarded family." She would not let him forget it. Though her mother had not been wed to her father when he took her as his lover, she was his wife's sister and had been his brother's wife. Viv was illegitimate, but she'd been doubly related to her half-sisters and considered herself nearly their full-blood equal. "I must hold high the reputation of my loved ones." *And search out those who hurt them.*

"I do agree. Those of us who have returned have so much for which to be grateful."

I will be grateful when my duty is done. "Precisely my thought. But I think to exemplify by my good behavior the refinements of our shared past."

He shook his head. "A pity so much has been buried and forgotten."

"I wish to remember all who have gone." She put two fingers to her rouged lips and leaned coyly forward to allow a glimpse of her cleavage. "I should not say it aloud."

"You are safe with me, mademoiselle."

"Cyprien! You cannot keep the lady to yourself!"

A man approached them, boldly positioning himself so close to Viv that she inhaled his strong bergamot cologne. He towered over tall, lean Cyprien and smiled liked a prince who ruled the city. She had no idea who he was, but his good looks could enthrall many a woman. He wore his fashionable clothes precisely cut to his broad shoulders and trim thighs. His silky black hair complemented his bronzed Provençale complexion. But his flashing dark-blue eyes told her that he was a shrewd man who could strike her down with one blow.

In her reverie, alarm colored a memory. She had seen this man before.

Her host smiled with stiff displeasure at the interruption. "Mademoiselle, allow me to present Monsieur René Vaillancourt."

His name meant nothing. Only his stance—and her memory of his handsome face sent fire through her blood.

He gave a slight bow. "I am honored, mademoiselle. I have been very busy lately and have not seen your performance yet, but I understand you carry it off with aplomb."

"*Merci beaucoup.*"

"Perhaps I will come next week?"

What was he expecting? A complimentary ticket? An invitation to her dressing room? Inwardly, she flinched, afraid all at once. "Come whenever you can, monsieur. We are there five nights a week."

"Indeed." He possessed a thin baritone, but he used it on her as if she were his servant...or his pawn. "And you perform for how many weeks?"

Her skin prickled at his tone. "Until the end of June."

"And afterward what do you do?" he asked with an arch of his elegant black brows. He sounded as if she had no right to go anywhere.

She could not get away from him quickly enough. He was rude. "I will go to Neufchateau."

"Really? Why? What is left for you there?" he asked.

Recoiling, she dropped open her mouth.

Cyprien smacked his lips as if he'd had enough. "The lady wishes to see her home, René."

"Of course she does." The man bowed. "I realize it now."

She gave him what small smile she could summon. Then he excused himself.

"I apologize for his rudeness, mademoiselle. The fellow thinks he runs Paris."

She could not take her gaze off him. "Does he?"

"He is the deputy chief of police."

"Ah," was all she could manage in her horror. Smooth, well-dressed, debonair René Vaillancourt was police—and a snake.

"Think no more of him." Cyprien took her hand and led her to look up at him. "I am here to bring you new delights."

Laughing, she leaned toward him and gave him a glimpse down her bodice. She wanted a barrier between her and Vaillancourt. "Onward, then!"

But she needn't lure Cyprien. His eyes were already eating her up. His lips were wet, his mouth already salivating. And she knew why, too. Her full breasts were one enticement. The other was the latest rumor about her. And she had not fabricated it. The whole of it was true. In fact, her majordom implied today that the first consul liked such tales told abroad of his masculine prowess. Or in her case, the man's greater attention to his work than to her.

"I trust you, monsieur. There are so few true gentlemen." She sniffed. Bonaparte was one. Certainly he had not exhibited anything to her other than his boorishness. That she was glad of it and proud she'd escaped his bed were added boons. Vaillancourt was a different breed of cat.

"The rumor is damaging to the fellow who was rude. You saved yourself."

Cyprien spoke of Bonaparte. She nodded. "A lady must. I hope others see it my way."

He was so bold as to lay a hand on her cheek. "They do. I do. Now you will allow me to repair all of your sensibilities, *ma cherie*. First, a little wine." Cyprien arched a thinly plucked silver brow, and a footman appeared. He swept two crystal flutes from the tray and placed one in her hand. The touch of his fingers to her own repulsed her.

She would not show it, and looked deeply into his tiny eyes and leaned toward him like a coquette. "I am hungry too."

"What would you like?" he crooned, his tone salacious, and her skin prickled.

Not you, was her first thought. Then, before thinking, she blurted, "Beef."

And he took it as risqué, throwing back his head to laugh. "Well, *voilà!* If you wish such sustenance, I can give it to you. Come."

She swallowed hard as he led her through an inner vestibule and into a small octagonal room with mirrors from floor to ceiling on each wall. "Oh, this is spectacular!" *And not designed for dining, is it?*

His beady eyes widened with pleasure. "A room of many delights. Tonight it is to showcase my chef's supper menu."

"How grand!" She could guess what the room usually showcased. Charmaine had been succinct with her instructions about many in Society, especially Cyprien. But to Viv's relief, tonight the round supper table at the center of the room was piled high with hot and cold dishes, small crudities and rolls of meats dressed in herbs and spices. Pastries in pastel icings and gateaux dripping in chocolate and raspberry sauces were arranged in colorful display. The offerings on the platters could feed an army.

"Astonishing array," she managed, and patted Cyprien's arm. But her instinct that he'd accept her gesture as friendship was wrong. He swung around before her, two hands now to her bare shoulders, and pressed himself against her. She stared at him, shock chilling her. "I—I'm sorry, monsieur. Did I give you the impression—?"

He leaned over her, towered, in fact, and moved one hand from her shoulder across her bare chest to lift her chin. "You are no innocent."

His whisper only served to make her heart beat like a drum. "Please..." She tried to pull away, her fright no pretense.

He grinned, the satyr, and put his palm flat against the bare skin of her chest. "Charmaine, *ma tigresse*. I have heard of your preferences."

Viv was no tigress. But her sister had had her hungers—and satisfied them liberally. Viv had known there were those in Paris who might catch her in their claws, thinking she was Charmaine.

"*Ma belle*, you are excited."

Terrified.

He settled his hips against her own. "I am complimented."

"Monsieur." She felt his interest rise too high and hard against her skirts.

He pressed closer, his personal musk, thick and cloying, making her gulp back despair. "You are no virgin."

"*Monsieur*," she said as she stiffened and stared him in the eye, "neither am I some lamb to be led to your lair."

"Forgive me." He backed away, chastised for now. "I was too enraptured and stand corrected. In the flesh, though, you are quite irresistible."

She smiled, giving by her ease a sense that she forgave him. "You are kind."

"Many a man would love to describe your beauty in detail."

She looked up into his cool little eyes. Pretending to find him attractive was a chore. "Few have said the right words."

"I wish to try."

She hoped she blushed. "I cannot be rushed—or ignored."

"Clearly. What we hear of the other night in the Tuileries

tells us tact and kindness are required."

"I must know a man well," she said with a frown. "So many assume a lady of the theater can be charmed quickly and offered delights for an hour's worth of her time."

He squeezed her hand. "*Ma cherie*, I would take from dusk to dawn."

"Monsieur Montagne!" a male voice called him.

"Monsieur, so good of you to have us!"

She hung in Cyprien's arms, grateful for the disruption, shocked because the only sound ringing in her ears was the bass voice of Tate Cantrell. *How could that be?*

She looked over Cyprien's shoulder at none other than Tate with another man.

With a smile of her relief, she stepped away from her captor.

Both men strode forward. "Monsieur Montagne, *bon soir*," Tate said.

"Ashley and Appleby, of course, you are welcome," Cyprien greeted them in a hearty fashion that told her the Frenchman knew both well. "And I wonder if you have met Mademoiselle de Massé?"

"*Bon soir*, mademoiselle." Tate took her hand. "Indeed we have met. I am delighted to see you again. My friend Lord Ashley does need an introduction, Monsieur Montagne."

Viv fumed. She did not want Tate here to see her at work among these people. Must he be everywhere? Following her. Riding with her? Here she was striving valiantly to show a few of her acting skills. She politely responded to the formalities.

Ashley spoke up. "Monsieur Montagne, I came tonight because I thought you and I needed to get on with our initial discussion of a few days ago."

"Ah, Ashley, you English may discuss business on a night of pleasure, but here in Paris we frown on it."

"But if Bonaparte and our Ambassador Whitworth argue like they did the other night, we may not have the chance to discuss the five or six percent more I may now offer on those Lyon silks."

Cyprien's brows arched, and with a look of regret at Viv, he extended a hand toward a small collection of chairs. "How can I refuse?"

When the two had left them, Viv let out a breath.

Tate's arms came around her from behind. "That was close."

She clamped shut her eyes and allowed herself to relax into the refuge of his embrace. This was so much more than a friendly embrace. His hold was definitely amorous. Viv was stunned but lost to his tenderness.

Tate's subtle fragrance drove away Cyprien's flowery cologne and Vaillancourt's heavy bergamot. For just one moment, she could rest here.

"You are fine now, sweetheart." He held her securely to him and pressed his lips into the hair on her crown.

She pulled away from the temptation to remain. "Thank you. He became troublesome."

Tate lifted her chin. "Do you know what he is? What you're—?"

She was recovered, and a fool to have sunk into Tate's embrace. He might be her savior at the moment, but she did not want him chastising her. "I know what I'm doing, yes."

"Getting yourself raped?" he seethed.

She caught her breath. "Not if I can help it."

"Sweetheart—" He stepped forward.

She evaded him. "Don't."

"Don't stop wanting to save you? Whatever in hell this is!" He waved an arm to denote the crowd beyond.

"I do not want your salvation."

"But you need it. They are nothing like you. They are without any bounds and will do whatever they wish."

"Stop following me. Stop tormenting me!"

"I won't. You are precious to me, and—"

"Am I? How good to know." *Precious but never loved.*

"Let me help you. I can. I will. I have always wanted to give you all you desired."

She sniffed. Oh, the arrogance of him. To think she'd take him as hers, when all he felt was duty. Angry that he pitied her, she lashed out at him. "You failed."

Her accusation froze him. But only for moment, then he pressed against her. His body was a shield she could stand beside to fight the world and all its tragedies. But he'd never loved her…only stood by her because he believed he owed her and her family for not rescuing Diane.

"Viv, sweetheart, I came to find you last year. You were gone."

"Too bad." She covered her mouth, lest he hear the sob that rose in her throat.

He anchored her to him, his arm around her waist a band of iron. "My year of mourning was over. I came to ask you to be my wife. To tell you all I wanted for us. All I wished to propose we have."

Ironic, wasn't it, that when she finally stopped hoping he'd ever want her, he'd come to claim her and offer her a loveless marriage? Simply tragic, but none of that could ever be.

She stepped from his arms.

He cursed under his breath. "You won't stop this…this lie?"

"No."

"Why not?"

"You would die!" *Oh, hell.* What good could come of his knowing that? She shook her head and took one stride away.

"Viv?" He held her wrist. "If I could die, then you would too."

"I must cultivate these people." She swallowed all her tears and anger. She shook back the tendrils of blonde curls obscuring her vision of his ravaged features. God, she had hurt him. Hell surely awaited her for that. He had suffered enough for his failure to get Diane. "And I will do it. You will not dissuade me."

Impossible man, he caught her elbow and stood so close her head swam with his nearness. "Why not?"

"I have promised!" she blurted. She hated herself for divulging that. But she shook him off.

"Promised what? To whom?" he called after her, his voice that of a hopeless man searching for salvation.

She understood the feeling. But she would not allow the negativity to stop her.

"Retribution," she threw at him, and he balked.

She could not wait for his reaction and headed for the vestibule, the grand salon, and those she had to court. She stared out at those assembled, then glanced over her shoulder at the exquisite man who had always been her champion and was now her nemesis.

TATE SEETHED AT her word. Retribution was so scurrilous an ambition. He took his carriage home that night, went to his library, and had his man bring up tea, sandwiches, and a good bottle of brandy. Then he sat at his desk, naming all whom he could think of who had ever hurt her or her family.

Tate had come into their lives early in 1791 when he was wandering the Continent, tired of his travels and not wishing to go home. He went to Neufchateau. The vicomte received him like long-lost family, which indeed he was. Tate was a distant fifth or sixth cousin by marriage of a Massé girl to one in his line.

But the vicomte, for all his many lascivious ways, was a gracious host and loving father. That he had also been a man who had loved many women, not all of them his wife, was a matter of public gossip in his little estate in the east of France and in Paris. In the capital city, he kept his grand *hôtel particulier* and a smaller house on the rue du Four. That townhouse he had purchased for his last and favorite mistress, Madeleine de Massé, the sister of his wife and the widow of his brother. By Madeleine, whom he always claimed was the love of his life, he had wished to sire males. His ambition was not so much to get a boy who would inherit, because under French inheritance laws, a bastard could never do so. But the vicomte wished to prove his manhood by getting a boy from Madeleine. The lady loved him and did not care he used her for a broodmare. Alas, by his wife, his other women, and by Madeleine, only females were his progeny.

Of the three children, Tate considered Diane, second born, the wisest and drollest. Charmaine, the eldest, self-indulgent and mean. Vivienne, the daughter of the vicomte and Madeleine, naturally disarming and, yes, vivacious.

Awash in the memories of that first day Tate met them all, he took up his glass of brandy and allowed himself a generous draught. Vivi, as he had called her when she was younger, was all energy as a child. Her mother had adored her. Her father had held her up—to Diane's agreement and Charmaine's envy—as a model of fealty. Spirited, inquisitive, industrious, loving her dogs and her animals, Vivi enjoyed her childhood on her father's lands. The revolution had robbed her of that—and so much else.

But Vivi had blossomed in England. Free of the fear of attack by rabble, she took to the care of the family cottage and the nurturing of her animals. She sewed, she knitted, she cleaned and cooked. Charmaine exerted herself very little. Vivi cared for their mother, who was increasingly despondent and later crippled, body and soul, by what terror she'd witnessed. Through it all, Vivi grew into a favorite among the Cantrell tenants. A favorite of his.

Now as an adult, his Vivi had grown into her fullness, exquisitely lovely with that rippling river of platinum-blonde hair and sapphire eyes, a graciousness of form and function that could make a man weep to hold her.

That she should now be considering some sinister act was totally against her character. With all that had happened to her family, Tate could identify causes for retribution. Yet that was more than ten years ago. So much had changed in Paris since then. Many had died. Of disease, despair, chaos, and war. He hated that she would indulge in it.

But whom would she hurt?

The list was short. Two people seemed a paltry number, given the enormity of the trauma they had suffered that night in ninety-two, before and afterward. He was certain there might be more who were complicit in the arrest of the Vicomte de Neufchateau and the attempted capture of all in his family. Many Tate could never name, let alone trace.

One he knew was dead. Alfonse Jarre, the banker, had called in the vicomte's loans and created such a scandal about it that the Committee of Public Safety put Neufchateau on their condemned list. The vicomte had decided his family should leave France, and he would see them off himself before he fled somewhere else—he told no one where. But the committee and their gendarmes were dogged in their search, found him north of Paris, and hauled him back to the guillotine.

The other person Tate remembered whom Viv might want was the former scullery maid who worked in the house of the rue du Four. The young woman had taken to offering herself to men. One Tate thought may have been a gendarme. Told by the majordom to rid herself of him, the maid did not. And to now find the least important servant who worked in the house ten years ago would be most difficult. Was the woman still in Paris? Was she even alive? Who would know?

Aside from those two, who might Viv want? He did not know.

But he would try to learn. For Viv to ponder their destruction was nigh unto laughable. Yes, certainly she portrayed herself as an actress. Worse, she dubbed herself as her older sister, a virago. An exact opposite, black to white, up to down.

Still Viv had somehow insinuated herself into Charmaine's life as an actress. Whether Viv had worked in London as Charmaine, he had no idea. But here in the Théâtre de la Gaîté, Viv received sterling reviews for her performances. That, he attributed to her love of books, an odd combination of cookbooks, medicinal books, and plays. Furthermore, Viv had managed her charade to date because she was far from London.

Yet like him, some canny person could spot the differences. Many British came to Paris to enjoy the sights. One discerning person could see that off stage Charmaine de Massé was too sweet, too charming, too selfless to be real. They would ask. They could probe. Their curiosity might lead them to search for Charmaine.

But Tate had no idea what the two sisters had contrived.

Or was he suspecting too much? Was Charmaine not involved in Viv's scheme? He could not imagine otherwise. Viv was never one to plot deception.

Why now?

Why here?

The only answers he had were obvious ones. Viv did this now because of the treaty. She had Talleyrand's approval and could cross the border into Paris freely. She'd not been able to do that prior to this. But then, Tate knew her strength of will—and the immense challenges she had lived with all her life.

The odd thing was, until the age of twenty-one, when last he saw her, she had accepted what she had lost with a stately equanimity far beyond her years. She built a life for herself in the cottage on his estate. With her animals around her, she sold eggs and butter. She wrote little instructions on housekeeping she intended for new wives. Though she had not yet secured a publisher, she planned for it and kept writing. She wanted to be known as an English lady who wrote useful articles by which young women learned efficiencies and found satisfactions in their daily lives. *Fine Ways to Run a Household*, she titled her works. "A loving home will sustain a person through all vicissitudes of life," she had often said.

She had made her own loving home, even if her mother and Charmaine could not or would not appreciate it. And though Viv accepted *what* she had lost—land, home, money—she had taken years to accept *whom* she had lost.

Tate understood that. Terrorists had taken her father. Illness and heartbreak had felled her mother. A mob had captured Diane. He, who had been her friend, however, had disappeared from her life the day he was forced to marry another for money.

He had never become more to her, not because he did not wish it. Since she was sixteen, he had wished for her in his arms as his wife. But his father and his debts and his diabolical negotiations with an heiress's father had cast him from Viv's life from that day forward. Irredeemably.

The knowledge roiled him.

He downed the last of his brandy and stood. But none of that, he vowed, would block him from trying to save her from herself. Or regain her good graces.

Or kill his love for her.

Chapter Six

S HE SET HER mare to a walk. The mid-April morning was bright and gay. Would that she were able to absorb that. Acting required more than she ever knew. She preferred to be herself, by God. Some people could remain who they were all the time. Look at her surly groom. Crabby, no nonsense, spiffy attire, the smell of soap, a pistol at his waist, Fortin was up and working. The man had an approach to the world that worked for him. Would that she could imitate him.

She let out a laugh. Hair loose, stern face, well dressed, good cologne—she felt powerful with a pistol that Fortin had been so kind as to purchase for her in her saddlebag. She was happy at last night's success with one search. Her frequent evenings at Cyprien Montagne's house had not yet yielded his two distant cousins, the new administrators of Jarre Bank. But she had information. One by the name of Sylvain, said the gossip sheets, was in the country. The other was ill.

She'd get one of them sooner or later.

She rejoiced too Vaillancourt had not attended any of those entertainments at Cyprien's house. The man, according to the gossips, was busy at home cultivating a stubborn woman to become his mistress. Whoever she was, she could have him. Vaillancourt made her flesh crawl.

Viv trotted ahead, smiling, loving her solitude. But at the far corner, just as a carriage turned, her peace dissolved. And lo unto her, Tate sat atop his horse. The man sprang up everywhere! And not just out here on her morning rides, either. The theater, the soirees she attended, even Cyprien's!

Drat his persistence. She had summoned enough gumption to add a new feature to her investigations this morning. With him beside her, however, she would not go. He'd hector her about her reasons, and she would not hear the end of it.

"*Bonjour*, monsieur. Do you never rest?" She went on, never stopping for him, as they took the shady Champs-Élysées.

Good humor was his hallmark, ease in his own skin the element that gave him levity and popularity. "I am well, thank you. How was your visit to Madame Récamier's salon last night?"

The beautiful and impertinent lady who had made short hair and simple toga-style gowns the Parisian fashion was married to one of Napoleon's favorite bankers. The first consul rarely liked men of money, so this affection was one both Récamiers worked to their benefit. Known for her lavish soirees, Julie Récamier was one whose invitation one did not refuse. To appear in her salon was to ensure one became at once the talk of the town.

"I was honored to be invited." Viv clicked her tongue to her mare and rode on.

Her groom politely dropped back in deference.

"As was I," Tate said when he caught up to her.

She gave in to the need to look him over. He looked marvelous for so early in the day. He'd complemented his charcoal-gray habit this morning with a bronze waistcoat edged in gold passementerie. His robust complexion was a glory. She wanted to brush her fingers across his ruddy cheeks and sink them into his wind-blown locks. The man had always looked like a colorful feast. He was delectable.

You cannot lick him today, Viv. She glanced away.

"I noticed you spoke with a certain banker last night," he stated.

She knew it was a question. Armand Vernon of the Bourse was an older man who last night came without his wife. The pleasant fellow was no lech when alone—and he was also of no help to Viv. "So I did."

"Do you take up only with financiers?" He smiled, but his expression was strained.

She gave him a leveling look. He had no right to judge her. She'd trade barb for barb. "Did I rob you of time with him?"

He grinned. His lips, rich and full, formed words that lured her from her aggravation with him. "You rob me of more than that. Well you must know it."

He sounded like a suitor. She wrestled down her foolish hope. "Good. Keeps you on your toes."

"Tell me your secrets, *ma petite*, and I will cease and desist."

"Ha!" she burst out. "That, I cannot afford."

He trotted close. "Then you are stuck with me."

She turned to argue with him, but he urged his horse to a stop. Then, with a tip of his hat, he bade her good day.

Surprised at his early departure, she admitted to herself she was relieved, but disappointed that she could not spar with him. She brightened, choosing the better of her plans.

"Come, we return to the stables," she said to her groom.

What she needed to do should best be done soon, when the street markets were open. She'd also go on foot for this expedition. She had to take the chance that Tate was done stalking her for today.

For this, she wanted to go alone.

As THE SUN rose in the sky toward nine in the morning, Viv strolled her neighborhood street market near the old abbey. She had ordered her personal maid Alice to her work, and instead called for one footman and her kitchen maid, Suzette, to follow.

The footman and the young maid were Parisians. The maid would provide the cover of knowing precisely what was needed to be purchased for the day's menus—and how to haggle the price of it.

Viv had come this way on foot only twice before this day. She had tried to walk the street ever since she settled into her house in March, but had postponed it. Curiosity had finally overcome her. She wished to see her former home.

Only twice this past week had she and the maid walked in front of the house. Both times Viv forced herself to behold the house for one more minute than the last. Here in the shelter of a shop doorway, she was away from any audience.

Here she did not have to pretend she was anyone other than who she was. In her bones, she was slow to vengeance. She knew that of herself. So she pardoned herself for her tenderness and delay. She would take her vengeance in her own time. Her own way. Heartened, she did not hide the tears that welled in her eyes now as she gazed upon the front door.

A flash of Tate's expression grinning at her this morning buoyed her. He would applaud her coming here. That had her smiling as she paused directly across from the house where she once had laughed and frolicked.

The five-story townhouse looked in good repair. How it had survived the assault of rioters who looted and burned so much of the city, she did not know. But it had good moldings on the windowpanes. All were intact. The creamy Parisian stone looked worn, but then, the house was more than one hundred years old. The stone on the street level had been washed lately. She would be proud to live here. Had been happy to do so...until that horrible night when all went wrong.

"*Mademoiselle?*" asked Suzette. "You like this house?"

"I do, Suzette." *I do.*

"Do you wish to see it? Inside? It is to let."

"Is it really?" Viv saw no sign in the front window. "How do you know?"

"My mama is a friend of the majordom who is the caretaker. If you wish, I can rap upon the door and ask?"

"No, no. I have no desire to take a lease. I like our house. Very much."

Suzette, like all her staff, knew her family history. Viv had read the stories herself in the gossip sheets. The trials and tribulations of the French actress Charmaine de Massé were often reported. Her servants might not know the full of the tragedy that occurred there, but it was enough for Suzette to wonder if Viv might wish to take over the house.

"I could introduce you, the famous actress of the ancient Massé family. Anyone would be proud to allow you to walk through, mademoiselle."

Viv wavered, her lips parting in eager anticipation.

The girl's blue eyes mellowed as she read Viv's expression. "I can do it, mademoiselle. Shall it be now?"

"*Oui*, now." *Before I lose my nerve.*

The young woman crossed the cobbles. Her basket, full of tiny potatoes and spring asparagus, swung with the sway of her hips.

The motion mesmerized Viv. Courage was a delicate cat, lured by peace, inspired by rabid desires.

The maid stepped up to the door and pulled at the filigreed iron-worked bell. She paused, glancing back at Viv, then smiling.

But minutes passed.

Suzette rang again.

No one came.

Viv nibbled her lower lip.

What would she do here, anyway? Survey what was left? Cry that the house was empty? Gasp that the Jarre family had retained Mama's furnishings—or destroyed them as cruelly as they had all in the family?

Viv hurried to her maid and took her arm. "Another day, we will return. Another time."

FLUMMOXED, TATE LEFT Viv that morning and, instead of going home, steered his horse to rue Saint-Honoré. Kane would be up—he rose early. His wife, Augustine, was great with child and would not be able to receive anyone for quite a while. Kane and Tate would break their fast together, as they often did.

Tate also knew that Godfrey, Lord Ramsey, was at odds and ends lately. He did not sleep well and often joined Kane and Tate for breakfast. The reason for Ram's insomnia was one Tate had recently learned quite by accident.

Ram was recently estranged from Madame Saint Antoine. Tate had not known that night in February, when they were all at the theater, that the reason for Ram's odd behavior was due to the despair Ram felt at the loss of the lovely widow whom he adored. Their breakup was not recent, but it left a vast crack in Ram's heart.

Work offered Ram many salves. Tate went about his with a similar lack of zest. Kane offered advice to his two friends with their professional worries and a respite from personal ones.

Tate looped his reins around the iron fence outside the door to Kane's house and stepped up to pull the knocker.

Kane's majordom, a resourceful Florentine named Corsini, promptly appeared and welcomed Tate inside. "I'll have our groom see to your horse, my lord. Allow me to show you to the library. Lord Ramsey waits there too. Lord Ashley will attend you both shortly."

Once there, Tate was startled when Ram took one look at him and his expression fell.

"Not happy to see me?" Tate joked.

"Not that at all, my friend."

"What bothers you?" Tate watched Ram as he walked toward the window and clasped his hands behind his back. "From the look on your face, I'd say it is not that our ambassador and

Bonaparte continue to carve each other up for dinner lately."

"Not that, no." Ram faced him. His cerulean-blue eyes flared wide, the wry humor about politics dying as something more disturbing replaced it. "Something has come to my attention lately. I have time on my hands…and I reminisce more than I should. I really should have put the pieces of this issue together for you long before this, but I have been, shall we say…distracted?"

"Very well." Tate took a chair, comfortable to be in such old, familiar company. Whatever it was, he trusted Ram. "It cannot be that bad."

"I have no idea. You must promise to tell me."

"Anything." Tate lifted a hand. "Let's hear it."

"It occurs to me that I know a few things that you should. The whole matter may be of no import to you. But we work in puzzles and missed chances. It might be useful."

"Go on." Tate reached for the coffee service Corsini must have provided earlier for the morning meeting.

"I am in my own house lately in rue d'Orleans. This is the one I let when Kane and I first arrived here last April. Soon after that, I left Paris to search for Madame St. Antoine."

Tate knew how the lovely redhead had disappeared from Paris for many months. She had left the city early last spring. When she returned in July, she came with Ramsey but soon parted from him. Ram, who had never married and never shown any permanent interest in a woman, had cared for Madame St. Antoine with an undying passion. Kane had told Tate the story, not to spread tales but to inform him of Ram's occasional dismal moods. The full story of Ram's affection for the lady was not one Tate wished to press either friend to reveal. Ram, usually so forthcoming on any matter, had never shared much about his *tendre* for Madame St. Antoine—and Tate knew him well enough not to intrude, nor to embarrass him by asking.

Ram turned toward him. "I accompanied Madame St. Antoine for a few weeks last spring in her journeys in the countryside. Last summer, we returned to Paris, as she and I both had reason to report here."

That was new information to Tate. Was Ram implying that Madame St. Antoine was an agent? For Kane? Or for someone else? Surely she would work for the Crown or some entity opposed to the Consulate, else Ram would not have, as he obviously had, fallen in love with the woman.

"For a while, we lived in a house in Saint Germain. Near the abbey. On the rue du Four."

Tate regarded Ram with new interest.

"It was once the home of the Vicomte de Neufchateau, one he purchased for one of his mistresses. Often, he lived there with his whole family instead of in his mansion on the right bank."

The hair on Tate's neck rose. The house on rue du Four was the very one he himself had lived in with the Massé family before he accompanied the women in their flight from the city—before the vicomte fled Paris, was caught, and returned to it. The mistress for whom the old vicomte bought the house was Vivi's mother, Madeleine. "I know it well."

Ram flourished a dismissive hand, appearing as if he thought Tate's stillness implied the house meant little to him. "In any case, after Neufchateau was chased down and sent back to Paris and the guillotine, the banking family Jarre bought the house from the government."

At the mention of the family who were related to that roué Cyprien Montagne, Tate sat forward. He did not like the alarm that rang in his ears. "The committee confiscated the properties of those they condemned to death."

"They did."

"The house could be used as government property or sold to private citizens who had enough money. The Jarre family wanted the prestige of owning such a house. The vicomte even complained that Monsieur Jarre told him that," Tate went on, remembering how the vicomte disliked the resentful, gray-haired banker. He frowned, angry that he had not thought of the Jarre connection to Montagne. But Viv had been to Montagne's house often. He'd seen her, been there too. Three times now, she had flirted with the danger that Montagne might hurt her. Drug her. Rape her.

But going nonetheless…so that what? That she might cultivate Cyprien? Or come across the old man Alfonse, who'd testified against the vicomte? Tate was fairly certain he'd read the little bugger was dead.

He rose slowly.

Ram went on, apology in his manner. "I only lately recalled that you told me years ago some of this story of how you'd been here in Paris and had to run from the Paris gendarme. But you seemed too devastated to talk about it in detail—and I never asked specifics."

"It's true I was disturbed about it and did not wish to speak of it. Only lately did I tell Kane more about what happened here in ninety-two." Tate needed more information. "What else do you know about the house? Those who own it?"

"The caretaker for the family acts as the majordom. A good man. Fair and kind. I liked him. Might you wish to talk to him?"

"I might," Tate said, speculating what niggled at the edge of his memory. Why would he meet the majordom? To learn of his connections to the Jarre family? Find old Alfonse's young successor before Viv did? If she even wanted him at all!

Ram tipped his head in consideration of Tate's thoughtfulness. "If you wish an introduction, I could do it."

Tate nodded. "Yes. Yes, I might. What is his name?"

"Gaspard."

"I do not know it."

"He never mentioned being related to the Jarres. Only employed by them," Ram said.

Tate nodded. "Not unusual. These townhouses on the left bank were not as elaborate as the mansions on the right bank. But still they are fine edifices, some untouched by mobs and standing with all their fine furniture intact." Many of them, whether owned by the government or vacant, needed the careful touches of those who knew when a roof needed repair or a cellar cleared of rats. "To withstand the tests of time, the houses need experts to look after them properly, and so many of the old retainers were carted off to Madame Machine or were frightened off."

"Let me know if you wish to go. Mademoiselle de Massé, too," Ram offered. "I'd be happy to do that for you."

Tate pondered whether Viv would wish to visit. But why would she? It would be a walk through the hell of her last days in Paris. Wouldn't it?

But such an act might jar her to give him further evidence of what she did here in Paris.

Her "retribution" sounded dark. And such evil was never in her nature. He knew what terrible consequences a human could inflict on another when retribution was the goal. His wife Belinda, may God rest her soul, had earned all the evil from her own acts of revenge. He did not want Viv to suffer that, and hoped he might save her the sorrow.

Going to the house might then be a sound venture. It might soothe her. Restore her equanimity.

Or spur her on.

Chapter Seven

CRITICIZING HERSELF FOR her ridiculous fright at viewing her former home yesterday, Viv went with Suzette and the footman the next morning to market, then directly to the house.

The maid knocked again, and once more, no one came to the door.

"Perhaps he is away, mademoiselle."

"I will leave my card," Viv told her, and fished out from her reticule her silken card case and small pencil. She wrote upon the back of the good parchment of her desire to view the interior and ended with, *Please respond.* She expected that anyone would know where to find her rented house. The gossips published everything else. Her smooth, low voice, her penchant for *vin blanc* and chocolate. Even the hated fans.

Resigned to the lack of response from the majordom, Viv led the maid for home in the rue du Bac. The sun was bright, air fresh, their baskets filled with new white asparagus and fresh lettuce from the street *vendeurs*. All in all, still a good day. But as they paused before a window of Viv's favorite patisserie, she noticed in the reflection of the glass that a tall fellow also paused.

She thought little of it. Sometimes she was recognized in the streets. Most were respectful and stayed away. A few ventured forward to introduce themselves and praise her work at the theater. Those people were, for the most part, women out shopping with their maids. Unusual, but nonetheless, it happened. They tended to be well dressed and mannerly. Viv had no problems with their approach or praise.

But this man did neither. He dallied as long as she did.

"Let's go inside," she told Suzette. "I've a desire for a small gateau. Cook has so much to do to prepare for our afternoon reception today, she'll have less to bake for our guests."

In the shop, Viv took her time. The apple tarts were of a thousand delicate puffed pastry layers. The tiny creme-filled shortbreads were iced a bright pink today. She sailed around the shop, glimpsing her follower now and then as he lounged on the corner. Crossing and uncrossing his arms, he seemed to give the appearance of one who was lost—or bored. But when she and Suzette emerged, Viv led them down a parallel street to home.

Few walked this lane, and so she could hear the man's footsteps on the cobbles.

At a wine shop, Viv paused, and so did her man.

She could not lose him. She did not try. She led her maid home and, inside, gave her cloak to her majordom and asked both to remain a minute. "I must speak with you." She beckoned them toward the window to the street. "Stand away from the drapes. You see this man in dark blue with black top hat?"

The fellow was so silly—yet so helpful—as to remain on the corner, and within sight of her house.

"Note his looks." Swarthy coloring. A morning's growth of beard already, at half nine. Large, dark eyes. "He followed us from the market today. If he appears again, you must write down when and how long he observes us. Notify others in the house to his looks so they are aware if they are followed by him too. Come to tell me of every instance."

They both agreed.

"I will not countenance any of us being threatened."

⇒⟫⟫⟩⟨⟨⟪⟪⇐

HOURS LATER, READY for her first afternoon guests, Viv decided she had concentrated on her shadow long enough.

Whoever he was, she did not know him and had not met him. He was dressed as a gentleman, one with enough means to be clean and pressed but not *à la mode*. Who he was, why he tracked her, she had no idea. If he was a curious theatergoer, all well and good. Instinct said that he followed her for a reason. Yet he did not attack her. Not like those ruffians on the road near Rouen. She now had done what she should and made her staff aware of him. That was the whole of it.

At her resolve, she nodded to herself in the mirror and allowed Alice the last touches to her hair. Little rouge today was necessary because of the effects of the glorious pale pink of her new gown. The décolleté was discreet, fit for midday. She had no need to flaunt her proportions during daylight hours. In truth, she had no wish to display them at night, either. But then, for those invited today, she might still catch a fish.

She rose before her dressing table, heading for her sitting room and the hall when Alice called her back.

"Your fan, mademoiselle?"

"I don't need it, Alice."

The maid smiled and pressed her lips together in that look which said she knew better. "You always have it to hand when you entertain."

"Ah." *Do I? Drat.* "So many details."

The maid had been with Charmaine for three years and knew every nuance of the actress's habits. Fans in public, silk chemises, fine gloves to match gowns, cognac in her morning coffee, men, certain men, demanding but discreet, with specific sexual appetites. None of those delights had ever been counted among Viv's particular joys.

She held out her hand for the fan. *"Merci beaucoup, Alice."*

"De rien," said the young servant politely. During her tenure, Alice had learned some French from her mistress, and for this venture to Paris, she had agreed to accompany Viv. She knew only that Viv was to take Charmaine's place here in France and that she was to go with Viv everywhere and ensure her safety. That was all the maid had been told.

Viv took her staircase down to her first-floor salon. The house on rue du Bac was a four-story townhouse built decades later than her former family home on rue du Four. Rented by the theater manager for Charmaine on her written instructions, the house was completely furnished. Charmaine had required a house ready to be used as an abode and as a place of entertainment. She required a staff to manage the place. Thus Viv had a butler or majordom, *châtelaine*, footman, housemaid, cook, scullery maid and Suzette, the kitchen maid.

She entered the salon and inhaled the drama of its appointments. Surrounded by pale green walls, the gilded ivory furniture was from the last century. In various shades of green to darker jades, the upholstered settees and chairs grouped together to enhance conversation. Viv preferred her little cottage gathering room to all this folderol, even though she admired its beauty.

"Is it all to your liking, mademoiselle?" Her majordom hovered by the threshold. An older gentleman of pleasing personality, Monsieur Allard Franck was a chubby little man devoted to his work. Her staff ran happily on his every word, and efficiently too. She could not say the same for her châtelaine, Madame Clery, who had few words and no smiles.

"Indeed, Franck. Please thank Cook and the staff for the array of dishes. I am certain the French will admire the pastry and the British the creams."

"We expect eleven today, mademoiselle."

"A full drawing room. Wonderful." She clasped her hands together. "List for me once more those who have responded."

He began with the ladies who had accepted. Two were wives of Bonaparte's generals, another a widow of a French *comte* who had been a friend of her father's. The last were a mother (also a widow) and daughter, both a lively part of this year's social circle and both in search of husbands. The others were men, many married, others not. Most she had invited because they held high government posts and indulged in Society events to garner useful gossip. They knew how to carry a decent conversation, little of which focused on themselves. One was a dashing young widower, a vintner whose estate was in the Loire valley. Viv liked Luc Bechard and had invited him because he injected life and color into any salon he entered. She planned to go to Luc this afternoon if her conversation with Cyprien Montagne became difficult.

"A good mix for today," she told Franck. She fluttered the damn fan. For once she felt natural using it.

She had no reason to be anxious. The afternoon began well, everyone enjoying the diversity of company, the wine an added aid to conversation. Cyprien Montagne took his time attempting to get her alone today. Perhaps he did not attempt to seduce women when the sun shone. Truth was, the man had invited her to three of his dinner parties and to two of his entertainments. She had attended all, heaven help her. Each time he had become even bolder, alluding to his desire to become more than friends. If she could ignore him, she would. Alas, she needed to be in his house and his company if she were ever to chance upon the likes of the Jarre brothers.

"Excuse me, mademoiselle." Franck appeared before her. He looked perturbed.

"Is there a problem, monsieur?"

"If I might have a word, *s'il vous plaît?*" He nodded toward the hall.

She strolled with him.

"We have an uninvited guest at the door, mademoiselle. I understand he is a family friend, but I hesitate to admit him. He insists you will welcome him."

Though she suspected who this bold person might be, she

asked who he was. She need not have. She did not have Franck bar him. Nor did she scold herself at that weakness so much as welcome the relief he brought by his presence. Tate represented such an old touchstone of safety that, no matter how she wished him gone, she could not rob herself of the assurance of his company.

"I see, Franck. Do welcome Monsieur le Comte upstairs. I know him quite well, and I think he is acquainted with many here."

Tate had evidently mounted the stairs right behind her man. Tate came strolling in, joyous in his coup, looking superb in stamped sapphire wool frock coat and Pomona-green silk waistcoat. Making her heart sing, he brought such light and air into her day.

"You are happy to see me," he said with a roguish smile, and bent close to kiss her hand.

"You flatter yourself, sir." She tossed off the allure of the lush touch of his lips to her skin and sent him a spirited lift of her brows. "Hungry?"

"Famished." His gaze devoured hers.

"Come have your fill," she said with a laugh. He was a man for suggestive conversations.

"I intend to."

She swallowed her guffaw as she walked with him to her buffet. "What will you have?"

He stilled, his blue eyes with those bright green shards absorbing her. "Everything." He cleared his throat. "I am here to save you."

"From myself?"

"And any who would carry you away."

His chivalrous words made her heart beat faster. Ever had he been her knight. "None from my own home, surely."

"Some"—he paused and found Cyprien paces away—"are wily."

She should not succumb to his endearments, and so she countered, "Do you not have serious work to do?"

Her footman appeared and offered him a flute of *vin blanc*.

He took it and raised the glass to honor her. "I am here, doing it. But I admit that I have challenges with my work, as few of my counterparts want to do business. I am often dismissed as if my cravat is too simple."

She examined the elaborate twists and twirls of his blinding white neckcloth. "They are fools. My compliments to your valet." Her gaze drifted up to the caress of his large eyes.

He drank, his lips moving with sensuous appeal, his tongue darting out, wet and intriguing. "And mine to you."

His words hung in the air like gentle kisses.

At last she roused. "Shall I introduce you…?"

"I care not for anyone else."

"Tate," she managed, as her whole being flooded with the desire his bass voice imparted, "you are here to be sociable. Conduct business, *oui*?"

"No. I am here only for you. To protect you from…anyone. And to invite you to come with me to rue du Four."

She blinked. That was the last thing she thought he'd say to her. "What? Why?"

"Don't you wish to go?"

"But…yes." Did he know she'd been there? She'd seen him following her on occasion, and he admitted it, so…

"I want to go, too, Vi—mademoiselle."

"To relive it?" She quickly tried to cover his near mistake.

He noticed a movement of others toward them. "Yes. I think it best. And I have news of it."

"News?" she asked just as Cyprien Montagne joined them.

"*Bonjour*, Monsieur le Comte. Good to see you."

"And you, monsieur."

Cyprien had already greeted Viv when he arrived, and so the conversation among them easily passed to lighter topics. Her cook's pastries. Attendance at her performances. Bonaparte's increasing antipathy toward the accomplished British ambassador, Whitworth, and his tirade against the man in public a few nights in a row lately.

"It worries me," Tate said. "This peace is fragile, but it can offer us so much if we can agree on increasing commerce between our countries. Don't you agree, monsieur?"

"I think, monsieurs," Viv said with a grin, "much as I love a good discussion of money, I leave you to discuss trade and shall attend to my guests."

TWO HOURS LATER, her receptions completed, the guests drifted out. Tate had whispered he would adjourn to another room to talk. She'd told him to ask Franck for her small sitting room. Behind Tate came the last to leave, Cyprien.

Ever gallant—and opportunistic—he lifted her hand and pressed his cool lips to the back. "*Merci beaucoup*, mademoiselle, for the afternoon. I have enjoyed myself very much."

"I am delighted, monsieur. Please come again. I shall do this each Monday. I love good company."

"As do I, mademoiselle. I give my annual masquerade in a few weeks. I have sent my invitations this morning and a special one to you, but this is my personal one." He put her palm flat to his cravat and held her there. The intimacy revolted her. "Come, *s'il vous plaît*. I know it is an evening when the theater is lit. Come after your performance. You will add such beauty to the party."

"You are kind. Is there a theme?"

"The glories of Rome." His beady eyes blazed with mischief.

She tipped her head—a real ingenue could not appear more naïve. "That calls for a simple gown of cream."

"Draped supplely over your perfect curves, mademoiselle."

A hand to her cheek to hide her anxiety, she feigned joy at the compliment and gushed, "Now, monsieur, you must go home, lest my complexion become a permanent blush."

She waited until she heard the last of Cyprien's remarks to Franck drift up the stairs. Then she headed down the hall to her small salon. In a brief conversation, she'd told Tate to find the room as others began to leave the house.

She hurried along the hall, bypassing the staircase down, eager to see Tate and hear why he too wished to go to the house in rue du Four.

TATE SAT IN a chair reading, little Louis snuggled into him, draped over his thighs. She liked this room. Cozy with only two chairs and a chaise longue, it had one wall of bookshelves. The tiny room was made for one who liked to read. Viv spent much of her free time here. She was filled with a sense of déjà vu seeing Tate in a cozy chair with her little pet. Tate and she had always shared a love of books, plays, and animals.

As she walked in, Tate got to his feet. Louis scrambled to find a new comfortable position in the chair.

"Don't you always marvel how animals remember people?" she said, proud of her pet.

"Those who love remember who loved them, no matter the years that have passed."

His words felt like a reprimand of her recent behavior toward him. Unsettled, she sought to bring him to the issue at hand. She sat on the chaise longue. "Why do you wish to go to rue du Four?"

"It would be helpful to remember—"

"Those who loved us no matter the years that have passed?"

"That," he said, his rich jade gaze examining her with sweetness, "and what happened that night."

She sucked in a breath. "I have not forgotten a thing."

He gazed at her long and hard as if to question that, then took the space beside her. "Are you certain?"

"I do not forget the who, what, and how of that night."

His thigh warmed hers. His words were a tender balm against the chill of remembrance. "I recall the color of your gown."

"Blue with tiny white stripes."

"Diane's was—"

"Green," she said with distaste. "Emerald muslin."

"You and Diane reined in Charmaine."

She tipped her head. "The speed with which you jumped from the carriage to get Diane."

His jaw flexed. "You mean the way I failed. The way the gendarmes hurried her away to a waiting tumbril. Diane was so brave, cursing them, angry. They knew her name. Her full name."

Viv caught her breath. "They called her by name?"

"They did."

"I didn't remember that! How could they know it?"

"I have asked myself that for ten years. Our own carriage was hired. We had no escutcheon on the door."

She was confounded. "We were four women in that carriage with you. Mama, yes. But who would know we three girls?"

He nodded. "Two who looked exactly alike…"

"Charmaine and me. But Diane was the one who was different. Not blonde, but with copper hair."

"None of you wore fine clothes," he said.

"On the contrary—Charmaine wore her pearls," Viv said with distaste.

"And sat on her gold Louis," he added, "like a queen on her throne."

"She didn't have all her gems," Viv said, bitter about her sister's never-ending greed.

"She kept harping on that. Even your mother did not pine for jewelry that day."

"No. Just my father. That's all she wanted." And would never have him near her again.

"I am surprised," Tate said with a frown, "you have not gone to the house before this."

"No. I—I've been busy. It takes time and energy."

He stared at her with sorrow in his gaze.

But he did not ask once more why she did this. For that, she was grateful. The assurance of his presence flowed over her. "I do want to go to the house, Tate. If you come with me, we can recall more than if going alone."

He took up her hand and put it to his lips.

She grew melancholy. "Do you think the majordom will let us in?"

"I do. A friend of mine whom you have not met rented the house months ago. He knows the current caretaker."

She nodded, eager now and relieved to go. "So too does one of my maids."

Tate drew her closer. "We are resolved, then."

His hold on her sent rivers of remembrance through her, of other days and nights when he had touched her. All in friendship. "We are."

He stood, her hand still in his. "Tomorrow, then? After we ride?"

She laughed, happy he would join her and thrilled he did not let go of her hand. She got to her feet. "Why not?"

"Why not, indeed." He stood too near, his scent too alluring.

She sought to recall her training as Charmaine. Her older sister would never allow a man she did not want so close. "On...on second thought, not after we ride. All of that is so public."

"You worry others may hear of it?"

I wonder if my shadow may find it interesting. "Yes. Gossips will read of it, remark and make us into lovers."

"We know who we are," he murmured, and those memories of long ago rose up to draw her gaze to his lips, her fingers to curl in want of him. "We will appear to be two old friends who make a journey together to the past." He put his other hand to her cheek. "The present can be so much more fulfilling than the past."

She pulled back. "Can it?" *I find it more terrifying.*

"To be together once more, it will. Give us the chance."

"Why?" To be with him once more created so many problems. She could not succumb to his charm, and she took a step around him.

He caught her wrist. "When I went to find you on the estate last June and you were gone, I left a letter. You did not answer."

"I did not know you were in England, nor that you came to see me. I...I have not returned to my cottage since last spring." That was true. But did she tell him too much? Reveal in her tone how her heart ached to learn this now? Now, of all miserable times, when the admission changed nothing.

"I long to tell you now what I wrote in my letter."

Her gaze flashed up to seize his. She should not ask. She should not want to know. But she did. "What did you write?"

"An apology."

"No, no apologies! You've given enough!"

"For the years I had to leave you, yes! For my father's demands. The marriage I could not postpone or annul or even end through divorce."

His marriage that showed her how she was so wrong for him. How she would never become his wife. "Tate, you are not responsible for what others have done."

"It made hell for us, for you, so yes! I will say this. All of it. All that kept me away. Now Belinda is dead, Vivi. I did what I must by all the rules of Society and I kept away from Norfolk and you for a year. It appeared I mourned her...but I do regret it was less than that."

Tears sprang to her eyes. She could not see him. But oh, she felt the iron bands of his embrace, the drum of his heart, the fine marble of his male form, and, yes, even his raw desire for her.

She clutched him. The man she'd adored since she was a girl. The man she'd admired and yearned for lo these many years. He was free now. A widower. A man untethered from the woman whom his father had chained him to with wealth untold and threats fantastic.

He lifted her face with both his hands. "I looked for you last spring because I wanted to tell you everything new and bright and possible then, but you were nowhere to be found. I went to George Farland."

The man whose proposal she'd once considered taking. A tenant of Tate's. A fine farmer. A fine man. One she could not marry because she did not love him. "Poor George."

Sorrow suffused Tate's manly features. "He did not know where you'd gone. I searched and found Charmaine in London. I caught her in her townhouse just as she was moving. But she said she did not know where you were."

Viv winced. Charmaine always knew where Viv was. But it was news to Viv that Tate had gone to Charmaine, asked for her, and her sister had turned him away with no details.

He thumbed her tears away. "I searched, my sweet Vivi. I wanted to tell you this. Tell you more. Everything I have wanted to say for years!"

Viv stared at him. Charmaine could not tell him last spring where Viv was, lest the news ruin their project. So of course Charmaine had turned Tate away with no information.

Tate's voice caught as he moved to embrace her. "But I have found you now. And I can say what I have wished to tell you for years. I value you. I admire you. I need you and I will not lose you again."

Overwhelmed, she caught her breath.

He took her lips. His were warm and firm. He parted hers with a brush of his tongue to the seam. He darted his tongue inside, claiming all of her.

And for once, she let him have her, for she would not, could not, deny him or herself. Her lips molded to his with all the years of longing for him gone with the pressure of one kiss, and two, and another. Her arms bound him closer.

On a gasp, he bore her down to the chaise, her back to the

silken damask, her legs open and his between hers. His kisses were stark and deep, fast and luxuriously wicked, his flesh searing hers.

This was what she had wanted from him since she was sixteen. She could not have enough now. His lips on hers. Her hands in his silken hair. His fingertips stroking her throat.

She gazed up at him, shocked she had him in such passion after so many lonely years. But she could not have him. Too much had changed.

She pressed her fingertips to his lips. "We must stop."

He shook his head. "No. Not now that we have each other again."

"We do not have each other." *Cannot now.*

He reared back on his elbows and shook his head. "Let me be clearer, then. Last year, when I came to tell you I was free, I came with a special license." He ran his fingers through the tendrils of her hair. "My darling, I came to marry you. I want you as my wife. I want you as my own."

She stared at him, proud of his choice, furious at her own. "I wish…I wish I'd been there. But I was not, and now…things have changed."

She'd fallen in love with him years ago. She was young, naïve, giving herself to fantasies, assuming she could have him. Thinking she was worthy, even though she was no one and poor. But his tenants suffered from his father's bad management with floods and fires, and famine too. The man demanded Tate marry a girl he'd never met. Viv had been left alone to survive her mother's creeping madness and death. To see Charmaine leave her with promises of fame and fortune and a prompt return. Viv had raised her chickens, ducks, pigs, and herbs. She'd confided her woes to kind old Fred, her donkey. She'd sold her eggs and chicks and herbal remedies. She'd survived alone.

And to learn that there could have been an end to her strife last spring was suddenly no salve to her wounds. She had gone from her little house, her friends and her animals and her herbs and garden. Left them to her purpose. Now she was committed here in this hellish city. Cursed, she must be, to have found some peace, only to be drawn back into chaos.

She pushed him away. "Stop. We must."

He slowly let her go. His features, awash in confusion, turned stern. "I will not."

"We have no future." She rose and brushed at her skirts. *Not with what I plan.*

He shot to his feet. The look in his eyes grew dark with longing as he encircled her waist with both arms. "We can take it now. Our path to happiness is clear for the first time in our lives. I adore you, Vivienne. Since you were young, I laughed with you, was at once proud of you, who you were and what you were. And this—this imitation of your sister is nothing you can easily do and get away with, because you are and always have been a terrible liar."

"You are wrong."

"I will prove it. Tomorrow morning," he said as he straightened his waistcoat and shot his cuffs, "we take our ride. Afterward we visit rue du Four."

He strode toward the door, then faced her. "We will face the past. Then we will see what the man who follows you thinks of that."

He knew about that man who stalked her! She opened her mouth to warn him off.

"Yes, I discovered him long ago, my darling. I have others following him to his den, wherever it is he hides. We will discover whom he works for. So we ride in security everywhere we go. Then, in hope for a brighter tomorrow afterward, we inspect rue du Four."

She set her jaw and would have argued.

"But I will hear no more denial of what we are to each other. None."

Chapter Eight

HER EUPHORIA AT Tate's declarations drifted away like the ripples in the Seine. She watched the river rush past as she took her town coach to the theater late that afternoon and admitted that she was overwhelmed with dread of what she now had to do.

Viv diverted herself with the task that had long eaten away at her. Now she must make haste. She had to prepare. Going to rue du Four was the first step.

She took the groom's hand and nearly leapt from the coach in her haste. Louis was tucked under her arm, wiggling to be let down.

Alice harrumphed and scurried along behind her into the backstage entrance door. The English maid was rigid in her daily chores, and when it was late afternoon, she preferred to sit and nap. Today, Viv had other plans.

Her nerves had been a jumble since her encounter with Tate earlier. The house was dark tonight, but she decided to go to the theater to talk with the manager. She had one thing in particular to discuss with the man. He'd delayed doing her a favor, and though she did not need the service immediately, she would soon. Since she had kissed Tate, she had to hurry her actions, find her marks. His presence everywhere all the time told her of his dedication to following her and discovering her plans. She also had to dampen her delight that Tate had come looking for her last year—and kill her anger that Charmaine had not told him where she was.

Was that another example of Charmaine's cruelty? Or had her sister been wise to deny Tate any knowledge of where she was? Viv went from one conclusion to the other.

By June of last spring, she and Charmaine had already decided on the outline of their plan. Viv was well on her way to impersonating her sister. She'd convinced the manager of the London theater where Charmaine had opened in a new production of *Romeo and Juliet* that she was indeed the acclaimed star who was known for her ethereal French beauty. She'd also convinced him that she would disappear each night into her own world—and her solitude had to be complete.

Charmaine retired to the country with another name and a new maid. Viv was launched as the star who would accept the offer to return to Paris and appear in the land of her birth in a play by Molière.

"Good afternoon, Giselle," Viv bade the house seamstress who sat at the rickety table near the backstage corridor. Alice trotted along behind her. "Is Monsieur Lamond in his office?"

The old woman raised her pinched gaze from the hem of a wine-red cloak she sewed. "*Oui, mademoiselle. Il est ivre comme un putois.*"

Drunk again? *Why am I not surprised?* "*Merci*, Giselle. You need more light to work on that cloak. Come, I will give you two more candles from my room."

"*Non, non. Ce n'est pas nécessaire, mademoiselle.*"

"It *is* necessary, Giselle. We'll do better than one candle. Come with me." She hooked her arm through the old woman's and lifted her up. The lady had a crooked posture and wobbled whenever she walked. If her feet and legs did not do well for her, neither did her weak eyes. She needed every bit of help she could get.

"Mademoiselle, *s'il vous plaît*. You go too fast for this old woman."

"My apologies. Alice, will you take Giselle's other arm and escort her to my room? Light all the candles for her. And yes, get Giselle's mending and let her do it in my dressing room."

Viv left them at the turn for Lamond's hideaway. He liked to be invisible. Actors, he claimed, wanted the moon, and he had only stardust to give. A frustrated thespian, the man gave speeches worthy of a candidate for prime minister. Viv had seen many in her day try for public office and counted them better actors than many she'd seen on stage.

Sidestepping the coiled ropes and stage furniture piled on top of the other, she maneuvered through the close hall to the back wall. At the left was a makeshift old door, which she rapped upon. "Monsieur Lamond?"

"Go away."

"It's Charmaine de Massé, monsieur."

He grumbled and groaned. "Wrong day, madame."

He always called her *madame*. She shook her head. "Monsieur, only a word, please."

He grumbled more. Then his door swung open on its creaky hinge. Ordinarily a good man to deal with, when drunk, he was a bore. "What might you want, eh?"

"Might I come in?"

He waved an arm in elaborate circles. "You're in now, *chatte*."

In his cups, he could be crude. She had no energy to chastise him, only to get what she needed. So she sat.

He put his jowly face near hers, pressing his lips together as he curled a brow and established that, indeed, this was the lady of the hour. "Not open tonight. Why're you here? Hmm?"

Her eyes watered at the sour alcohol on his breath. "I wondered, monsieur, if you been able to get any of those medicinals we spoke about?"

"Medicine. What?"

She cleared her throat. "You agreed to purchase for me a few tinctures at an apothecary you frequent."

He lowered both brows and let his tongue bathe his lower lip. "Hmmm. *Apothicaire?* Did I?"

"You said you knew of a good one in Place Royale."

"*Oui.* Not Royale. Vosges." He stood taller, his head bobbing as he scanned the walls of his littered cubbyhole.

Meanwhile, Viv was bitterly recalling that Bonaparte had changed the name of the famous Parisian square to the part of the country which had paid their taxes to keep up the Corsican's army. "The apothecary, monsieur? Did you see him and buy my—"

"No. Haven't"—he hiccuped—"seen him. Haven't."

She sighed, but smiled at him. "Perhaps if you were to give me his address?"

"Why not, eh? Wait. Don't go." He went to scribble on a loose scrap he had on his little desk. "Know a man came looking for you this morning?"

"No, I did not know. A patron, was he?"

"No. Didn't look it."

"No?" *Who, then?* "Why not, monsieur?"

"Not dressed. Very..."

She pressed her lips tighter at his hesitance. "Very what, Monsieur Lamond?"

He snarled his lip. "Gendarme, I'd guess. Sharp. Cagey. Off, I'd say."

"A city official looking to cite us for breaking some code?" She ventured at that because the government was known for suddenly deciding some play or newspaper or street vendor was infringing on new orders of banned topics. Bonaparte and his men pretended they were such freedom-loving republicans, when in fact they issued edicts ever more frequently limiting the rights of speech and publication.

Lamond wiggled his nose as he thought over her premise. "*Peut-être.*"

Maybe?

Her mind ran back to the fellow whom she discovered tracking her this morning. "What did he look like?"

"Black hair. Tall. Skinny as a pole."

Her fellow or not? "Did he leave his name?"

"No. No, no, no. Left like a bird." Lamond held out his slip of paper with the address of the apothecary.

"Merci beaucoup." She slid it from his shaking fingers and bade him adieu.

Collecting Alice and Louis, Viv climbed back into her waiting carriage. She'd only created more mysteries for herself coming here.

She glanced at Lamond's handwriting. *2 Blanc* was all he'd written.

Wonderful. What help was that?

TATE HAD NOT slept well, and the horse the stable master assigned him this morning was a massive stallion who had a mind of his own. Tate had long since given up training unruly animals—or men, for that matter. He left horses, cows, and pigs to those who knew how and what they needed. As for men, Tate believed he chose those who were his friends, male or female, with a shrewd eye to their ethics, and those who did not match his own were irrelevant to him.

But this horse this morning was under strict orders to mend his ways. The animal had already kicked up his hooves and affected a faster run than Tate anticipated. The horse almost unseated him. Which would have been a fine mess, if Tate had broken a leg. "Or my arse. So you see, sir, I have no time for your shenanigans. I am here to woo a lady who is most recalcitrant. If you will not help, I will walk you on a lead."

As if the brute understood, he shook his noble black mane and trod on like a gentleman.

Tate soon saw Viv turning off Pont Neuf toward him along the river. She wore a bright pink riding habit, trimmed in bold fuchsia. The little hat perched on one side of her head was a perfect adornment to her white-blonde hair and sublime complexion. Her blue eyes danced with wickedness when she saw him.

Had she thought well of what he had revealed yesterday? God, he hoped so. That event when he went to her cottage last year, found her gone without word among her friends of her destination, had left him bereft. Even Charmaine did not know where Viv had gone. Afterward, he'd accepted another set of secret assignments from Scarlett, if only to fill his mind and ignore the loss that could send him to the bottom of a whiskey bottle. And then a year later, on yet another assignment, to suddenly see Viv appear in Paris was a jolt to his system.

And now it was a benefit he would not waste.

She was here, for whatever reason. She had kissed him. More than once. She showed signs she had cared for him despite his failure with Diane.

He'd felt the power of her kiss, the eagerness of her fingers in his hair, her nipples hard and yearning against his chest. His Viv might be portraying her sister, but his darling did not feign her desire for him.

It was real. It was right. She could be his.

"Good morning, mademoiselle." He tipped his hat to her and, with a nod at the dour-faced groom riding behind Viv, smiled at the woman he adored. "A lovely day."

"Indeed," she bit off.

"Bad night?"

"Terrible."

"Wish to discuss it?"

"No."

"Very well."

They rode on past a few shops and greeted a few early morning riders. His horse made a few approaches to hers in what passed for his interest.

"Your horse," Viv said with a wrinkle of her brow, "likes my mare too much."

"He is incorrigible. I do apologize. He's given me a fit already this morning. The best I can do is tell you we should return to our stables and walk instead of ride."

"No walking," she said with a surreptitious glance to her far right.

He checked her view. Then the other side. "I see nothing untoward."

She swallowed and shook her head. "Good. About *him*," she said, and widened her eyes to emphasize whom she meant, "everyone in my house knows his description. I made them aware immediately."

"Wise." He gave another glance left, front, to the right. No one matched the fellow he had seen previously.

Viv slowed her horse. "He or someone has also been to the theater to inquire as to my whereabouts."

Tate bristled. "Who told you this?"

"The theater manager. In his cups, he was, but he retained enough sense to remember to tell me."

Tate noticed no one following her. No one loitering outside her townhouse. "So do you think he is the same fellow?"

"I'm not sure. The description the manager gave me left much to be desired."

He rode quietly for a few minutes. "Let's stop at that café ahead to our left."

She faced him, her pretty pink cheeks gone ashen. "I am afraid, Tate."

"Not to worry, my darling. I am with you. Let's stop and have a coffee and pastry, shall we? Then we'll look at anyone who may have more interest in our coffee than we do, eh?"

"LET'S GO," VIV told him minutes later. "I don't see him."

Tate checked on her groom. The man sat at another table, and the shake of his head told Tate he did not see anyone matching the description of the fellow.

Tate and Viv returned their horses and her groom Fortin to the stables, then continued down the thoroughfare toward rue du Four.

On their way, numerous pedestrians walked toward the abbey. As it neared the hour for morning mass, the bells tolled and the square was alive with the music of them.

"I never thought to see the likes of that again," Viv said to him as they passed the entrance to the church. "So many hated the priests and their hold over people. They killed hundreds of them so brutally that same day they came for us. How do they go to mass now? How can they pray for the souls of those gone before when in fact they destroyed them with knives and hatchets?"

Tate took her arm and pressed it through the crook of his elbow. He patted her hand. "Bonaparte opened the churches for masses months ago. He needs peace, and so do the people."

"They grew tired of their persecution, did they?" She scowled. "How good of them."

Tate understood how she could vilify those who had come for them that night years ago. "They missed their God and their reason to live."

She sniffed. "God has nothing to do with the reason to live."

Such cynicism from her shocked him. "You used to believe that love was the best means to a happy life."

She snorted, impossibly sad. "Did I?"

He stopped to put his arms around her. They stood near the turn into rue du Four. He cupped her cheeks. "My dear Vivi, I have no idea what you are doing here in Paris, but it has changed you in ways I do not understand. I want to hear you say you believe in love again."

"A noble endeavor, sir."

"To which I am devoted, my darling." He dropped a sweet little kiss to her lips and silently led them both toward the house they both had known so very well.

SHE PUT A hand out to stop him from approaching the house. It rose above her, five stories tall, serene, stately. Built at the turn of the previous century, the facing was of that special Parisian white stone from a massive quarry north of the city that all prestigious architects bought. The elaborate scrolling above the door in the lintel was of grape leaves entwined with the petunias and geraniums of the east.

Now upon the broad front step, Tate gazed at her with compassion. "Pull the bell."

Of course she would. She reached across the delicately carved front door, now a curious emerald green.

They waited.

"The caretaker may be on holiday," she told Tate, anxiously tapping one foot to the cobbles. "He did not answer yesterday or the day before."

"We can return if he does not come today," Tate said. "It is important that we are here."

But someone called within the house. A lock turned. The door swung wide.

A tall, gray-haired man stood there, his benevolent smile the warmth Viv recalled—not from him, for he was new, different from their previous servant, their majordom. Dear heaven, what had happened to their man? To all in the house who had served them so well? She had not thought of them. Not until now. Had they fled? Were they hunted? Had they died because they served tea and did the laundry and cooked the meals for the family of Vicomte de Neufchateau?

Viv ridiculed herself for her lack of concern for them. A hand to her mouth, she muffled her cry.

But there was more that stunned her. This man, this major-dom before her, for surely he was the caretaker of the house, looked familiar.

Viv caught her breath. She swallowed hard on a vague memory. Could it be that she knew him?

Her mind raced to match his characteristics to those servants she'd known in the past. His nose was terribly large, his eyes bulging. His wiry gray hair was tamed but barely so. Still, he was quick to smile, and his pleasant look seemed the true essence of his nature.

He exchanged a few introductory words with Tate, then his pale gaze traveled across to her once more.

"We have come to ask if we may see the house," Tate explained. "May I present the daughter of the former owner—this is Mademoiselle de Massé."

Viv glanced at Tate, who evidently could not bear to call her by her sister's name. A good thing, given the circumstances. Putting that aside, she smiled at the majordom.

"I am honored, mademoiselle," the man greeted her with a sudden broad grin, then took her hand to lead her over the threshold. His gaze flowed over her with the kindliness of an uncle. "Come," he pronounced delicately, as if he invited her into a fantasy.

And he did.

Like a butterfly drawn to a fragrant flower, Viv went. One foot before the other, she sailed into a phantasm of what had been.

"I am delighted you have come. I read that you appear at the theater nearby, and I did wonder whether you would wish to see the house."

She tore her gaze from the familiar graceful architecture. "You are most gracious, Monsieur...?"

"Gaspard, mademoiselle. I am honored to welcome you."

They stood in the foyer. The elegant, wide, white-stoned

foyer, and the winding staircase up. The ones she and the others had run down to flee.

That night, Charmaine had been in a rush to leave and carried her pearls and small gold necklaces in her case. Barking at Diane, Charmaine had held her head high, superior as ever, but acting as if she had not a care…

The image of Viv's oldest sister dissolved.

"The owners told me we have few pieces of the original furniture," Gaspard told them as they climbed the steps to the first floor.

"The owners?" Viv asked.

"*Oui*, Monsieur Jarre," he told her.

"The bankers." *The ones who increased the interest on Papa's debts and turned in my father to the Paris Commune.*

"Exactly." Gaspard spoke as if it were unimportant and so far in the past. "They bought the house from your father."

She blinked. That was not true. The house became the property of the state after Papa was guillotined. Jarre had bought it from the government.

"And in here," Gaspard said, opening the doors to the salon, "only the drapes are original."

Viv stood, her mouth open at the sight of sky-blue damask drapes against the curtains trimmed in ivory Chantilly lace. Her mother had adored these drapes, which kept the cold out in winter and the heat away in summer. The chairs and settees placed strategically around the salon were nothing she remembered.

"Would you like to go upstairs?" the majordom asked.

Tate deferred to her. "Would you?"

She swallowed. "Indeed, I would."

Up they went to the third floor. Two tapestries hung, but they had been slashed at two corners and not repaired. One had a burn mark as if from a candle's flame. All the art was gone, including the portraits of her father and mother, even the one of Viv with her two sisters. Gaspard led them into the small salon dotted with three bright chartreuse chairs. There her mother, father, and Viv would often sit when they were in town and Papa had no obligations at Versailles, or later, after the storming of the Bastille, when he was not sitting in the first National Assembly.

Further along was the girls' bedroom. The frilly pink and white of the room was now painted over with pale blue, but to Viv it was as it had been that terrible night. She grabbed the bedpost as a vision swept over her of the three of them here packing. She saw Diane folding her dearest blue and green gowns. Charmaine was sniping at her.

"Monsieur Gaspard, did you ever hear of some group called the Bonnet-Rouge or…or…"

He nodded, a solemn look in his eyes. "Bonnet-Rouge Section, it was. *Oui*, mademoiselle. Many knew of it. All in that tribunal lived in this part of Saint Germain. They are gone now, thanks to God. They were ruthless—notorious, in fact. They worked with the local police, those in the Croix-Rouge—the crossroads in this faubourg. Together, they sent many to their deaths with only a few minutes of trial."

Tate took her hand. "Why do you ask?"

"Diane had gone earlier that day to watch them hold a trial. Char—Charlotte was our maid." She made that up to cover her blunder of the name. "She was afraid Diane went to watch them too often."

"Who is this Diane, mademoiselle?" Gaspard asked.

"My sister. She was abducted that night from our carriage. We…we never saw her again."

But more about that night disturbed Viv. She could not put her finger on the point, either. Meanwhile, Gaspard ushered them around to the master bedrooms and her father's little study. Then the tour was done and the three of them took the staircase down.

In the foyer, Viv had to ask if Gaspard had any news about the former servants.

"A few. My mother's cousin was your majordom. He is gone now these past five years. Aside from him, I know only two. Your mother's personal maid lives with her son north of Paris in Compiègne."

"And the other?" Viv had to hope he might know about the scullery maid, whom she and Charmaine often talked about as being the one who informed on the family's departure and got the Section's *sans-culotte* hoodlums to harass them as they left the house that night.

"Ah. Gatel. Once one of your family's maids. *Oui.* Jocelyn Gatel. She worked for your mother and afterward for the Jarre family here for many years. Promoted, she was, to first kitchen maid. She is pensioned now. Crippled."

Thrilled to know she still lived, Viv could not find any compassion in her soul to pity her. "Do you know where she lives? I would love to visit her."

"Ah. A fine idea. She would welcome you, I am certain. She likes a smile. An old friend."

"You have her address?"

"I think the house agent knows it. I will try to get it for you."

"Wonderful. I can return tomorrow to get it. Will that be convenient?"

"The house agent is not the generous sort. He may take persuasion."

"Does coin help persuade him?" Tate asked.

"Sadly, *oui.*"

"Allow me, then," Tate said, and reached in his pocket for a few shiny new francs.

"*Merci.* He will appreciate it." Gaspard gave a rueful smile. "When I get the address, I can bring it to you, mademoiselle."

Tate and she left with many thanks. He accompanied Viv home, strolling slowly as they both absorbed how fine a reminiscence it had been to visit the house.

"No one follows us," she said, having examined the pedestrians all around them.

"Even if our man does, you are protected. You are not to worry about being attacked."

"I'm not," she confessed. "Perhaps it is because you are with me."

"Perhaps that is a sign you need me with you all the time," he said with a smoldering smile. As they approached her front door in rue du Bac, Tate paused and took her hands in his. "Look at me, please. What is it about the scullery maid that compels you to visit her?"

"She was friendly, too friendly with a man whom Diane said was a runner for the local Bonnet-Rouge tribunal. Yet I overhead another maid say her lover was police. I must learn who he was— and if he informed the local police that we were leaving that night."

His gaze turned hard as stone. "What merits it now if you see her?"

"I must hear her explanation, mustn't I?" She gave him a lift of her chin in defiance.

"No."

"But I will."

He winced. "I will come with you."

"That is unnecessary."

He clutched her hands. "I will not let you go alone."

"I do not invite you."

He traced the arch of her cheek with a fingertip. "But you trust me and you should want me for this—and for more. I am your best shadow, my darling. I promise you no one will hurt you ever again."

Chapter Nine

S HE LOVED HIS response. She hated it. Now, as they waited for Gaspard to send her the address of the scullery maid, Tate was everywhere Viv went! To parties, the theater, cafés, even her modiste appointments. Tate Cantrell lived like a genie in her mind with memories of his gallantry and his regard of her and her family—and she could not cast him out.

Tate also invited himself to her afternoon receptions. He was one of the dashing British envoys in Lord Ashley's group. But there was also the added familiarity he presented. Somehow, someone had remembered that he had once lived with her family in the country. The news spread in the gossip sheets. A few ladies, enamored of his irresistible good looks, asked about him. Often. Was he of good stock? Rich? Well regarded in Britain?

Oui, he was all of that. And when he came and filled her small salon with his beguiling wit, Viv was filled with pride. She kept him at arm's length. She wished him not too discerning, not too close, yet not too appealing to any other ladies.

But many weeks now into her theatrical engagement, she felt enough ease with the *beau monde* that she could pretend a few of them were her friends. She lured them with Charmaine's airs, and the sham seemed easy. Too easy. The most important of these fraudulent friendships was to Cyprien Montagne. Tate did not attend all of those parties where Cyprien was, but when he did not, he awaited her in his hired carriage outside Montagne House. Still he would comment on Cyprien's interest in her. Plus he looked tired.

"You do not sleep well, do you?" she asked him a few evenings later when he appeared after the theater at a musicale hosted by Julie Récamier. Tate wore stark black and white tonight. The somber color gave rich contrast to his sun-kissed hair and rich complexion, but did nothing for the dark circles around his eyes. She longed to kiss them closed and let him rest.

"I cannot rest when your life is at risk." His magnificent jade eyes said he worried—and he craved her.

She longed to satisfy his hunger but did not trust her burgeoning desire for him. She need only look at him and want to unwind his cravat and slide off his frock coat. Imagining his long, muscular perfection naked on creamy sheets was becoming her most favorite fantasy.

She understood the anguish in his eyes and on his lips. It mirrored her own. She yearned to kiss him and make his heart light. But that would mean she'd give up a part of herself, and eventually, she'd disclose her plan and ruin it. Yet, growing so much closer to him by the day, she felt herself distancing herself from her hunger for vengeance.

Instead, tonight, she availed herself of the buffet, a cracker with *foie gras* here, a small serving of soufflé there.

He followed.

She knew he wanted news of the address for the scullery maid.

"I have not had word from Gaspard on the address we want." If she had learned it, she would have tried more earnestly to find the apothecary in Place des Vosges. But she could not escape Tate's devotion to tracking her every move, and she did not want him to piece together what she planned. He would not be proud of her. But then, of course, she was not proud of herself.

"I assumed that was true," he said as he took a few offerings from the elaborate feast.

She picked up an empty flute and allowed a two-foot-tall cherub, carved in ice, to pour from his ice chalice a lemonade. She took a sip, noting how two ladies put their heads together to admire her dashing Englishman.

But not mine, *is he?*

"Don't you have work to do of your own?"

He noted the two who looked his way and turned to give Viv a true smile of satisfaction. "I do try. Even here with the banker whom the first consul loves most, I find the man does not wish to speak with me as often."

"A shame," she said, and meant it.

"Truly, for money is a valuable asset, more delightful in peace than war. It is what I contribute to the friendship, but sadly, I cannot win if I am not permitted."

Viv admired him, his expertise, his dedication, his devotion to his cause—even his trying to save her. But Bonaparte's vehemence killed Tate's ability to balance the pound with the franc. She put a hand to his sleeve. "Some good intentions are ruined by others."

He covered her hand with his warm one. "Are yours?"

His perception riveted her. He knew her too well.

She'd allow him to learn more about her, too. "Yes. My good intention was to come to Paris and learn what happened to my sister. I have allowed all my past heartaches and grievances to rise to the fore. I learn I have little stomach for vengeance. I fear that makes me a coward."

He came near, his lips by her ear. "I think that makes you wise."

She cringed. "But I want answers. And with them, I still want blood. That is not wise, Tate. It's evil."

"Let's look for the answers and deal with the evil after all else is known."

Viv drove Tate quite insane. The business about the house, the maid, the infamous Bonnet-Rouge tribunal—it was all so sordid. What did she derive from remembering? Reliving it all?

He knew.

Her statement of retribution was the desire she bore to punish those responsible for that night they fled Paris. But what was her plan to implement it?

That sparked horror in him. She knew not what chaos she created.

So the morning three days later, when he followed her, and she went not to the corner market, nor to the house on rue du Four, but to the tawdry stalls under the quays of the Pont Neuf, he could not decide whether to be alarmed or relieved.

Her destination was the renowned two-century-old square on the right bank. Decreed by Henry the Fourth as the newest improvement to his capital city, the Place des Vosges was the square of residences and shops facing a green park. The houses were the same size and frontage, with similar materials and quality. The harmonious appearance of the houses, all of the same red brick and the same number and size of windows, had quickly become a favored location for the aristocracy. Inside, they could decorate as they wished. Outside, the buildings were not to be changed.

At first when Viv alighted from her hired carriage with her maid and a footman, Tate surmised she meant to visit a friend. As she walked along the colonnade, stopping here and there as if in thought, he realized she searched for something.

Whatever it was, she ducked into a small shop on the eastern wing and emerged ten or so minutes later. She talked to no one and carried no packages, only her little reticule. Her journey perplexed him.

"You worry, friend." Kane cocked a brow at him as they sat

facing each other in Kane's library on rue Saint-Honoré the following afternoon.

"I do." They had just finished an analysis of what to do about Ramsey, who had sent round a note and begged off their regular meeting today. Their mutual friend and colleague, so prompt, so dedicated, was in a coil performing his latest assignment. He had nothing new to report.

Kane explained that in January, he had assigned Ram to follow a French émigré who was sent to Paris by Scarlett. Ram's duty was to track if the lady met with any officials in the government. Scarlett had questions about the trustworthiness of the woman. Ram had continued to trail the woman on her journeys throughout Paris, but he'd sent word this morning to Kane that for the next few days, he was incapable of tracking her. Might Tate substitute for him temporarily?

"Scarlett questions if the woman is a double agent?" Tate asked, and put his coffee cup and saucer on a near table.

"She does."

He must not disappoint their spymaster. "I can do it."

"Thank you. I have another, if by taking this on you will destroy your schedule."

"I can do this for a few days." He employed two men to follow Viv when he could not. That meant he could help Ram. "Who is the lady?"

Kane stood and took from his desk a large piece of parchment. "Here she is."

The sketch was of pencil, hastily done but exquisitely precise. The subject was a lady, young, with pouting lips and sultry, dark eyes, and beneath an elaborate turban, she had a wealth of short golden curls. "Who is she?"

"Madame Albert duPre."

"Lovely. I've never heard of her."

"She is also Mrs. Clement McAllister."

Tate grimaced. "I do not know of her, either."

Kane gave a laugh. "Have you heard of a Baroness

Bergheim?"

"Ha! Never."

"The lady has money to burn, slips around Paris like fog, and has met with two of Bonaparte's generals. In private. Follow her if you can. We'd love to learn where she lives."

"I'll do my best. Who did the sketch?"

"One of ours."

Tate was appreciative. "That artist might be able to learn more than we can. Madame Turban, here, sat for long enough that our artist caught her in her glory."

"Discover what you can. Report to me. Ram will take over again in a few days, he tells me. But I must now warn you our days here in Paris are numbered. Take care of those in your house. Wrap up your work."

"That, sadly, is easy. These days, the atmosphere from the Tuileries spoils whatever I try to accomplish. I can hardly secure appointments with bankers. As for my other occupation, the lady is stubborn. Her engagement ends the last week in June. Seven more weeks." Tate had told Kane about Viv's recent odd activities.

Kane crossed one long leg over another and brushed a hand down his thigh. "A woman with a mystery is a lady who brings a man more trouble than a morning hangover. Your day never improves."

Tate shifted in his chair. "I hope she returns home with me before my hangover gets worse."

"She should go home to England like the rest of us." Kane turned sour. "I will be frank. In case you suddenly must leave and need a friend or two, I have suggestions."

Tate frowned. "Go on."

"Augustine is the niece of Countess Nugent. I assume you have heard of her?"

Tate certainly had. "I met the countess briefly when I was invited a few weeks ago to Julie Recamier's house." The countess was a Society leader of the highest caliber.

"She is English," Kane continued, "but has lived in Paris for many years. Leading a remarkable life, she was the old Duc d'Orleans's mistress. Both the countess and her adopted daughter, Madame St. Antoine, were in Carmes Prison together with Josephine Bonaparte."

"That, I did not know."

"The countess and madame owe their affection for Josephine to that terrible period. Inside, the women rallied around each other to survive." Kane winced. "Madame St. Antoine is the lady whom you met in our box the first night we attended the theater together."

"I remember her. Lovely woman. I also read her dossier before I came to Paris. Scarlett gave it to me. So I know she is English by birth, the adopted child of Countess Nugent, and the widow of a French vintner."

"Madame St. Antoine also left Paris last spring fearing for her life when the deputy chief of police was after her."

Tate had met that man at Montagne's house. "Fouché's assistant? What *is* his name? Vaillancourt. René Vaillancourt. Yes, I have not met him, but I hear he is a dignified creature. Dapper. Evil sort, I hear. Which proves that looks deceive, eh?"

"Indeed, they do. After madame disappeared, I assigned Ramsey to find her and protect her. He did. Madame became Ram's very, very close friend. But they are now parted. She is here in Paris, in her own house."

That explained Ram's mercurial moods. "Does that mean Vaillancourt has no desire for her any longer?"

"Oh, but he does. Vaillancourt has made threats. I do not know them all. Neither does Ram."

"No wonder he's at wits' end."

"Exactly," Kane went on. "But since she has returned to Paris, Madame St. Antoine has remained out of Society. I do not ask why. But I do want you to know that she has great influence. She, like my wife, is also friends with Josephine, Bonaparte's family, and many in Society, including Julie Recamier."

"Surprising."

"Indeed." Tate stared at him and said at last, "Most especially because madame works with us."

Tate sucked in a breath. But this revelation of Madame St. Antoine's role was unusual for Kane unless he had another reason. "So you tell me all of this so that I know about madame in case I need friends or…need to help a friend."

"Yes. Countess Nugent is a mystery to me. But she is bold, honest. Madame St. Antoine, I expect, will remain in Paris. If you need help, either lady can be useful. My majordom falls into that category as well."

Corsini? The Italian with the sunny disposition who kept order in Kane's household like a wizard? "I see. Now all this is in preparation for your anticipated departure from Paris just in case things go foul?"

"If this treaty dissolves before our eyes, you know we British will be persona non grata at the bat of a lash."

"I will be ready." *I must ensure Viv is ready too.* "Passports. An escape route. Money."

⇶⫘

THE FIRST OF May dawned bright and warm. Viv was more open in her conversations with Tate, but she put her mind to her plans and how she might change them. She had many problems, most of them ones of her own doing—or lack of it. Her promises to Charmaine were too many. Her sister had once been a harpy, but she had loved Diane and was outraged at her loss. But could Viv *poison* someone? She doubted it, had always doubted it. Perhaps that was why her failure to get arsenic at the apothecary shop had irritated her, but not destroyed her. She let that go and looked on the highwaymen's theft of her reticule with the little vials inside as a good sign. Still, she forced herself to buy two new ones.

Meanwhile, Monsieur Lamond failed to get a better address

for the apothecary. She let that drop. All he wished to do was attempt to get her to extend her run. Ticket sales were excellent. The house was sold out. But the truth was she did want to leave France. The memories Paris engendered had only renewed her sadness over the loss of her family and increased her desire to go home. Home to England. To Norfolk. To peace…and perhaps more with Tate.

She could be his mistress, his tenant who visited the manor house. That would make her similar to her mother. A woman who loved a man despite all Society said against it. But that was not in her nature either.

She shook that off and returned to her own line of thinking on returning to England. If she went back without results, Charmaine would be disappointed in her. Or rather, her sister would be furious with her.

Though Viv was proud she had no desire to find another shop where she'd acquire arsenic, she still owned the little pistol that her groom Fortin had purchased for her. She kept it in her reticule at all times. Or when they rode in the mornings, she tucked it in a small saddlebag. She had always been comfortable with a gun. A woman who knew how to use one could do much damage.

Her remaining two issues were the lack of an address for the scullery maid and her need to meet a Jarre banker.

One asset she had was that Cyprien Montagne pursued her. At least twice a week, he appeared at the same parties as she. The man followed her like a dog. She would never give in to him, but she had to keep up appearances to be invited to his own soirées.

She had learned from Cyprien that of the two administrators of the Jarre bank, the one who controlled it was his distant cousin, Sylvain Jarre. That man, a few said when asked, was now approximately thirty-three years old. He was therefore the age of one of the men she thought the scullery maid might have seduced.

Rumor said Sylvain was currently away visiting the century-old Vauban French forts along the Atlantic coast. He'd been there, Society gossips speculated, to assess if he would finance Bonaparte's newest venture. That, she presumed, was fortifying the coastline in preparation either for an attack on Britain or repelling one from Britain.

"It amounts to war, doesn't it?" she said to Tate when he rode with her one morning.

"That becomes more and more likely," he said with a bitter tone.

She looked back to see Fortin was out of earshot, and gave the man a lift of her chin that meant he should remain far back. "I understand the first consul will soon sell much land in North America to the new United States."

"He will," Tate said with a grimace. "Tomorrow or the next day."

"So the Americans will own most of the continent?"

"They will," he said. "Millions of dollars they agreed to pay for it, too."

"Interesting. Which means the first consul will not only become richer, but by selling it, he proclaims that he does not wish ever to fight over land so far away."

Tate sighed. "True."

"Only land close to home."

He gave a sad laugh. "If you ever get tired of portraying your sister, you could work with me."

She eyed him, and for a moment, she wanted him—and to surrender. "Oh, Tate, I am tired of this."

He blinked at her frank admission. "Come home with me," he said in so mellow a tone she could hear her own heartbeat.

"I wish I could," she said quickly, and looked ahead.

"You can, sweetheart."

She shook her head. "She'll be angry."

"Charmaine should come do her own dirty work."

"She can't."

"You mean she won't."

"No. She's ill."

He stopped his horse.

Viv had to pause in order to look back at him. There was no reason to keep the truth from him. "She's dying, Tate. She could not come here."

"I see," he said, blinking at the revelation. Then, at once, he was angry. "She sent you here in her stead to carry out her wishes to learn the truth—or to exact revenge?"

"*My* wish is to learn the truth."

He sent her a rueful glance. "Viv, I cannot stress this enough. Things grow worse with Bonaparte. We have few hopes this peace will last. When it collapses, we must run for the coast and the channel. Come away with me. Pack now. End this escapade."

"No! I cannot. I may have given up on hurting others. But I must know who hurt Diane!"

"*Ma cherie*, whatever…" But his words were lost to her because she trotted away.

That afternoon, she sent him a note via her footman. In it, she told him not to join her any longer in the mornings. She gave him no explanations.

But she knew the reasons. She was too sensitive to her own failures—and too drawn to him. To everything about him, in fact. His patience. His devotion.

She had to do without it all. If she succeeded in her plans— no, *when* she succeeded—she trod on dangerous territory. Old members of the commune were still in power. Perhaps even those in the Bonnet-Rouge tribunal or the police office in the Croix-Rouge street crossing. She would not have Tate near her. Once her work was done, he would be tarnished for paying attention to her. She would not ruin him—or have him die because of her.

The next day crawled past. And the next.

Where was Gaspard with the maid's address?

She sent Alice to the theater, declaring she was ill and could not perform that night. Her absence would allow the understudy to take the role. Viv had better things to do than portray a young girl who died for love. She would die soon for revenge. Alone.

She shivered.

That afternoon, when the kitchen staff sat in their kitchen for their early dinner, she changed into a pauper's costume she'd taken from the wardrobe at the theater. Out the back door she went. Coins in her pockets, she walked toward Pont Neuf looking for someone who could fill her little glass bottle for her *étui* with arsenic.

THE NEXT TWO nights, Viv saw Tate at every party. She went now even after a performance. The more she was out and about, the more she became acquainted with those she sought. But acting five nights a week took the starch out of her. The next morning, she was always limp, depleted. Anxious. And she needed to rest, restore her confidence in her ability to do this. Lying took such energy. She had never known how Charmaine had done it year in and out. Even reveled in it.

Viv's consolation at each event, however much she would never tell him, was seeing Tate. He was accepted by those in French Society as one who had lived in France before the chaos of the revolution. He had fine manners, spoke perfect French, and dressed like the wealthy aristocrat he was. A member of the diplomatic entourage of the Earl of Ashley, Tate was celebrated as an informal envoy of importance. He continued to cultivate bankers, and so it behooved her to join his little circles of conversation. Now and then, she heard a snippet of how well the Earl of Appleby did attempting to negotiate the impossible transfer of francs to pounds. If he did not speak of money, he spoke of fashion and Sèvres china, the cost of a fine pink and jade Aubusson and bolts of Lyon silks. To every widow and debutante, he was a dashing bachelor, a widower with money, land,

and panache. He might be English, but with all those other qualities, he was a young girl's dream—and an older one's desire.

Once mine.

Viv admired him that evening at Monsieur Lenoir's. In a sumptuous embroidered midnight-blue frock coat that complemented a waistcoat of gold, he attracted the attention of most of the women. To them, he returned polite regard. Viv set her teeth, feeling the nip of jealousy, the bite of need. Especially when she found him focusing on her, time and again, with those marvelous jewel-toned eyes of his. His look was an embrace she ached to wrap around her.

"You must not look at me so often," she told him too gaily in passing.

"I warm you," he crooned. "How reassuring."

"Stop." She could not help the hot flutter in her stomach.

"Never."

She had to act like Charmaine, so batted her lashes at him. "I go to play cards."

He came close, his bass voice a breath of temptation. "Come home with me instead."

She would have swayed against him. But she was Charmaine here, wasn't she? So she snapped shut her fan and pressed the tip to his waistcoat. "We have no more to say on the subject."

He grabbed her fan and held. "You bid me end my morning rides with you. We now will speak at night."

She tugged at the ivory sticks. "I will not speak at all."

He gave over. "Actions only now."

He threw down a gauntlet to her? So be it. She had things to do that had nothing to do with him.

He held her wrist. "I am yours. You are mine. Always."

Then he let her go.

An hour or more later, she sat at a circular table in the card room and trained her eyes on her hand. Yet she felt Tate's gaze fall on her. The heat she'd glimpsed in his jade eyes resurrected the blaze she'd felt years ago when first she fell in love with him.

She was naïve and just turned sixteen. He was a dashing twenty-one.

That was lifetimes ago. When his father was alive. When the man ran the Appleby estate into neglected ruin and debt. Before his father demanded Tate marry for money.

She shifted in her chair. Her eyes fell closed. She'd loved Tate forever and played no coy girl when he needed a friend and a confidante. That he discovered she was a young woman who adored him had astonished him. But he had taken her in his arms and kissed her with such tenderness that she remembered the feel of him, the might of him, the kindness of his claim for many, many years. Yet, all too soon, he was gone. He had been told to marry a stranger whose fortune allowed him to buy plows and horses, repair tenants' cottages, build bridges, and improve roads.

Did he care for her as a friend? Or someone to love and cherish? She'd never learned.

Meanwhile, he'd been the perfect gentleman. He stayed away from the manor and gave directives from London. He did not return home. Not when his father died. Not when Viv's mother did. Not even after Charmaine went to London and left Viv alone. So utterly alone.

She inhaled and considered her miserable hand. She sat taller, appraising this older, more mouth-watering Monsieur le Comte who would not leave the room. Who did not stop making eyes at her and marched over now and then to tut at the cards in her hand.

He had never become her lover, but he had always been her friend. His handsome lips had never whispered words of love but assured her of help, sustenance, a cottage and a plot of land. She should be content with what he had given her. What he gave her here. Protection. Friendship.

Why did she want more from him?

He was as appealing as ever. More so. Older, even more confident than the young man who'd run away from home, he had now a manly swagger that came from years of ruling over his domain, enriching it with hard work, then leaving it to his tenants to enjoy the rewards. He was a treasure, an enigma, too. After all, how many men left the comforts of their inherited estate to traipse the Continent to secure commercial success for his country? And spy for it, too?

She applauded him. Treasured what he had become. Why could she not savor him? Just a little, as her lover?

She was older, wiser. Gone now was the young woman who dedicated herself to raising her chickens and ducks. Gone was the lady who'd taken positions as a tutor of French to young girls. Yes, she had learned to live without him.

But her gaze returned to Tate over and over. She threw reason to the wind. She'd hungered too long for the sight of him. Thirsted too long for his regard. So long deprived, she admitted she was ravenous. So long denied, she could take what he offered. Nearness, care, affection. Oh, yes, she could see herself touching the long column of his throat. Nuzzling the hollow beneath his ear. Kissing those lips she had longed to learn and memorize. She could satisfy herself easily. Tonight, even.

But could she walk away?

He drew near. As if he measured each step he took, each smile he bestowed, he took his sweet time maneuvering around her table. Then, just his luck, one of the players at her table declared his final loss and stood to leave.

Tate asked if he might join.

The others welcomed him, some jokingly declaring they wanted him for the cash he might bring. The ladies bade him sit down. Their reasoning included victories of their own with him in other entertainments. Viv watched while it happened. One lady scooted her chair close to his. Another jutted out her breasts, already generously displayed above her silk and lace.

But Tate sat close to Viv and played his cards.

The rascal.

He was good. Always had been. Better than her.

He won the first hand. His knee pressed hers when she made

a poor move, his hand to her thigh—but briefly—when she played well.

But the play went on. The others grew careless, drowsy with wine and the hour. Tate inched nearer. The heat in her legs, the need to press them together, had her jumping out of her skin. He pressed his palm flat to her thigh…and inched up her skirts. Her heart raced. Her *chat* grew wet. He patted her leg and pulled up the last of her petticoats. His fingers were smooth, sliding among her secret folds, parting her so easily she was certain the others at the table could hear her liquid desire for him. But then at once, he turned toward her, looking at her cards, his fingers seated deeply inside her, stroking her little nub.

She gulped.

He grinned. "You have a good hand."

"And you, monsieur?"

"A better one."

"Pardon me!" She jumped up before she came on his fingertips. "I must find the ladies' retiring room."

The other four waved her off.

She scurried away, hoping to find cool water to put to her brow. Or wine, even whiskey, to allow her to wash him from her mind.

But she was no sooner in the room, checking behind the painted screen and finding it thankfully vacant, than she relieved herself, brushed down her skirts—and there he stood!

"*Mon Dieu*, Tate! Do you follow all ladies to their toilette?"

"Only you," he crooned, his smile erotic and eager.

She headed for the washstand. He came to stand right behind her. Close. So close that the churning desire he'd ignited in her loins with this antics under the table set her aflame now.

Her eyes drifted shut, and she fought for a semblance of sanity as he pressed her back into his embrace.

She felt rather than heard him sigh.

This was torture. Did he intend to raise her skirts and give her the fullness of his attentions? Her body ached with need of release. She squeezed her thighs together, wanting to ask for his affections and hating that she'd give in to him.

But he made no move to fulfill her need. He only dropped tiny kisses to her shoulder. "Since when do you play cards?"

Melting at the pressure of his lips on her skin, she could not drag her eyes from him in the mirror. "Since an hour ago."

He smiled but narrowed his gaze to a squint. "You hate cards."

She curved her shoulder, feigning the ploys of a *femme fatale*. "I've changed."

"Charmaine is a genius at counting them."

"A cutthroat," she blurted, using her father's term for his oldest child. She inhaled Tate's essence, his truths, his admissions that he cared for her. Her head reeled at the combinations.

He ran a fingertip up the arch of her cheek and buried his lips into the hollow behind her ear. "You won't win, darling."

Lost to his touch, she closed her eyes and swayed in his arms.

He turned her to him and brushed his lips on hers. "You'll lose your money, sweetheart. You'll hate that."

The spell broken by mention of money, she snorted. "I won't lose." *Not at any of it.* She flipped him an insolent wink and spun to leave. "Watch me."

He caught her arm. "I am, my darling. And you have never even known how to play! At cards or deception."

"I'm older. I have had so many lessons. Chess, archery, guns. All of them by so many teachers—"

"Not all were hideous," he whispered, and caught her to him, his palm to her cheek. He brushed his lips on hers, and she felt herself surrendering, going up on her toes. To taste him, she drew closer. "Some were glorious."

Some were irresistible.

His jaw set in frustration, he growled as he turned her toward the mirror. "Look at us there."

She rebuked herself for enjoying his possession of her. Finger her, kiss her, hold her, fight her. He showed each time he was her man. Hers. She shook her head, ignoring his command. If she did meet his gaze there in the glass, he'd see in her eyes how she wanted more of him—and should not be so foolish as to want. Not now that she had this purpose.

He dropped more tiny kisses to her throat. "It is how we are meant to be."

"A fantasy." She tried to step away.

He secured her to his frame as his arms crept around her and his hands bound her breasts. "Years ago, we were both so young. We had barely begun to find our own inner selves, and how we cared for each other."

She never wanted his embrace to end.

"I wanted you then, sweetheart."

Tears scalded her eyes.

He stroked her throat and lifted her face so that she had to look at the two of them. "I came to you that summer to ask you to marry me. You were, I think, all of sixteen."

Through tears, she pleaded with him, "Tate, do not say this."

"I will go on. I will not argue with you. I will instead say what I have hidden in my heart for so long I can scarcely count the years I've lived without you. My darling," he went on, his lips near her ear, his voice a mellifluous enchantment. "Let me take you home. To England. To Norfolk and Cantrell Manor. Let me show you what I have always wanted to share with you."

She enjoyed the image of him—delectable man—reflected in the spectacular oval mirror. His hair disheveled, dipping over his broad brow. His eyes, promising sensual pleasures his fingers surely complemented. His lips, broad and lush, luring her. If she turned, she could have his mouth. His arms. Him.

But she pushed away—and he would not let her go. "This is who I am now."

"Not her. Never her."

"Yes. So very exactly her."

His eyes turned black with denial. "Looks are only skin deep, especially when comparing your oldest sister to you."

"She and I…share much." *The anger, the pain, the losses.*

"This is so dangerous. Someone can discover who you really are."

"Someone? No. Only you, I'd say."

He set his jaw. There was the determination again that defied her. The anger that deterred her. "Tell me how you plan to kill the scullery maid."

She groped for an answer.

"How?" He cupped her shoulders. "Shoot her? You cried trying to shoot a goose!"

"Stop." Tears of anger blotted her vision.

"No? Not shoot her? So you'd poison her? Charmaine would know how to deliver a dose. But you? You have no idea how to administer a poison!"

She could not stop her tears, but saw Tate opening his arms to her. Grateful, sad at her lack, she went to him and told him the one thing she did know. "I must learn what happened to Diane."

"Then learn, and take what you can in the knowledge."

"I have not heard from Gaspard with the address of the scullery maid."

"Very well. I will go tomorrow to rue du Four and ask him about it. If he has it, fine. If not"—he sent a hand to the air—"then that's the end. We go home."

She would not allow him to bully her. "I won't—"

But he kissed her in a crushing declaration. "A lie. I taste the proof on your lips. I shall see you tomorrow at the turn for Pont Neuf."

Then he bowed like a gentleman—and left.

AFTER A FEW minutes in which she cursed his stubbornness, she returned to the game.

That night, after one in the morning, she'd won a pot with no money, but one small ruby ring and three slips of paper. The first promised a prize-winning racehorse, another was three cases of fine cognac, the last a week in the man's Loire chateau.

She tore up that last one, nonetheless declaring her night a success on two counts. First, she had met a late arrival to the party and the card game. Monsieur Sylvain Jarre was the controlling partner in his family's bank. He was young and darkly debonair, but everything about him was small. His eyes were beady, his nose a pencil, his hair thin, and his stature shorter by an inch than hers. However, he clearly had heard of her. Moreover, he had a desire to pursue her. She invited him to her reception on Friday, three days hence.

Second, she'd also controlled her maddening impulse to kiss Tate Cantrell more than once. *It was once, wasn't it?*

She lay in her bed an hour later, breathless, panting, and admitted she could not deny herself the final sensual relief he had refused her.

She had to count small victories, yes? *C'est la vie.*

She needed all she could get.

⧽⧽⧽⧼⧼⧼

TATE FOLLOWED HER home in his own carriage. Anger ate at his good nature. She defied him at every turn. What did he have to do to make her see that she had to leave with him or she would die?

Chapter Ten

May 8, 1803
Passy, Paris

TWO MORNINGS LATER, as Viv sat at her little breakfast table, she received a note from Gaspard with the address of the scullery maid in Passy. It was Sunday, a day for rest, but she could not let that stop her.

She sent her footman immediately to Tate's house to notify him of her receipt of the address. *Please come,* she had written. Those two words, she knew, he would take as acceptance of his help and her need for him. So, yes, that much she did want from him. She would wait to declare what else, if anything, she must do to satisfy herself before she gave in to his plea to leave Paris.

Within minutes, via his own footman, Tate responded with a note. *I will arrive at nine o'clock at rue du Bac. You will never walk alone anywhere ever again. Loving regards, Tate.*

He called for her on time, and they left immediately. "I hired a public cab for us. No need for us to be flamboyantly conspicuous."

"You're right," she said as she took his hand and climbed up into the fiacre. As hired carriages went in Paris, this one was relatively new and clean. But the street was crowded with servants and shop people shouting as they loaded and unloaded lorries. "What is going on here? I've never seen Parisians so loud and irritable."

Tate sat opposite her, his jade eyes so beautiful and consoling. "They are frightened."

Fear crawled up her spine. "Of what?"

"The end of the peace."

She took another look at the throngs. "Now? Today?"

"Within days, certainly. The British ambassador plans to leave Paris."

"And what of your friend, Lord Ashley?"

"He and his wife have departed. Another I cannot find this morning. His majordom has not seen him since yesterday. I worry what has happened to him. So you see, if a favored diplomat can disappear in this city, others can too."

"You?"

"Why not? I have my passport papers ready, but I am uneasy, as they may be worth less than the paper they are written on." He stared at her, stiff and forbidding, with more warnings unuttered. "I will not repeat myself and become a nag."

She was grateful he did not harangue her once more about leaving. He did know when to leave off. She turned her face fully to the window and viewed the results of the animosity between Bonaparte and the English ambassador. Some in the street were cross with their servants. A few yelled in English. Others in French. Women dabbed at tears as their trunks were loaded onto the backs of traveling coaches. Dogs ran amok from house to shop and toward the Seine.

Viv pulled the collar of her pelisse up her throat. She caught the fright of those trying to run for safety. "I am glad we do this today, Tate, and I am thankful you come with me."

The carriage wound along the Seine and south away from it, into smaller and dirtier alleys. Tate nodded to her as if to imply he understood her concern at the change of circumstances here.

The air grew foul, thick with the odors of wine and decaying vegetables, urine, and the detritus of human life.

Tate frowned. From his waistcoat pocket he dug out a metal object and slid it over his knuckles.

She stared at him in awe.

"This turns the odds in my favor."

Undoubtedly. One swing of his fist and a jaw could break.

He shifted in his seat then leaned over and patted his boot.

Something else there?

She blew out a breath. A knife, she imagined. "Have you spotted the one who follows me?"

Tate winced. "I have."

She'd pondered who her shadows might be and what they wanted. "If he is going to steal from me or abduct me, he has had many chances."

"Clearly—"

"He intends to do neither," she finished for him.

"*They* do not," he corrected her, and a muscle twitched in his jaw.

"They?"

"They are a team. Perhaps four total. They take shifts. Usually six to eight hours and a new man comes on."

"You did not tell me." She was without breath.

"I did not want to worry you more."

She closed her eyes.

He came to sit beside her and took her in his arms. She went. Oh, she went. Chills made her clamp her teeth shut, and she nestled into his embrace.

"I have two of my men following us this morning," he said so sweetly into her hair. "We are safe."

"I wish we could learn who they are and where they come from."

"Indeed. They are very used to this cat-and-mouse business," he said. "They know how to dodge and weave. They change clothes, too."

That did not surprise her. "They're not poorly dressed, either."

"They have coin which they use to dart into a crowded café or into a private room. Therefore, they must receive money on which to operate, as well as a decent wage."

She stared up at him. "So they are not base cutthroats hired off the streets. They're employed gainfully by someone to do this."

He arched a brow. "The question is, who is that someone?"

She shivered. Whoever masterminded this was crafty and had a goal beyond hers and Tate's comprehension.

Their fiacre idled to a stop.

She clutched Tate's cravat. "Post a man to the front door. Can you signal one to do that? And…and another at the corner across the street."

He cupped her cheek. "My darling, my men are very good at this. They are everywhere."

"But you cannot be certain."

"I can."

"How?"

He brushed tendrils of her hair from the arch of her cheek. "Did you see them when you went to the Place des Vosges?"

She gasped. "You had me followed then?"

"Or when you decided to dress as a pauper and seek out an apothecary in the Marais?"

Her mouth dropped open. Her shadow—correction, shadows—had followed her for weeks now. They did not follow every day. Or rather, because they were a team, she did not spy them every day. Nor could she detect them at night.

She sat back in the squabs and collected her thoughts. The interview ahead with the maid required her wits. She would not be afraid of the shadows, but stand in the light of her own desires. She'd talk with the scullery mind and be done with this. She was not gaining ground elsewhere—meanwhile, the world had caught on fire and headed toward war. In her reticule, she had her smelling salts in her little *étui*. Another vial, too, was filled with

Charmaine's usual dose of laudanum. Viv was prepared as much as she could be without a dose of arsenic.

The coachman opened the door and Tate got out.

She looked outside at the crumbling old building before them.

By the time she stepped to the cobbles, she'd found her strength. Old hatreds did not die. They simply festered in one's heart.

"Darling," Tate murmured to her as he took her hand and they gazed up at the half-timbered shack before them. "If this is not to your liking, we can leave."

"No. I am here." She patted the collar of her pelisse to her throat. "Knock and ask if Jocelyn Gatel lives here."

He rapped on the door. Minutes stretched. No one came. He knocked again. Another minute passed before, inside, someone dragged a foot across ancient, creaking floorboards.

The rough-hewn wooden door inched open. A shriveled gremlin squinted up at Tate. Curiosity had the little person examining him head to toe.

"*Bonjour*, madame—are you Jocelyn Gatel?"

"Who wants to know?" The little owl of a lady spotted Viv, and shock had her drawing back.

He stated, "Mademoiselle Charmaine de Massé."

Those watery eyes grew big with shock. But with the bat of a lash, she sent Viv a shrewd, sharp look of greed. "Come to see me after all these years? So noble of you. So kind." Her words implied nothing of the sort. She leaned on the handle of the door and swept a hand toward the inside.

A waft of putrid air hit Viv like a hot river. But she planted her feet more securely. She'd come this far.

The ugly little creature punched her black cane into the floor and craned her neck at Viv. "Why've you come?"

"I have come to visit you, madame, and see to your health." *And not.*

Confusion lined the ugly spotted bird's already wrinkled

brow. *"Oui?* You?" Her mouth dropped open in surprise. "You come to help *me?*" She slapped a hand on her knee and cackled.

"Why not?" *I can. I will. If you help me.*

"Come, girl!" The woman spread her white lips to show small black teeth. Viv felt the scourge of her rotten breath upon her face. "Come inside, then, if can hold your stomach."

Viv stepped across the threshold, Tate beside her—and the stench brought up her gorge.

"You can smell my mother there."

Indeed. The woman sat like a corpse in a ragged upholstered chair that Viv would say had belonged once to the house in rue du Four. Her spidery hands to the armrests, the old lady had the complexion of the dead, a few wisps of white hair sprouting from her bald head, and a gown that clung to her emaciated form like a wet rag.

"She never rises from the chair. So that's why you smell her. Does all her living there, if that's what you can call it."

Viv held on to her sanity by a thin thread. "Sad," she offered.

"Stupid. She should die but lives to drive me insane. What do you want, mademoiselle? To give me money? I'll take it. How much?"

"I did come to help you if I could."

The little owl licked her thin lips. "What do you want for the gift of a coin, eh?"

So a transaction was expected. Greed was good. "I thought you might tell me about what happened to the other servants in our house." That was a lie. But Viv had to improvise. The woman was no simple-minded hag, but one who was still canny, despite the squalor in which she lived.

"You got coin for them too?" She crossed her bony arms. "Lucky you. What do you do for that money? Did your papa give it to you? Did he even live? Ha!" She looked Viv over like a man buying a woman for the night. "Pretty, still. Good breasts. Clothes, too. Earn them on your back?"

Tate cleared his throat.

The owl sneered at Viv. "What do you want, Charmaine?"

The woman did not read newspapers or gossip sheets. She had no money for such frivolous things. Therefore, she had no idea who or what Charmaine de Massé had become. And of course, she was rude to address her by her given name.

Viv did not care what Jocelyn thought of her. "Tell me, Madame Gatel, do you know where our other servants are now?"

"Most are dead. The majordom. The chef and the châtelaine. Your mother's maid lives north somewhere... Why? Want to give them money, too?"

"I am grateful for their service to us, and I wanted to give all of you a token of my appreciation."

The owl blinked at Viv, greed giving way to gratitude. "*Merci beaucoup*, mademoiselle. Not many care for those who washed and fed them."

Now there was a spark of melting regard of which Viv might take advantage.

"Did you not have a beau?" Viv said with concern. "Someone you favored?"

"I did. Smart pig, he was. Is still."

"Did you not plan to marry?"

"Marry?" Jocelyn scoffed. "The likes of him marrying a maid?"

"It happens. Especially after the revolution. All classes marry now whomever they—"

"Not him. Too high and mighty, he was."

"Really? Who was he?"

"Then he was police. Still is, but grander, you know?"

So not a sans-culotte *for the commune or the Bonnet-Rouge Section.* "In the local police?"

"*Oui.* Handsome devil."

Viv's heartbeat picked up. "And now? He still lives?"

"Ah, *oui*, he does. *Quel enculé!*" Jocelyn muttered.

Viv knew the obscene insult and put a sneer into her next words. "Was he really?"

"An asshole who rose up fast after I"—Jocelyn jabbed herself in the chest—"I helped him!"

I always suspected you were doing more than kissing him. "He was not appreciative of your help." Viv shook her head as if to commiserate.

"They do not prize a woman," Jocelyn said with a sour glance at Tate. "Like this one, do you?" she prodded him.

He only stared back at her.

The woman sniffed back her irritation that he did not respond. "Men take women. Then throw them away."

"What happened to your man?"

"Him? Oh, crafty, he was. He had a friend who was the concierge of Carmes."

"Carmes?" Tate murmured, as if reflecting on some fact he'd heard.

"*Oui*, one of the gaols," Jocelyn said. "My man and this warden ran the prison like a *bardello*. Bribed women, raped them. Two devils."

The name of the prison struck a bell in Viv. Charmaine had once talked of the Paris prison near rue du Four where she thought Diane might have been sent. Why Charmaine would know about such a place had always perplexed her. "Carmes is a prison?"

"Worst kind. Even Madame Bonaparte spread her legs in there to survive."

Viv wanted to be sick once more. She had to know the name of this man! "And he used that to become a rich man, did he?"

"Used it to become Fouché's man."

Fouché. "The Minister of Police? He works for that man?"

"His deputy."

"Vaillancourt." Viv recalled his name, his tall and elegant good looks, black hair, and cut-glass-perfect cheekbones. She had met him once at Cyprien Montagne's. Vaillancourt had acted honored to meet her, a sophisticated gentleman out on the town who fawned over her success as an actress and spoke of some vague remembrance of her father.

"But you knew him."

Viv's head spun.

The maid frowned, perplexed. "You wanted me to tell him you would have him."

Viv could not move. She licked her lips—and she panicked. Where was her acting skill now? What should she say? "I cannot recall."

The woman looked at her as if she were the dumbest person to have ever lived. "It's what you paid me for. To get him for you."

"Get him? Oh, oh, I…" Viv shook her head, frightened she had destroyed her act as Charmaine. "I really do not remember."

"You paid me to keep him happy." Jocelyn hitched her arms on her hips.

Viv could barely breathe. "I did?"

"*Oui!* Do you play innocent with me? Ba! You liked his looks." The old woman preened. "You told me to tell him about your sister, the one who was always running up the street to watch those animals in the Bonnet-Rouge."

Viv's stomach turned. Charmaine had ordered this woman to watch Diane as she went on her expeditions to watch the tribunals.

Tate was beside Viv at once, a hand to her arm.

Jocelyn wiped the back of her hand over her nose. "*Oui*, he had his friends watch the house, too. Just for you. But then you look a pretty piece to offer a man. Paid him well in *chat*, did you?"

Tate growled at the woman.

Viv could only stare into the past. Wouldn't Vaillancourt want to arrest her father? What good was Diane to him?

But…but then…

Would this woman lie? Why? For fun? To see me—or rather Charmaine—squirm? But what good would it do to make this up now? Charmaine wouldn't pay the woman more for lies she made up here years later.

She had to speak. Sound logical. Sound like Charmaine.

"I…I do remember him now. Handsome man."

"*Oui.* A real *chevalier.*" Jocelyn cursed. "René Vaillancourt. Bastard."

TATE HAD VIV'S arm curled in his as they bade adieu to Jocelyn Gatel. Viv held her head high as he and she turned for the door.

With a few words to the coachman, Tate climbed inside the carriage, sat beside Viv, and pulled her frozen body into his arms. He removed her little bonnet and opened the frog at the collar of her pelisse. Then, one hand to her cheek, the other arm around her stiff shoulders, he tucked her into the crook of his neck.

They rode in silence. She needed time to absorb the hellish revelations of the maid. His own conclusions he would hold inside until he had helped Viv put the news of Charmaine's betrayal and Vaillancourt's involvement into perspective.

When the coach stopped, he alighted first and, without a word, extended his hand to her. She came. On her face, a look of surprise soon melted to approval at the scene before her. His house, yes, it was. The servants' entrance. Those men who followed them—Tate's and the others—knew where they were. But few others would know. Protecting her reputation was the least he could do for her this morning.

She did not comment. She did not argue. She merely nodded at him and allowed him to lead her inside. Up the creaking stairs, they went round and round to the second floor.

He took her to his rooms. Privacy, even from his own servants, was most important to him today.

Inside his sitting room, he helped her with her pelisse and put to one side her little reticule. He heard the jingle of the metal and glass inside. Charmaine had taught Viv well how to imitate her, even carrying an *étui* filled with whatever Viv could buy in Paris chemists. With nary a word, he went to his dry board and poured them both generous draughts of good cognac. He gave her hers and caught her gaze.

"I don't know where to begin," she said, looking into the depths of her glass and setting it aside. "What she said was so...preposterous." When he had no response, she tipped her head in question. "You believe her."

He sat down beside her, but put his glass to the nearby table. "I do. She had no reason to lie to you today."

"Exactly. I took her by surprise. She had no time to dissemble." Her features grew pinched with disbelief. "The man she seduced was René Vaillancourt," she murmured, her dulcet voice a wreck. She stared at Tate. "I've met him."

"As have I." *He is the law, and here, above it.* "A dangerous man."

Her fingers curled over his cravat in a desperate clinch. "I am undone that Charmaine paid that woman to seduce him. How does one do that? And to trap one's own sister? I knew...I *knew* Charmaine could be... But not this. Not this."

Tate had always thought little of Charmaine. He should have sensed the enormity of her cruelty. "She knows no bounds."

"That is not...not who she is today!" Viv stared at him. "Or so I thought."

He threaded his fingers through her soft hair and stroked the fullness of her lower lip with his thumb. To respond with his disbelief that people never changed would not be helpful to Viv.

Terror stood in her sapphire eyes. "Vaillancourt took Diane to a prison."

"Carmes." Ramsey had told him a few details about those who had been incarcerated there. A living hell from which few emerged.

Viv opened her mouth, a memory flitting over her lovely face. "It is not far from rue du Four."

"If Vaillancourt was attached as a gendarme to the local police in the Croix-Rouge crossroads, he would have ordered her taken there."

Viv shuddered. "Why would he want her? Diane was young, fifteen, no threat to anyone."

"A question only he can answer. But I'd say he wanted to use her as a trade for your father."

"To offer up to Robespierre?"

"Exactly."

Tears welled in her eyes. "And what good has it done anyone?"

Tate curled her against him. He would not recount those lost to the horror of that evening.

"Even she," Viv said with a desperate groan, "Jocelyn Gatel, has not profited. After more than a decade, she is in poor health. Living in a filthy hell. Destitute. The ten francs I gave her before we left will do little for her for the rest of her life."

His heart melted. "You pity her. After all she revealed today. Amazing that you can do that, my darling. I must say you are a remarkably forgiving soul."

She took a quick gulp of her cognac, let it slide down her throat, then shook her head. "Forgiving? Not me."

He curled her against him and lifted her face. "You forgave me my failure to rescue Diane."

"Oh, Tate! Your intention was honorable. The odds were against you. We all wish we'd had greater success at some endeavors. Me too. Mama, who cried her heart out that she could not save Diane. Oh, to fail is…"

She shot from the settee and snatched up her reticule and pelisse.

He was behind her, his arms to her shoulders. "Where are you going?"

"A walk. A ride. A swim in the Seine!" She laughed wildly, then hung her head.

"I'll go with you."

She spun and stared up at him. "No! You have done enough. I must save myself."

"You do, my darling. You have saved not only yourself but everyone else in your family."

"Not Charmaine."

"Even her. You were thirteen when we left here. But in your soul, you were wiser than your years. You accepted that you were in another country without home or money."

"You gave us both."

"A pittance." He brushed tears from her cheeks. "You bought chicks and ducklings from George Drummond's mother. You planted herbs and vegetables."

"You tilled that field for me." Her tears stopped.

"A small service." He traced the arch of one elegant cheek. "You saw that another tenant was going to shoot a stubborn donkey, and you bargained with him and gave him five hens to save Fred. That wise creature has loved you ever since." *As I do.* "Through it all, you nursed your mother, who was gone to her own imaginings. And Charmaine? Well, even to her, you were her inspiration to take up acting. Meanwhile, you taught the tenants' children English history."

"Which they questioned because of my heritage."

He smiled and hugged her close. "Facts they spout to each other…"

"Yes, while fighting the Battle of Bosworth on the village common."

"With sticks and stones. Yelling at each other like ghouls." He grinned.

She curled her lips in a brief smile, but grief made her tremble and she pulled away. She ran down the way he'd brought her into the house to the servants' stairs and down through the servants' hall and the kitchen.

At the door, he caught her by her wrist. But she shook her head at him and pushed open the door to the alley.

His hired coach was still there. He'd paid the man to remain, planning to take her home himself. Congratulating himself on his foresight did not fill the ache in his heart that he could not comfort her in this sad hour.

Tate was faster than the driver to offer her a hand up into the coach. He lifted her chin. "Return to me. I will honor and comfort you in all good times and bad. I love you, Vivienne de Massé."

SHE SCRAMBLED UP into the coach, his words fire to her soul. The driver lashed the reins, and off they went into the sunny afternoon filled with the chaotic chorus of the city. Fleeing terror and war, death and despair, those in the streets looked like rabid animals. Viv remembered the emotion.

But today, she felt not their anguish.

She sat like a statue.

Tate loved her, and she was too obsessed with the machinations of Charmaine to respond. Tate loved her, and she had left him. Tate loved her, and she had not told him of her own desire.

She let her tears dribble down her cheeks. He had always been her friend. For years, he had been in her life for all the little things that had created her respect for him. He had laughed and dined with them in Neufchateau, teaching her a smattering of German and how to shoot a pistol. He had ridden with the family to Paris and helped them pack to flee Robespierre. He had escorted them to his estate in Norfolk. Given them one of his cottages. Some money. Hope.

He had been her ally, her comfort in good times and bad. Sending a physician to look at his mother. Plowing that field to grow the garden vegetables she so desperately needed to supplement their diet. Ordering another cottage cleared as the schoolroom. Building chairs and desks. Chuckling at the children who attended her village classes. Even taking part like a wild man in their reenactments of Bosworth.

She burst into a teary laugh at the memory of his wielding a sword of wood, pretending to be King Richard, dying to keep his throne. He was more her hero, her King Arthur, saving her family from ruin.

She pounded on the roof of the cab. She winced and did it again.

"Return!" she yelled to the man. "Return!"

Chapter Eleven

Viv BANGED ON Tate's kitchen door. She'd wake the dead if she had to.

A young girl swung wide the door. "Mademoiselle?"

"*Oui, je suis désolé, ma petite.*" *I do regret I am so slow to learn.*

Then Viv shoved her pelisse, her hat, and her reticule into the girl's hands, picked up her skirts, and ran up the stairs. At the second floor, she burst through the door and stood a moment, trying to remember which way she should turn.

On a whim, she went right and took the hall like the wind. She thanked heaven for snug slippers.

At Tate's door, she paused a moment to collect her thoughts. Then, without knocking, she turned the handle and marched through. He was not in his sitting room.

She strode for his bedroom.

Not there.

His bathing room?

No, not there.

His dressing room?

There! There he stood. His frock coat gone, his waistcoat too, he stood in his shirt, breeches, and boots. Shocked at her sudden appearance, he questioned her with those magnificent blue-green eyes.

"I...I return to you. I return to you," she said as she took a step toward him, "as you have always returned to me. In all good times and bad. With honor and the finest of intentions. I want to be here with you but fear I am not worthy of a man so wise and caring."

He'd grown wide-eyed at her words.

"I need you, Tate Cantrell." She gulped back tears that threatened to destroy the moment she meant to be a new beginning for them.

Not a breath did she take before he had her in his arms. His hands to her cheeks, he took her mouth. His kiss was a brand, his lips hot, fierce, and bold. He kissed her so deeply, he bent her backward in his arms. Fighting for air, she broke away but caught him by the nape and brought him back to her.

"I want to be with you," she told him between his ravishing claiming of her mouth. "Always. I can say it a thousand times, can't I?"

HE SANK HIS fingers into the coif of her hair and sent her pins flying. Her words were not love, but he could wait for them. "Say it each day, each hour. I will never stop you."

She had come back to him, and he would never allow her to part from him for the rest of their lives. She was his, and for the first time in his life, he could go on assured of hope she could return his love.

She rose and kissed him back with a fervor that had him gathering her closer.

"I love you, Vivienne. I will until I die. You are the finest person I have ever known."

"No, no. I am not." She looked tormented. Why that was, he would learn. With tender care, he would tease it out of her.

"I love you. You with your optimism. Your loyalty to others.

Your Louis and chickens and your ducks."

She gulped back tears. "And Fred."

"Dear me!" He laughed, even though he felt hot tears of his own form beneath his eyelids. "How could I forget Fred? The poor thing brayed at me like a vampire last spring when I appeared. He wanted to know how in hell I could be there and you were not. *Where did she go?* he seemed to cry at me. *Where did my darling girl go?* And I had no answers for him."

She hugged him closer. "I want to go home, Tate. I want to go with you."

"Do you, darling?" Now, like a rogue, he would ensure that—and so led her by the hand to his bedroom. Now it was his responsibility to show her how he adored her.

Viv followed him and stopped as she had not when she ran through before to scan the room. It was a grand affair furnished in heavy red and black Chinoiserie furniture. A century-old four-poster stood to one wall, a noble thing high off the ground. He wanted to be in it with her, forgetting the past, making new memories.

She dropped his hand and danced backward. "You'll make love to me now."

"Indeed I will."

"You'll show me how it's done properly?"

Wicked ideas inflamed him at the mere idea of having her naked and writhing. "Not so properly at all, I vow."

She giggled. He wanted to laugh with her, smile, embrace all the love he had for her that he had kept locked inside, far from his reach, far from her touch.

She paused in the midst of the carpet. "I've never done this with a man."

"A fact I will honor." He arched a brow and advanced toward her.

"I know how it's done, however," she said, waggling her finger at his clothes, "and without all these frills."

"Care to remove them from me?"

"Oh, I would. I've often wondered what was beneath all these layers."

He chuckled. The look in her eyes burned away any barriers to their union. "You have a few layers of your own."

She gave him a moue like a singer of a bawdy Pont Neuf vaudeville. "You may remove mine, after I'm done with yours."

He spread out his arms. "Go to it, then. I am eager, and the day grows short."

She shot a glance at the far window. "Hmmm. Not even noon, sir."

"But we have so much to do."

She put her fingers to his shirt and yanked it from his breeches. She hummed as she drew it over his naked shoulders and dropped it to the floor. At the sight before her, she licked her lips. His triceps and pectorals must have appealed, because she swallowed audibly. But as she ran her palms over each ridge and valley down to his hipbones, his patience died to an adventure in longing.

"You try a man's patience."

"Oh. What do you recommend?"

He hooted. "Want a description, do you?"

She batted her pale blonde lashes at him and flicked the top button of his flies. "I've never done this, so I need instructions. I won't know what to put where."

That aroused him as little else could, so he grabbed her and kissed her senseless. Panting, he vowed, "I know what to put where, my darling. I have things in hand."

"Oh! But I thought I could."

"What?" He looked confused.

"Have a few things in hand."

He gave her a sly look. "You steal my breath."

"Oh, marvelous. Because I was told that was allowed. I heard from my friend Kate Martin that a woman could have her husband's"—she cleared her throat—"*accoutrements* in hand and make him very happy!"

He growled. "And who is Kate Martin?"

"My friend, and one of your wise tenants."

"I see," he said as Viv unbuttoned his flies. "A fine lady. Married, is she?"

"Oh, yes." Viv sank one hand against the fullness of his aching cock and held him tight. "Told me all sorts of delightful things. And I have never been able to use the knowledge. Except on myself. Of course."

"You know a lot, then, about what you can feel?" he asked, ready to give her endless delights with his fingers, his tongue, and most especially his throbbing cock.

She put her lips to his and licked the seam. "I do. I hope you will make me feel better than that. It was…lonely."

He clamped her to him with one hand and stroked her collarbone with the other. Across the rise of her breast, he planted tiny kisses. She wriggled in his arms as he slid down her bodice to reveal one hard, pale pink nipple. "What we will do will always be together."

"Show me," she said into his mouth. "I cannot breathe or think or dream any longer without you."

Tate took her gown from her with care, though his fingers shook and his heart pounded. Her corset and her shift came next. She stood before him, her voluptuous breasts a treat he longed to savor. For a moment, she allowed him the pleasure of absorbing the sight of all of her, then she reached for him.

With a staying hand to her, he sat and pulled off his boots and stockings. Then he went to her, eager as an untried boy. For he *had* had women. An occasional romp, sometimes a refuge, but never one who meant to him more than the hour or the evening. He held Viv by the waist as she took down his breeches and his smalls. He stepped out of them, and she watched him as if she was memorizing each movement of his muscles.

Smiling in reassurance at her dazed expression, he scooped her up under her knees and back and laid her on his bed. With a slide of his fingers into the wealth of her silken white-gold hair, he pulled it free of pins and spread the waves over her throat and down her shoulder.

"You are so lovely, my darling. I have never seen any beauty to compare to yours."

Putting her heel to his knee, she slid her foot along his calf. "You are soft as satin."

"Not all of me," he said as she undulated and pressed her belly to the rise of his shaft.

"No. Some parts are beautifully hard." She wrapped her hand around his cock. "Beneath all that satin."

"You do me honors, my dear, and I have much to explore of my own." He cupped one pretty breast and sank over her nipple to lave it and suck.

She arched up. "That is…"

He sucked on her other breast. "Yes. This one too."

He ran his hand down her ribs to her waist, so small, her hips nicely wide, and into her nether hair, thick and wet with the desire of wanting him. "I have no words," he murmured as he sank his fingers inside her tight little channel.

She arched high into his embrace. "Yesss, there. Just…there."

"And here," he offered as he found her little nub, then tapped it and pinched it.

She panted. "That…"

He circled her clitoris and elicited another gasp from her pink lips. "Is wonderful."

"And I need…"

"More?"

"Yes!"

"This?" He positioned himself at her entrance and sank in bit by bit.

"Yes, and yes," she murmured each time he possessed her and retreated, only to repeat it all again.

Until at last, he was deep inside her velvet heat, and she clutched at his shoulders, rubbed her breasts against him, and said, "Yessss," one sweetly torrid time. Then, with artful care for the woman whom he'd treasure like this each day for the rest of his life, he brought them both the joy they had never before known.

Chapter Twelve

MAKING LOVING WITH Tate Cantrell left her in awe and yearning for more of him. After her first climax, she could not part with Tate and clung to him, astonished at the act and that she had finally had him as a woman takes a man she adores.

He made to move, and she complained. "I hate to let you go."

He rolled her to her back and took her mouth in a demanding kiss. "I never go far from you. I aways return."

With another kiss filled with yearning and acceptance, she did let him go. But he returned scant minutes later with warmer blankets that he curled around her shoulders. She watched him, still struck that he loved her, he was here, and they were one.

"You are a treasure." He caressed her cheek. "I can scarcely believe you're mine. But you are."

She luxuriated in the bedding like an animal nesting. "We will do that again?"

"Oh, yes. And soon."

She relaxed. "Not just once a day."

"No." He twirled a curl near her cheek. "Once an hour for many years."

She guffawed. "You will never work again."

He rolled over her, propped on his elbows, his enthusiastic

body rising to declare his interest. "I've worked for years for others. Now I'd say it's time I devote myself to my wife."

Her heart danced. "You'll marry me?"

"My fondest wish."

"Soon? Not here," she said, and pushed away thoughts of the necessary task before her. She could not marry him and begin a new life before besting all the devils of her former one.

"I think that would be difficult now. We could do it only if the ambassador married us, and he, I do believe, leaves Paris today."

"But I am not English. Catholic, too. That's a problem in the Anglican church."

"Never worry." He traced her lips and kissed her a thousand times. "We'll get a dispensation. You will be mine. And I yours. Never to part."

He made love to his fiancée then, with reverence because it was for only the second time in her life.

⊁⟫⟫⟩✕⟨⟨⟨⊰

IT WAS LATE afternoon when Viv roused from their bed and sat up. The sheets fell from her bare breasts, and the bass voice of approval from across the room drew her gaze.

Tate, naked as God had made him, sat opposite her in a large upholstered chair. One leg crossed at the ankle of the other, he crooked his fingers and bade her come.

"You were watching me sleep," she managed in a sleepy voice as she curled herself onto his lap, naked, and seeking only his warmth and his passion.

"I was. A learning experience."

"Oh?" She nipped his earlobe, inhaling his musk. "What did you learn?"

"You take up all the bed."

She shot back, pretending to be horrified. "I do not!"

He touched her nose. "You also snore."

"What?"

He demonstrated.

She pushed up, appalled. "I do not."

"I'm afraid you do, my love." He shook his head, severe and somber. "I simply cannot sleep with you."

She tried to leave.

He chuckled and hauled her back to straddle him. "I doubt I will ever be able to sleep with you, sweet Vivienne."

"You're making that up."

He filled his hands with both her breasts and swirled his thumbs on her nipples. He laved one and sucked the other.

She had her head thrown back, living for the feel of his tongue on her skin. "You have got to be wrong."

He scooted her hips up his thighs and probed her open folds. "I will never sleep again, my dear. It's this I'll be doing with you till the end of time."

She sank over him and gasped as he filled her completely. "Sleep is so unnecessary."

⤜⟫⟫⟫⟪⟪⟪⤛

"COME HAVE LUNCHEON," Tate whispered in her ear minutes later.

Viv put her fingertips to his lips and caught his searing gaze. He loved her. His declaration was the very one she had wanted all her life and never hoped to gain. He had bared his soul to her. She owed him the same. She would tell him, tell him all she could. *Save that one part that eludes me.*

A shared union—and shared life—meant she should not keep any secrets from him.

She sat up and took from his hand the red silk banyan he offered. She followed him into his sitting room and went to the credenza, where his servants had laid out a display of sliced beef, a cool cucumber salad, and sautéed asparagus and squash. She took a small plate and filled it, then went to sit beside him on the settee. Finishing quickly, she set her empty plate aside.

"I wish to tell you about my reason to come here to Paris."

His gaze consoled her. "Tell me quickly and we will be done with it."

Would that were so… "And afterward you will decide if you still wish to marry me." *If you still love me.*

"Nothing changes that, Viv. Nothing."

She dropped his hands and wandered about his sitting room, finding the right place to begin. Crossing her arms, she considered the tapestry upon the wall before her. Whoever built this mansion had had this fabric woven to portray the master of the house atop his white charger, his sons or retainers behind him in phalanx. All of them smiled. But they gazed at the carcass of a buck, strung upside down from a huge tree branch, gutted and bleeding to the forest floor. The deer was a sacrifice to this *seigneur*'s pleasure of the hunt—or his family's need for venison. Sport or survival.

She slowly faced Tate and smiled at him with all the yearning she had felt since she was a girl—and began her sordid tale. "Charmaine is very ill. Never to recover. She has been sick for years. A disease she acquired from her activities with those men she favored. She has been pregnant twice, perhaps more. I did not know then; I do not ask now. The babies did not live but for hours. They too carried this disease."

She ran a hand over her brow. Blind to the brilliant colors of the room, she saw her sister as she had the last time she visited. Charmaine, who once resembled Viv, now looked like a scarecrow from the fields. Her luxurious white-blonde hair was almost gone. A few tufts stuck out from her bald head. Her sapphire eyes—once large, brilliant, and bold—were hooded, red rimmed, and dim. She had her voice, that dark contralto that ordered everyone about. If it was a few tones lighter and held a rasp, Charmaine did not comment on it. That had been days before Viv had left for Paris.

"She asked me to come tend her last spring. That is why you could not find me. I had left Norfolk, and she told me to leave no word lest others find where I had gone and trace her. She wanted no one to know where she was or why she secluded herself.

"I arrived in a new house she had rented on the edge of Richmond. I nursed her, paid her bills. Finally, to earn her wages to support us both, I agreed to impersonate her last winter. By then, she was so ill she could not work. She lured me, saying she needed the wages. About two years ago, she had begun to give me money, not that I needed it. But she had to give it to me. She had debts, you see, even then, and I was to pay them as I could. Then at Christmas, I agreed to be her double.

"I could do it. I was capable. After all, I was the one who used to make up the plays and demand that she and Mama and a few of your tenants do the parts. I could be Juliet or Desdemona. Odd, you know, last winter she was to star in *Macbeth*, and oh, did I love portraying that tragic lady." Viv fisted one hand. "Charmaine got what she wanted."

"None of it good," he said with bitterness.

She nodded. "So you realize that, like her and those fellows there, I can have a taste for blood." She tipped her head over her shoulder at the tapestry.

Tate shook his head, adamant. "Lady MacBeth also went mad. It was not her nature to kill. Nor is it yours."

"Perhaps not. But there are times when I can taste victory like that…" Viv whirled on him. "Can you imagine what it was like to live with the question of what happened to Diane? To wonder if the maid told the police that we were going to leave that night? To ask yourself what you could have done to prevent her from being taken from you?"

His eyes went dead. "I do know that well."

The force of his words hit her like a wall of stone. Her reminiscence had not been meant to make him regret the past.

Yet he still did mourn. "I have spent my life castigating myself for the failure to capture her. I ran from the carriage that night. I ran like a fiend. She was just before me, hurried along by two men. Were they police? Or soldiers? I did not see their clothes. In the melee, I could not tell who they were, what they were. I knew only that they rushed her through the throng. That others parted for them. That I was left scrambling to catch up—and I never could. Finally, near a high wall—a convent? A church? A government office? I cannot remember where it was, what it was, but the two men rushed her inside a door. Massive, it was. It was not wood but iron, and it clanged shut. In a moment, Diane was gone…and I could do nothing. Nothing."

Viv went to him, her arms around his sagging shoulders. "I am no assassin. You are right. I have not the will. And you?" She ran her fingers through the thick satin of his hair. "You, my darling, are no failure. You tried to save her. You *tried*. The odds were against you. We cannot blame ourselves for those things we tried to do. It is important to mark that we tried. It is vital we praise ourselves for attempting to change our lives. Most often, I venture, we can."

"So then you agreed to impersonate Charmaine and come here in her place. But you told yourself you would learn what you could about that night."

She hated to tell him the rest. But she must. "I was so…angry at Diane's loss! In and of myself, I was aggrieved. And yes, living with Charmaine did that to me. Listening to her rant and rave. I became more spiteful and vindictive. I was rabid to take her place and hurt anyone who had hurt Diane. Who had hurt us. My entire family was gone, and soon I would lose Charmaine as well."

She inhaled and cleared her mind. "Then suddenly you were here, before me, questioning me, warning me, helping me see that…see that I am not one who can exact retribution without conscience. I am not that strong."

"No," he said, "you are not that perverse."

"When I go home and tell her what I've learned, she will

accuse me of believing others' lies. She will deny it all. Then she will accuse me of being weak."

"She should declare you brave, braver than she. But then, she serves only herself, Viv, and never sees what she truly is."

She nodded. "You are right. Of course."

"Now there are a few facts more you can discover about what happened to Diane."

She let her head fall back and stared at the frescoed ceiling. Above them, cherubs cavorted around a carousel. Oh, to be so carefree and laugh like that. "Yes. With what the maid has revealed, now I can go to Vaillancourt and ask what he did for Charmaine and the maid." She scoffed. "Do I have the courage? No, no. But I have the curiosity. *That*, I have in abundance. And I have the need to know. To confront Charmaine. But then, it is a risk, eh? Will he even let me in to see him or answer my questions? Will he answer? Ha. He has no reason to. He could deny it all and show me the door."

"But if you went with more proof of what he did, he might not be able to deny you the truth."

"I have no idea where to get that."

"I do."

She rounded on Tate with wide eyes. She could not imagine how he'd know. "Tell me."

"A friend of mine is acquainted with a lady who was in Carmes."

"The prison?" she whispered in awe.

"Yes."

Viv blinked. A memory crossed her mind, and so did anger—and she quickly defined why she was agitated. "Charmaine had once talked about a Paris prison near Saint Germain where she thought Diane might have been sent. I always wondered why she would think that."

"Perhaps she had heard much about the place," Tate offered.

A hand to her mouth, Viv made an ugly sound. "Or she knew Diane had gone there."

Tate could only stare back at her, sorrow in his gaze.

"And this lady who was in Carmes? Who is she? Can we speak to her?"

"The English Countess Nugent, Cecily Struthers-Sumner. Well known to Society."

"The woman who was mistress to the old Duc d'Orleans, the liberal Bourbon prince who was guillotined?" Viv asked.

"You have heard of her, then?"

"Who has not? The duke was one my father knew and worked with. I had no idea the countess still lived in Paris."

"She does. A close friend now of Josephine Bonaparte. Both of them survived a sentence in Carmes."

Viv could not catch her breath. "I must call on her."

Tate stood and took two strides to take her in his arms. "I will go with you."

LATE THAT AFTERNOON, Tate saw Viv to her home in the same unmarked old carriage they had used to go to Passy. They had agreed on a few things. First, he would talk with his friend Ramsey and ask for an introduction to the infamous Countess Nugent, then write to ask for an audience with her.

While they waited for the woman's response, Viv agreed to prepare to leave Paris. She would order her household staff to begin to close the house. She would also order Alice to return home tomorrow, and take little Louis with her. Viv told the maid she must not go to visit Charmaine, but take rooms in London to await her mistress's return. She gave her an address of a small hotel near the city, respectable and quiet. Alice would want to wait for Viv to travel with her, but Viv had no idea when or if she could meet with Countess Nugent. The maid and Louis were to go. Tonight, however, Alice and another upstairs maid would pack Viv's trunks and the majordom would make arrangements to send them via barge toward London. The address they were to be sent to was Tate's house in Berkeley Square.

"I will perform tonight," she told him as the carriage stopped behind her house. "This is too late to cancel. After this performance, I give my notice. Come here when you know more about when we might meet with the countess."

He kissed her to seal their agreement. "Have a valise ready and sew your passport into your clothes."

"Into the hem of my shift." *Like I did more than a decade ago.* "I will."

"I will call for you tonight at the close of the play."

She beamed at him, the novel security of being with him enveloping her. "Thank you. You will stay the night with me, I hope. I do not wish to lose you now that we have found each other again."

"Never worry," he whispered. "We are one; the world is right. That will not change."

Chapter Thirteen

TATE ORDERED HIS coachman to Ramsey's house in rue d'Orleans. But Ram's staff were in an uproar.

"We are dispersing, Monsieur Appleby." His majordom looked exasperated. His hair was on end, his cravat a simple mess. "My master has told me to close the house."

"Do you have any idea where he is?"

"No, monsieur. He said goodbye to me in a most formal way days ago, and I had the impression I was not to ask where he went or why, and not to expect to ever see him again."

Then, to Tate's surprise, he said, "But I am glad you have come here. Do you need money, monsieur?"

Tate was flummoxed. "Why do you ask?"

"Monsieur le Vicomte told me if you called, or if two other gentlemen who are his friends came here, and you needed coin, I should give it to you. Come with me, monsieur."

The man promptly took him to his own apartment beyond the formal foyer and extracted from a large wall safe some gold coin. "For your escape, monsieur. Vicomte Ramsey took what he needed, and you are to have a share, too."

Tate was grateful for the gold, which he would use if he had to. It could substitute for any failure of French francs. Not everyone, especially peasants, liked paper money. They distrusted hard-coin francs too, marked though they were with the visage of the French first consul. Tate shook his head. A bad thing, when one led a country where even the money was distrusted.

"One thing more before you go, monsieur," the majordom bade him. "If you need more help of any kind, le vicomte told me to remind you of another upon whom you may call. That is the man who was the majordom of your other friend, Comte de Ashley."

Kane's butler, whom he and Ram had trusted implicitly, was Corsini, an Italian of many talents and many friends. "*Merci beaucoup*, monsieur." Tate paused and smiled, of a sudden remembering Kane's advice about whom to trust—Corsini, Countess Nugent, and Madame St. Antoine. He'd call upon them all for help, if need be.

Tomorrow, Tate decided, he would go to Kane's former home in rue Saint-Honoré and learn if Corsini was still in residence. He went home straight away, ordered up supper on a tray in his sitting room, then sat down to compose a long letter to Countess Nugent. In it, he introduced to her the actress Charmaine Massey and told of the young woman's desire to learn more about the fate of her sister, who may have been sent to Carmes Prison. If Diane had been there, might she also have been there at the same time as the countess? Tate appealed to the lady's love of justice to receive Charmaine and tell her any details she might know.

The woman had made a reputation for herself in London and in Paris. She was once the young mistress of the Prince of Wales, but that man had married her off to a sickly, simple-minded creature, all to cover the prince's infatuation with the nubile young girl. Soon after the marriage, the countess disappeared from court. Many speculated as to the cause.

But many months later and a widow, she appeared in Paris. Suddenly she was the talk of the town—and the mistress of the Duc d'Orleans. That man, though a Bourbon close to the throne, increasingly voiced liberal causes. Later dubbed Philippe Égalité for his sentiments, he nonetheless was carted off by Robespierre to the guillotine. She was sent to Carmes.

But her friendship with Josephine Beauharnais saved her...and her young charge, a girl Cecily had saved from her parents' poisoned marriage. The girl was Mademoiselle Amber Gaynor, later to wed and become Madame St. Antoine. That lady was the one Tate had met at the theater that night he discovered Viv acting as Charmaine.

Countess Nugent had long been heralded as a beauty. But she was also wily enough to befriend dutifully those in power. She also saved her reputation by never openly consorting with any other men—and saving the fortunes her two famous lovers had bestowed upon her. She was, despite war, famine, and inflation, a woman worth millions.

That night, when the play closed, Tate was at Viv's dressing room door to escort her home. At Viv's house, she took him straight away to her suite.

"My men surround your house and mine. No one comes in or out whom we do not know," he'd assured her as he slid off her creamy silk negligee and led her to her bed. There they took down each other's clothes and made long, slow love to each other. He slept as fitfully as Viv, worried about the details of escaping Paris. She, however, pondered what she had learned from the scullery maid. Her contemplation was dark, and he knew in his heart he must not probe, nor lure her from it. The maze of her relationship with her half-sister was a journey only she could take. She must find her own way. Tate knew she would.

THE NEXT MORNING, he finished his coffee, stood, and bent over Viv as she remained at her breakfast table. He raised her chin and dropped a warm kiss to her lips.

The night had been theirs, sweet and intimate, the newly found refuge from the storm of their past and their present. The morning, however, swiftly brought their attention to the details of their departure.

He cupped her cheek. "I go to find a man who will help us leave the country quickly. I will return to you when I can."

Viv loved the shelter of his arms, but knew she should not deter him. "Yet if Countess Nugent arrives, you will want to be here."

"I do, but if I am not, so be it. Those things you need to know from her, you must ask. Then report to me later, when I return." He put his lips to hers once more, his kiss the vital reassurance of a new life for them both. "Ask her for all the details. Anything you want to know. I think the lady will be forthcoming. She has not survived the terrors of this country's violence without a clear vision of others and herself."

HE RETURNED TO his own house to oversee its closure. He double-checked that Kane had departed Paris. He went to Ramsey's, too, but that man had not returned to his house.

His friends were truly gone. It was time he and Viv left France.

But first, they would wait for a response from Countess Nugent.

He prayed they would get one—and quickly.

AFTER TATE LEFT her, Viv bathed and dressed. She spoke with an upstairs maid when a footman hurried in. He brought on a silver salver a rectangular parchment, fragrant with a perfume of freesias and roses.

At once, Viv broke the seal on the letter. The letter fell open. The fine script confirmed that the correspondent was a lady of repute.

My dear Mademoiselle de Massé,
I write hurriedly today to invite you to call upon me. I do this recognizing you may be preparing to leave Paris. The current political situation between our two countries certainly deteriorates. I do think it prudent you leave.
Before you go, however, I ask if you might spare me an hour of your time?
Might you visit me this morning at eleven o'clock? I realize the hour is soon and early for calls; however, time grows short for you here and I wish to be helpful.
Please reply at your earliest convenience.

Yours sincerely,
C

THE COUNTESS LIVED on Île Saint-Louis in a very fine *hôtel particulier* that rumor said was purchased for her by the old Duc d'Orleans, her former patron and lover.

Viv stood in the foyer handing over her gloves and reticule to the lady's majordom. He ushered her up the winding stairs to the first floor, and as she went, she marveled at the exquisite Carrara marble statues in the niches and the tapestries upon the curved walls. The bouquet wafting through the air at each bend of the stairs spoke of lemon and orange that stirred Viv's senses and made her pine for rue du Four and what might have been had the mobs never gained power.

The butler showed her down the hall to the open double doors of a grand salon. The walls were a soft lime, the moldings of a lemon cream, while the overstuffed Rococo chairs were upholstered in bright emerald with tiny yellow *fleurs-de-lys* and the settees were in eye-popping amethyst. The colors stirred one to open one's mouth and exclaim at the beauty. Of course, as the main drawing room of a lady of Society, the aura inspired one to conversation.

"Welcome, mademoiselle." Countess Nugent walked toward Viv, one hand out, another on a cane.

"Thank you," Viv said, smiling, taking the lady's offered hand. "I am delighted to be here and honored at your invitation."

"Please come sit down, *ma petite*." The lady had a regal elegance to her stride, despite the cane, and a smile that could warm any stranger to become her most loyal friend. "I ordered for us *petit déjeuner*. Forgive me for asking you to attend me at such an early hour. But I fear you and I need to discuss much, and do it quickly."

She looked wearied, the lines around her green eyes denoting she was older than her forty-two years. She was exquisitely lovely, with naturally pale pink cheeks and cropped coal-black curls, all the fashion. She was a dramatic figure, tall and sensual, showing her bosom and long arms to perfection in a supple jade silk gown. In her oval face, the most expressive elements were her eyes and lips. But her eyes were dim with some recent sorrow and her mouth was thin with strain. She stood slightly stooped, leaning upon that cane.

The countess led them to the amethyst settees that faced each other. As she walked, the lady drilled her cane into the fine lime-colored carpet. "Do please be seated. I will serve you, if I may?"

"Please do."

The lady sat and began to pile a plate with the delicacies of cold shrimp, tiny crepes, and glacé strawberries. "I apologize for my cane. I... Well, I have had a stressful family situation occur in the past days. The result is that I have been weakened by the madness. Unwell, truly, if the truth be told. There are too many unruly situations in our city, are there not?"

The countess blinked, as if trying to rally to some challenge and could not match her reputation as a renowned hostess of Parisian *beau monde*. "I slept late this morning," she rattled on as she handed over Viv's plate. "I have not eaten yet this day, and I hoped you might like a few delicacies."

The woman repeated herself. Whatever had happened to her, it had shaken her confidence. That made Viv doubly grateful for her help, even if she hated the delay in the pertinent conversation of Diane and Carmes. "I would be most happy to do so, Madame la Comtesse. I have heard your chef is a master at his work, and I am eager to try anything you put before me."

"Good. I like a woman who admits to a strong appetite." The countess cocked her head to one side. "I see you are no fainting flower."

Viv managed a true smile—and found fun in the fact that she'd acquired that hunger assuaging Tate Cantrell's. The countess would find amusement in that, if she knew.

"I have wanted to meet you, mademoiselle. I knew your father and your mother."

Viv managed a polite nod at that. The lady had met Charmaine and Diane's mother. Not her own. Her own mama had never ventured into Society after she became the vicomte's lover.

"How wonderful, Madame le Comtesse." Viv had to carry this off and hear about those she had lost. "Do you remember them well?"

"I do, indeed. My friend the Duc d'Orleans and your father were quite close for the last few years of their lives."

How smoothly the lady spoke of the chaos in France during the beginning of the revolution.

"They were close. Orleans was fond of your father, credited him with many fine ideas to change the taxes and levy them less on the poor."

"As I remember, yes, Papa was devoted to restructuring the

burden of taxes."

"A major cause of all the unrest, yes, it was."

At that moment, the majordom appeared, carrying a large silver tray filled with small dishes of eggs *au gratin*. Behind him marched a footman in stark livery of blue and gold trim. That man carried another tray with an urn for hot chocolate. A third appeared with pastries and small tarts the size of Viv's thumb.

"One of each of those?" The countess's green eyes glowed over that idea.

"But of course." Viv would not refuse her hostess.

When they were sated on a few delicacies, the countess began. "I've wished to meet with you from the very start of your visit here in Paris. I have not had my usual number of soirées lately. Challenges with family, you see."

Viv was reminded of what she had read in the gossip sheets about the return of Amber St. Antoine to Paris, that lady's affair with Tate's friend Lord Ramsey, and St. Antoine's apparent secrecy since her return. She merely nodded, silent.

"However, I was eager to have you here with me and my friends," the countess said. "But after the first consul invited you to his bedroom suite, Madame Bonaparte could not in good grace receive you, and she always attends my parties. Hence, I could not invite you here."

"Please you need not apologize for that. I do understand."

"I hated the gossip about that incident with Monsieur Bonaparte, but I am proud of you for standing up to him."

Viv demurred. "Actually, madame, I stood up to his valet, Monsieur Constant!"

They both gave little laughs over that.

Viv had to add a few titillating details. "The first consul kept me waiting so long, I lost patience. But you must know that I did not wish to be his newest conquest. So I took the opportunity to leave him. I gave the excuse of my work. I am often exhausted by a performance and need my sleep to recover." *Plus, I was frightened to death.*

The countess grinned. "Madame Bonaparte adored the story."

Viv cast her a leery glance. "I am certain her husband did not."

The countess grew stern. "In fact, he was very unkind."

"To stretch the truth to say I was in his bedroom? Yes. So I heard it sung in a few vaudeville songs in the streets. But I was never in Bonaparte's bedroom, madame. I was in his secretary Bourrienne's!"

They had another small chuckle over that.

Viv could not contain her anger of the incident with Bonaparte. "In truth, I was very pleased to escape."

"You come from a noble and ancient family. No one should abuse you, my dear."

"Thank you."

"But I have brought you here today to tell you about a few who have abused those you have loved and lost. I am grateful for your friend Lord Appleby's letter explaining to me your desire to learn more about my time in Carmes."

Viv put her china and her serviette to the table before her.

The countess checked Viv's appearance, clearly looking for any indication of distress at the subject. Viv had girded herself for this, and she prayed she did not dissolve in tears.

The countess inhaled. "The world changes yet again now that France and England go to war once more. This conflict will be long, and time is of the essence for me to right a few wrongs, and save those I love and others for whom I care. You see, I loved your mother. She was a woman who loved well, regardless of Society."

Viv forced herself not to react to the lady's words. Truly, it seemed as if the countess spoke of her mother, Madeleine. Yet how could she? Viv was here as Charmaine...unless the countess perceived she was the half-sister. Tate would not have revealed that to her. Viv was truly bewildered, but could only continue her ruse here as Charmaine.

"I had great affinity with your mother in many things. What would she say about your attempt to learn the fate of Diane, hmmm?"

She would say that I have the right to know what happened to Diane. But no business doing Charmaine's work of revenge for it. "She would want to learn what you may know."

"So then, it is only you and your young half-sister left of your family. What was her name?"

The sister who is more than half? The one everyone forgets suffered as well as the others. Viv bit her cheek. "Vivienne."

"*Oui.* That was her name. Little Vivacious! Does she wish to know what happened to Diane?"

"She does."

"It is not a pretty tale."

"I did not expect it to be."

"Very well," the countess said. "For your happiness, to answer whatever may be a question in your mind about the past, I will reveal what little I know.

"Your sister Diane was a darling girl. Charming, strong, impervious to the threats of the guards. She was a beacon of light to many. She took up for all of us and all the sorrows we bore. She clamored for more food, better than the gruel they gave us. She wanted fresh water for us to wash with. She asked for time in the garden for us all, not for the flowers, because they were gone, trampled, but for the sunshine for our wellbeing.

"Sometimes, she was successful. A guard took pity on one or all of us. But more often they took advantage of any they wanted. Many young women were abused by these bastards who lusted for power."

The countess took a drink of her hot chocolate.

"Diane was lovely, delicate in face and form. She was healthy, and the concierge of Carmes was attracted to her. Much too enamored of her. But she did not care for him, and ridiculed him.

"My own child, a young girl I brought up in my household, knew your sister better than I. If she knows more, I am certain she would tell you."

"Madame St. Antoine?"

The countess nodded, her lips thin with dismay. "Exactly her. My bright, good girl. I know she would help you if she could, but I am afraid she is ill. Very ill. So very…incapacitated that she may lie dying."

"Madame!" Viv took the lady's hand. "I am so sorry."

"Yes, yes. Thank you." The countess reached into a tiny pocket of her gown and took out a handkerchief. She dabbed at her tears. "Forgive me."

"Nothing to forgive, madame. Nothing." Viv squeezed the woman's slim fingers. "I do not wish to upset you more. But I must ask this."

The countess contemplated Viv with tears in her eyes. "I know what you want."

Viv glanced at their entwined hands.

"Diane often talked about her memories of that night she was taken from your carriage. She was quite clear."

Viv sat stock-still. This was the part of Diane's fate that caused her to go numb. Today she had to listen and remember. She could not block out her own failure. Somehow she had to hear this and accept what she had done—and failed to do.

The countess wiped her cheeks. "Diane remarked that the crowd called for her. The one with the red hair. Not the blonde girls. Diane knew she had been targeted. She knew not how. She knew not why. But she was.

"She recalled that a young friend of the family ran after her. She heard him call to her. She said she looked back and saw him. He was then a viscount—he is this friend of yours, the Earl of Appleby, who wrote to me?"

Viv smiled. "Yes. The earl is that same man."

"Diane had recollections that her younger sister's little dog— Beau, perhaps?"

"Yes, Beau," Viv assured her with a twist to her heartstrings.

"Beau jumped from the carriage too and ran after her. But

neither of them caught up to her. She was hurried away. To the prison. Straight away."

Viv's head spun. To hear that last detail, that Tate ran to save Diane, and Beau followed, always stopped her heart. Whenever she spoke of it with Charmaine, Viv lost her awareness of where she was, what she did. All she recalled was the fright of having lost Diane.

Her feeling was the fright of the girl she had been. Her regret was the sorrow of not having run after Diane's abductors. Such was her grief and self-criticism. Yes, she hated to hear it recounted, but was triumphant that at last she had confirmation that Diane knew Tate and Beau had tried to get to her. *Tate and Beau...*

"Diane said she never expected that anyone would leave the carriage to try to get her back." The woman's face held no rebuke.

But Viv felt the reproach like a slap in the face. For Charmaine, who had not moved an inch that night. Had not tried. And for herself! Yes, for herself, too! *All these years, I saw myself like Charmaine. A coward. Afraid to die, I remained in the carriage.*

The countess gazed at her with some small compassion.

"I am not proud." Viv spoke aloud for once in her life the words she had never uttered and should have. "I am not proud I did not help. I am ashamed, very ashamed."

The countess focused narrowly on her eyes. "You were a child."

"Thirteen!" Viv blurted, speaking as herself, not Charmaine. "I could have tried. I should have."

"You were young, tender, and terrified. You must forgive yourself."

"I—I cannot." *I have told Tate to do the same, and yet I cannot excuse my own failure.*

"Forgiveness is a gift we grant others. Often, we do ourselves the disservice of withholding it from our own soul. We are as human as the next, *ma petite*. Time will allow it. This I know."

"I am not certain of that," Viv went on, her heart pounding like a drum. She would declare to this lady, and now to all who asked, how cowardly she had been that night, never to try to save her sister. "You are right, madame, to look at me with a jaundiced eye. I am a wretch. And I do wish to make amends for what I did not do that night. I cannot bring back my sister. But it has haunted me, my other sister, and my...my Aunt Madeleine for what happened to Diane. We never knew. And so, if you do know, if you can say, would you please tell me what happened to our dear girl?"

The countess took a deep breath. "Diane made of herself a nuisance to the concierge of the prison. She was lovely, but used her wit and her tongue to bedevil him and the guards. She was often sent to a private cell in a corridor where those who caused trouble were sequestered. She was always demanding something, criticizing the guards and the concierge. The guards hated her and often tried to...influence her to stop her harassment."

"You mean that they beat her?" Viv asked, hoping it was not true.

"They did. She usually recovered quickly, though I must tell you, over time, she was weakened by them. But one day another girl was brought in, and they were merciless with her. I don't know who she was or what she did, but they intended to starve her to death. Your sister gave the girl her own rations. When the guards found that, they took your sister away. We never saw her ever again."

Tears rolled down both their faces then. They sat, crying silently together.

At last, Viv recovered her voice. "I would hope—with good friends and proper guidance, madame—that I might make recompense for the wrong done my sister. So I ask you if you know any names of those guards or of the concierge." *It might be wrong of me to want revenge when I cannot take it on myself for my part in this. But still, I want this.*

The lady shook her head. "No. I once knew many names, but

it has been years."

Viv pressed her handkerchief to her mouth and tried to accept that this was the end of her search.

"But I do know the name of the police who brought your sister to the prison."

"You do?" Viv could scarcely believe it.

"Diane talked about him often. He came to see her many times. Whatever he told her of that night, she had reason to believe him when he said he was the one who had turned her in."

"Did he tell her how that happened?"

"Only that the one he really wanted was your father. To my knowledge, Diane never breathed a word of your father's whereabouts. The man who arrested her was furious at that."

"Who was he? Do you know?"

The countess went white as marble. "He is a powerful man now. A man with whom few should tangle. Are you sure you wish to know?"

Viv took the woman's hand. "I do. Please tell me."

"He is the deputy chief of police."

Viv could not breathe. "Vaillancourt."

"René Vaillancourt."

VIV ORDERED HER coachman to take her to Tate's house. Her outrage was nothing to her grief, which was a caged beast in her chest.

She had always pushed aside thoughts of how she had failed to join Tate and Beau to rescue Diane that night, but now...now this knowledge that Diane had been so upright, and so abused, tore her in two.

Now, too, she had confirmation that the man responsible for Diane's imprisonment was René Vaillancourt. How and why that happened, she would learn. Oh, the scullery maid could cast blame. The countess could remark on it. But Viv now burned with the need to hear it all from the culprit's lips. Somehow, she would wheedle it out of the man. She knew Tate would want to be present. Indeed, she also knew that he would be a bulwark against anything aggressive Vaillancourt might say or do. She was brave, but to have Tate with her was also prudent.

Arriving at Tate's house, she balked when she noted the front door stood ajar.

She climbed down, but her attention went up the street, where two men scuffled in the road. One was a gendarme, and he wielded his club on the other man's back with a blunt precision resounding in the square.

Viv hurried up the steps of Tate's entryway. His majordom appeared at once inside, supervising two footmen who hammered nails into a large wooden crate.

"*S'il vous plaît*, monsieur," she addressed Tate's man, "announce me to your master."

"Mademoiselle de Massé." The man bowed. But his face was white, his manner stark with fright. "Monsieur le Comte is not here."

"No? Do you have any idea when he will return?"

The majordom's eyes went wide. "Soon, soon."

One of the footmen murmured something about the earl having learned who followed her around town.

Viv took heart. "He has discovered who is it who follows me?" she asked the majordom and the footman. "That's wonderful."

"*Oui*, mademoiselle. He said he will return as soon as possible. We here are to continue to pack up the house."

"I see." She bit her lower lip. "I will return to my own house, then. Please tell him I called upon him."

"*Oui*, mademoiselle. I am certain he will be with you as soon as he can."

But as she stepped outside, she stopped to note the scuffle of the two in the street. The gendarme had wrestled the other man to the cobbles. The fellow howled at the blows the gendarme delivered.

She turned back to the Tate's men. "What goes on here?"

The majordom looked like death had come for him. "That poor fellow is Mr. Winslow Aldrich, a neighbor who rented a house a few doors north. He is British, mademoiselle. And dozens of gendarmes have been in this street all morning, arresting any British who remain."

She caught her breath. "Enemies," she whispered.

"Hurry home, mademoiselle. Word is they march those men to prison."

"Carmes?" she asked.

"Carmes. La Force. Verdun. Who knows?"

She swallowed her fears for Tate. He must not be taken. He was her hope and her love. "I shall await your master at my house. Please tell him to come as soon as possible."

Chapter Fourteen

"MADEMOISELLE." VIV'S MAJORDOM, Monsieur Franck, appeared in her sitting room. He was so pale, he looked bloodless.

"What's wrong?" She looked up from her escritoire, hating the interruption. She hurried her letter to Vaillancourt inviting him to call upon her this afternoon. She would see him before she departed Paris. If he did not come to her, she would appear on his doorstep. Seeing that man was the last thing she would do in Paris. Her house was in order. She had even told her kitchen staff to make sandwiches, pack a bag of apples, and fill large flasks of whiskey. She and Tate would need them if they had to run for the coast without any delay.

"Two gendarmes demand you receive them. They come from Monsieur Vaillancourt."

She put down her pen. With a command to her heart to slow its drum beat, she rose. She was an actress today as she had never been before. Her courage was a slim hook on which to hang her future. But she would persevere. "Show them up to the grand salon." She took a step forward. "Are there more than two? Do others block the back door?"

"No. Only the two are here."

"Very well. You know what to do, all of you. Continue. Allow anyone who wishes to leave the house now to go."

Vaillancourt is questioning me. Marking me in the eyes of the public by sending his coach and his men.

"Mademoiselle, before you go. You must see these." He held out much wrinkled sheets of the day's gossip papers.

"Why? What?" She took them and skimmed. *Mon Dieu! Vaillancourt is a laughingstock?*

Astonished, she could not move.

Lord Ramsey had removed from René Vaillancourt's house Madame St. Antoine. This occurred last night or the night before. The papers had no date. But this they did proclaim: the English viscount had done so in the presence of many notable officials of the government. Talleyrand, for one, though not present at the scene, was not amused. Vaillancourt's superior, Joseph Fouché, upon hearing of the event, was furious at such treatment of a respected lady. Madame had been ill, so very indisposed, that Lord Ramsey had to carry her down the main stairs to his waiting carriage. To make matters worse, the gossip rags proclaimed with rage, the lady accused the deputy chief of police of poisoning her.

Viv stood in a quandary. What did this mean for her? Did this mean Vaillancourt would deal with her easily? Quickly? Or harshly? Would Viv's fate be vengeance for Vaillancourt's recent disgrace?

She could not know. Could not predict. She dropped the papers to a nearby table.

She would be strong.

She thanked her majordom profusely, and he turned on his heel. "Monsieur?" she called to Franck before he disappeared. "*Merci beaucoup.* You have served me well. All of you."

The old fellow had tears in his eyes. "Mademoiselle. An honor to serve you."

A glimpse of her boudoir told her she had made adequate preparations. Only her valise stood open. Her trunks had gone. She strode to her cheval glass and took one last look at Charmaine. Her nearest blood, her nearest duplicate, her tormenter and unfathomable nemesis.

Sticking a few pins to her coiffure, she flashed her eyes as Charmaine would at any challenge to her body or soul. A shot of iron to her spine, a bit of rouge to her cheeks, and the damn fan in her hand was all she needed to complete the transfer.

She snatched up her forest-green wool cloak that lay beside her valise. She'd chosen it for travel. The weather in May could be pleasant, and the fragrances of jasmine often wafted the air. The cloak was heavy for today, but if she encountered storms—or the chill of damp walls around her—the garment would comfort her. Heavy and plain, it would serve her well in prison if Vaillancourt sent her there for her arrogance to question him.

At the hall, she turned back and retrieved her reticule from her bed. Inside was the pistol Fortin had purchased for her months ago. So, too, did she carry the two étui, one with laudanum, the other empty. One never knew what one might have need of, eh?

For one moment, she shut her eyes. Charmaine would go into the presence of the deputy chief of police with her self-confidence and her bravura. No one got the better of her.

With speed, she took the hall and the stairs down to her salon.

The two men stood at attention in the middle of her grand drawing room. Their harsh blue-and-black uniforms offended her, and she allowed Charmaine, who took temporary quarters in her soul, to sniff at their impertinence to appear in her parlor.

"Mademoiselle de Massé?" One stepped forward. "I am to take you to Monsieur Vaillancourt. Will you come quietly?"

She swept a hand toward the foyer. "Lead on."

SHE WAS SURPRISED that the deputy's carriage took her not to the Hôtel de Ville and the offices of the police but to a house not far away in the rue St. Martin.

Why was that? Did Vaillancourt not wish others to know he interviewed her?

Arresting her would be simpler at his offices. But then, did he not wish to detain her? He had no justification for that. Still, he was the law and needed no reason, only desire, to see her off the streets.

She shut down her speculation. She would deal with him as he came, hear his reasoning as he articulated it. Dialogue meant to be met for what it was.

The two gendarmes alighted from the carriage and, one in front of her, one behind, marched her into the house. The majordom had opened the door for them, and greeted her with only a deferential look of frank despair.

The man, she surmised, had witnessed many scenes such as this, Ramsey and Madame St. Antoine only the most recent. Yet the butler was not inured to tragedy. She wondered if the man's master knew of his disapproval.

No matter.

"Monsieur Vaillancourt will attend you presently, mademoiselle."

She met his gaze with gratitude Charmaine would never exhibit. Why not? Vaillancourt would never know what honesty passed between them.

She was escorted up the stairs and down the first floor to a small room, wood paneled and overly warm. The man's office. Documents strewn across his desktop told the tale of a man who was not neat. Nor, perhaps, was he wise. Did he not wonder if she would steal documents from him?

Her gaze swept the rest of the room, and on the large, circular map table was a service of pastries and coffee. If that was for her, she expected either a man who wished to seduce her—or one who expected another guest after her.

The click of boots upon the marble tiles alerted her to her host's arrival.

She faced the doorway, waiting for him, serene as she had never been before, her hands clasped, her reticule, heavy with its contents, hanging from her left wrist...though her pistol was easily grasped.

And there he was—tall, imposing, and elegantly attired, each inch of his frock coat and breeches measured to a hairsbreadth of his lean, fit, muscular body.

Oh, yes, she remembered him well. A breathtaking, virile specimen, René Vaillancourt was a man to set many a woman's heart beating. But not Madame St. Antoine's. His trim figure, his grace, his flashing sapphire eyes, could enchant so many. *But not mine.*

Today, though, he had no starch to his shoulders. His eyes were swollen, as if he had wept. Did deputy chiefs of police have cause to cry over the loss of a woman they tried to poison?

Viv could only hope to use his indisposition to her advantage.

"Please," he offered with an outstretched hand and polite smile, "come sit and talk with me."

"*Merci beaucoup*, monsieur. I will stand."

"As you wish." He strode around her toward the silver tray and poured two cups of coffee. He held one out to her.

She shook her head.

"Very well." He took his coffee and strolled to a fine brown leather chair facing her. Then he crossed one long, graceful leg over the other. She had to admire that it did add to the impression he had this interview under his control. "I thought it best for us to meet and talk here. I am certain you understand."

The need for discretion? Perhaps. But she had to challenge him, didn't she? "I am intrigued that I am in your house."

Did he want the notoriety of her there? His reputation had so recently been tarnished by Lord Ramsey's rescue of Madame St. Antoine from his clutches that he could entertain a lady in his home.

"I am a busy man, mademoiselle."

"I can imagine." She gave him a smile Charmaine would have

envied for its sarcasm.

He put down his cup and saucer. Then, smooth as a tiger, he said, "You wished to discuss my activities with the police when I was younger?"

That he went right to the purpose did not surprise her. But then… A thought occurred to her. Was he the one who had men watch her? He had power, money, means. Yes. This was how he knew what she had done, where she had been, and whom she had seen.

"I do." She walked forward, nonchalance in her movement. Up close, he was a dreamy-looking man. A woman could walk into that aura and disintegrate. *Poof!*

"Well, ask what you do not know."

"You knew our scullery maid in the house in rue du Four."

He nodded, his fingers arched like a cathedral's steeple. "I did."

"You asked about our family. Wanting to learn when we would leave Paris. Where we would go."

"I did. I am glad the scullery maid was most helpful."

She grinned. He had followed her to Passy and Jocelyn Gatel's. "You planned for gendarmes to chase our carriage."

"Of course."

"And my sister, Diane, was your special target."

A smile curled those handsome lips. "She was."

"You are pleased with all that happened," she said as if it were a death knell.

"All of it went my way. *Naturellement, je suis huereux.*"

"You benefited from her detention. Were you praised? Promoted?"

"Indeed, I was. If I could not immediately arrest your father that night, I could get one of you." He shifted, frowning. "But I grow weary, Charmaine. You have told me what you know. You need to ask me what you are here to learn."

"Why did you take Diane?"

He narrowed his sapphire eyes at her. It was only a second,

but she noticed the surprise there. Then he lifted a palm. "Her copper hair? Ah. Easily described to my men."

She knitted her brows.

"But you knew that," he said.

She tipped her head. "We were three blonde women and one redhead."

"And a man," Vaillancourt said with distaste. "Cantrell."

Tate. Yes.

"Always a chivalrous addition to your family, isn't he?" Vaillancourt rose from his chair and strode to his long board. There he poured liquor from a stoppered decanter into two glasses. He approached her and held out one. "Take it. You will welcome it."

She accepted the silky crystal, cold as ice between her fingers.

"What else do you want to know, Charmaine?" His visage grew dark, his eyes slitted with evil.

"What happened to Diane?"

He got this odd mix of curiosity and humor on his face. "What do you mean?"

"Your men took her. Where? What did they do with her? Why my darling Diane?"

He burst into laughter. "I must say," he managed between chuckles, "you always were the most audacious woman. Even at sixteen, you had the guile of a female three times your age. How did your family survive the viper in you?"

Insult for Charmaine was nothing to the insult Viv inferred against her family. "How dare you."

He strode forward, toe to toe with her. "You came to me, my dear little wasp."

She shivered as he reached out and traced one fingertip down the arch of her cheek.

She pulled away.

His gaze grew menacing. "You wanted me, but only so far as you could use me to get rid of your sister."

She went to stone. *No,* her insides roared in denial. She glared at him.

"Your kisses, so sweet." He leaned over to whisper, "You thought yourself so divine that I would take those as payment for my service to rid you of Diane. You were surprised when I demanded money. And all you had was two gold Louis! What a self-serving little bitch you were."

Viv's anger flared as hot as Charmaine's would have.

"Your Diane was too pretty for you. Too smart. You wanted to offer me access to your sister as sacrifice for the family."

Charmaine had been jealous of Diane? *Surely not!* "If that were true, why hunt my father and bring him back to Paris?"

"If that were true?" It was Vaillancourt's turn to glare. "*If?*"

"Yes, why?" She took a step toward him, rage consuming her.

He stared at her. "You can remember hours of dialogue. Yet your memory really is so faulty?"

My memory? Her mouth fell open.

He gloated. Astonishment made his lovely eyes go wide. And then he smiled. Slowly. The look was that of angels frolicking on ceilings in a thousand cathedrals. Such a devil should never look so heavenly.

He took a long, leisurely draught of his liquor, all the while contemplating her as if he saw her for the first time. Then he turned away and walked to his window. "Have you packed to go yet? So many do. You want to be on the road before all the auberge are full, or you will have to sleep in your coach. If you can get one. Have you? Packed? Hired a coach?"

She blinked. He'd changed tone and subject, but she would not follow. "What did you do to Diane?"

He considered her as coolly as if she had asked of the weather. "I sent her to Carmes."

"That I know," Viv bit off. "What happened to her?"

"She died there."

She was hearing the words for a second time, but they were just as devastating. "How? Why?"

"She was impertinent. Always chiding the guards, insulting the turnkey. The concierge found her appealing, though. When she was not being snide. He found her…delightful."

The innuendo was not lost on Viv.

"I know you have been to visit Madame la Comtesse Nugent. So be not coy with me. I am certain the lady would be as forthcoming as she could about your sister. But it was not the countess who was Diane's friend—it was Madame St. Antoine."

The lady's very name sounded like a prayer from his lips.

"I have not met her."

He threw her a look that could kill her. "I know."

Lost in some euphoria of remembrance about St. Antoine, Vaillancourt spun to a window and stared out. He scowled at those in the street below.

"Amber knew that Diane befriended many in the cells. She told me how she had watched your sister give her own bread and gruel away to those who were beaten or in need. Diane's generosity was the very reason she was taken away by the concierge. Your sister gave her own bread and slops to another who was to be starved to death. So then Diane was caught, marched to the courtyard…and shot."

Viv felt the last like a punch to her gut. A hand to her stomach, she stood but knew not how.

But Vaillancourt inhaled and, filled with some steely might, turned on her. "Why did you return to Paris?"

She managed to find words. "I had to learn about Diane."

"Why? You cared nothing about her before. Why now?"

"I…I was tormented by the lack."

"How sweet."

Viv allowed her indignation to swallow her sorrow.

"Don't give me this weeping sister act," he spat at her. "I know of what you are capable. So I ask again, why did you return to Paris?"

"I have to earn a living." She held her head high to say it. Damn him.

He tsked. "Sad Charmaine."

"I need not be insulted." She whirled to go.

"But you will need to know where Cantrell is."

She faced him, the swishing of her skirts the only sound in the room. "Tell me."

He gave her a mirthless grin. "After you tell *me* a few things."

"What?" She would play his word game and go.

He took his time. "Where did you disappear to last spring?"

That befuddled her. He already knew Charmaine had disappeared from London and the stage. "What?"

"How did I know you were gone?" he asked with a lift of his shoulders. Innocence dripped from his sly mouth.

Yes. How? Why?

"My dear *Charmaine*"—he said her name as if it were a curse—"of course I know you did not appear in London last spring as you should have."

Viv looked into his gaze and felt he had nailed her to the floor.

"Where did you go?" His blue eyes were the crafty slits of a snake.

"To a little house in Richmond."

"Why?"

"I was ill."

"Too ill to work?"

"Yes."

"Were you pregnant again and delivering a stillborn?"

Viv shuddered. He knew about Charmaine's scurrilous past, too. "No."

"Since when do you carry a pistol?" He smiled and waited while she closed her mouth. "Well?"

"Many years. I learned how to shoot when I lived in Norfolk." That was true, though of Viv, not Charmaine.

But how had he learned she carried a pistol? *Oh, of course.* The attempted robbery.

"You had me attacked on the road near Rouen. Those men were—"

"Mine," he said with satisfaction. "They were. Good fellows.

Know how to rough a carriage." He took two steps to stand before her and look into her eyes. "You carried laudanum and perfume in your little étui. Your pistol, too. And you were accompanied by your little dog."

She froze as his smile became utterly evil.

"Charmaine hates dogs. Only your little bastard sister keeps one. Charmaine has men. Many men. One or two at a time."

Viv locked her gaze with his and could have wept for all she had just lost in this room. Diane. Her own innocence.

"You are very brave, mademoiselle." He smiled with sad satisfaction. "To travel all this way to learn the fate of your sister. To come to…what? Kill those who hurt her? To kill me? But that is not who you are, is it, Vivienne?"

She expelled a breath. "I thought I could," she told him, and marveled that she had the means to admit it.

"Return to England, Vivienne. Tell your sister I still look for her. I will have her under my thumb, and soon."

She shook her head.

"No? You think not?" He bristled. "Why not?"

Viv opened her mouth, but the look in her eyes must have said more.

"Charmaine will not kill herself before I get to her for my revenge. Your oldest sister is a coward, Vivienne. So that means… Ah, yes. She is ill. Dying. Of the pox, is it? Cheating me of my satisfaction, is she, with her disease? But she failed in her duties to me. And I could not let that stand. She was valuable to me for many years."

"No!" Viv objected. Horror that Charmaine had spied for him made her blind.

"Oh, yes, she was. My payment for my services are very steep."

"You cannot mean that Charmaine—"

"I must say it for you? Charmaine is my agent, my tool, my toy. *Oui*, mademoiselle."

Viv could not breathe.

Vaillancourt preened. "Charmaine Massey was my spy in London. Mine. It was what I paid her for, and she was good. Until she wasn't and disappeared last spring."

He put a hand beneath Viv's glass and persuaded her to lift it to her mouth. "I promised you would need it. Drink."

She couldn't. "I don't understand."

"Why she worked for me?" He rolled a shoulder.

She smacked the glass on a nearby table and shook her head at him. "Tell me!"

He smiled. "Two gold Louis was pitiful payment."

"You needed more."

"It was my price for taking Diane. A good one, it was, too! I received information from Charmaine about London men in politics that few others ever got. I embellished my name, my reputation with my female agent in London. Charmaine was very good. I am sad to lose her. So gaining only you here instead, you see, is damn irritating. I cannot detain you. It gets me nothing. And I have had a recent"—he flourished a hand—"setback to my professional reputation. I dare not make another by turning in the innocent sister of my agent in London and having anyone learn that you are not Charmaine Massey, but her bastard sister, Vivienne."

Viv could barely think, let alone stand. But he had mentioned Tate.

"Go quickly, mademoiselle, before I change my mind." He swept a hand to the door.

"What of Lord Appleby?"

"Ah, yes." He grinned once with those dead eyes. "I have to salvage something from this disaster. If I cannot have the beautiful female spy who worked for the British against me, then I take one of the ones the British have sent."

"No. Where is he?"

"Why gone to Carmes, my dear. Where else would I send him? Carmes Prison."

Chapter Fifteen

VIV WHIRLED FROM Vaillancourt to the hall. To the stairs. Blind, groping to find a reality amid the nightmare the man painted for her, she struggled to go on. With each step, she felt despair grab her and squeeze the air from her. If he had taken Tate, she would find him. Free him.

But she made the staircase, seized the railing, and flew away from him and his vile words.

She rounded the landing, and at the bottom stood an illusion of hope.

She halted. Vaillancourt's boots on the stairs announced his presence behind her. She blinked at the sight before her. Then shut her eyes.

She opened them and confirmed what she saw. *No fantasy, this.*

Tate stood in the foyer, four men armed with pistols behind him. The majordom of Vaillancourt stood at attention at the foot of the stairs. He was wide-eyed, incredulous.

"Come down, sweetheart." Tate smiled softly at her, but then skewered Vaillancourt with his fierce blue-green eyes. "Come quickly, darling. My men and I have this under our control."

She took the last steps down to walk to Tate's side. He took her hand. Carefully, he stepped backward with her to the

190

entrance door.

"I suggest, monsieur," Tate growled to the deputy chief of police, "you replace your house guard. They need to be sacked for dereliction of duty. As for the men you trained to track mademoiselle and me, well, monsieur, I grant you that they are good. They eluded me for a while. But like the others, eventually they let down their watch."

He assisted Viv over the threshold, but at once turned back. "You will find it fruitless to summon any new men to guard you here today. At a time of my choosing, my men will disperse, but you will not know how many I still have surrounding the house and preventing you or any of your staff from leaving to sound an alarm."

One of Tate's men took her arm and led her up into an un-marked carriage at the curb. Tate quickly followed and sat down beside her.

A man slammed the carriage door.

At once, Viv was in Tate's embrace.

The horses raced away through the streets of Paris. She did not ask where they went. She had no mind to process the revelations of Vaillancourt.

Two armed men on horseback followed. The four who had been in Vaillancourt's foyer waited until the carriage left. Viv watched out a window and saw them disperse like fog as the carriage rounded the corner.

Tate gave her a once-over, then, with a hand to her cheek, he kissed her lips. "That is done. I see you thinking on what happened between you and him. Whatever it is, I do not wish to know now, or even later. It will be as you wish. But we are safe, we are guarded, and we must be away and out of the city."

She nodded, grateful for his unerring good sense. She could not fathom all she had heard from Vaillancourt.

Tate settled her cloak about her shoulders and smiled with consolation. "You have your reticule and cloak. Might you have on your person your passport papers?"

"I do. In my shift."

"Keep them there." He checked that his men surrounded the carriage, then turned back to her. "We go to Meaux. East out of Paris along the Marne. The roads west to Rouen and the Atlantic coast are flooded with refugees."

At sight of his frown, Viv thought of another route. "Why can we not go north? Through Picardy to Ostend and then sail home?"

"There are too many forts along that northern border. Those roads, too, are filled with those escaping." He shook his head. "An order has gone out to arrest all British remaining in France."

Viv stared at him. "I saw a man in the street near Vaillancourt's. He was attacked by gendarmes."

"It becomes ugly."

She clutched his hand. "You have your own papers?"

He gave her a slow, triumphant smile. "I have my British passport sewn into my coat. French papers for all to see in my valise."

"You pass as French today?" She knew his language skills were so good they made him sound like a native.

"You and I are Monsieur and Madame Alain DeLaCourt."

She had to smile. "Handsome creatures."

"Very. Now come here." He gathered her closer and pushed hair from her cheek. "Do you have your pistol?"

"The one Fortin bought for me? I do." She thought a moment. "And you?"

"I do. May it please God we have no use for them."

She settled into the security of his embrace and let his silent presence soothe her.

THEY SPED ALONG the Seine to a stable where they alighted from Tate's hired fiacre to change for another. But the stable master had no available carriage to rent to them. "I've a phaeton," he told Tate. "Old but sturdy. How long will you be out?"

Tate frowned. "I need to go to Meaux," he said in his best French. "My father is dying."

The fellow shrugged. "Ah, well, monsieur, you need to go to the auberge down the lane and buy passage in the next coach to that town."

"I cannot wait for a coach's departure."

"It will depart soon. In an hour. You will be in Meaux by dusk."

"Good. The name of the auberge?"

"The Fifth Cheese."

"I see. After the local delicacy?"

The man swept out a hand. "But of course."

THEY MADE IT to Meaux on the River Marne just as the sun set, about half past nine o'clock. Exhausted from the tension of their escape and from her confrontation with Vaillancourt, Viv welcomed the warmth of the cozy little quarters above the main gathering room. More than that, when Tate helped her out of her clothes and she his, she fell into the security of his embrace and the blessed silence of the night.

When she awakened the next morning, she opened her eyes to see him greeting her. Last night, they'd had no energy for more than comforting kisses. "We leave soon. I have bought two horses from the auberge. It is the only way we can go quickly. We must ride horseback."

"I will go with you in any way, at any time." She reached up to kiss him lavishly. "Anywhere."

THEIR JOURNEY THE second day took them further east to the next largest town along the Marne. Chateau-Thierry was a small town nestled along the banks of the river among stunning mountains.

Both of their horses had given their all, and soon would have been unable to go on. But the town appeared. Tate and she were relieved. He inquired about the location of the auberge the proprietor of the Meaux lodge had recommended. On a side street, they found it easily. That owner welcomed them in with wine, steaming bowls of *pot-au-feu* for dinner, and a straw-filled bed that was clean and wide.

Viv awoke the next morning to shouts in the streets. She sat up just as Tate was opening their door.

"Get dressed. We must leave."

"What is happening out there?"

"The French army escorts British citizens to prison. A long line of them."

She scrambled from their bed. There was not a moment to lose.

THE PROPRIETOR OF the auberge in Chateau-Thierry had a cousin who owned a farm along the road south. "There, monsieur," advised the man, "you may be able to buy one of his old pony carts."

As they headed down the farm road, Tate told her that they should not stay on the major thoroughfare east toward Verdun and the eastern border. "If the army herds British prisoners along that road, it is a dangerous one for us to travel. We will go southeast and head for Strasbourg."

"I was there once when I was nine or ten. A lovely old city along the Rhine."

Tate nodded, his features cramped with worry. "I have been there often. Recently, in fact. We will take a boat from a small dock north and call upon a friend of mine who, when last I saw him, lived in Karlsruhe."

Reaching Strasbourg was a trek through rolling, verdant farmland. Because they could not travel with the benefit of major rivers, their journey by horse or by carriage grew hot and tedious.

Viv worried over the cost. She had perhaps a hundred francs in coin in her reticule. "I hope we have enough money to pay for this."

"I have good coin, thanks to my friends. Never fear."

She had another worry. "The Rhine is shared by French and Germans. And if we are on it and Vaillancourt sends out men to arrest us, the French could sail the river to capture us," she said with trepidation.

"The Margrave of Baden would not countenance an invasion of his sovereignty by French troops. He and Bonaparte are friends, sad to say. But the German would object to such infringement of his boundaries. We will be safe. And my friend in Karlsruhe will help us find passage on a ship to sail north and home."

⟫⟫⟫✦⟪⟪⟪

FOUR NIGHTS LATER, they disembarked from a dock in the territory of the margravate of Baden. The trip to the capital was short, only a few miles to the center of the city.

Tate, who spoke excellent German, gave the coachman instructions. Viv, who understood only a smattering of the language, listened to Tate tell him to take them to Frederickstrasse, number ten.

"This friend of yours," she asked, more tired than she wished to show Tate, "he will welcome us?"

"Most definitely. Dirk—Lord Fournier—and I attended Heidelberg University farther north when were young. We learned how to fence and how to analyze soil. He will treat us like family."

"Fencing being the most useful of those lessons?"

He chuckled. "But of course."

The mansion of white stone and dark brown timber stood like an old gothic castle on the street. Beside other houses less royal, the four-story stood like a grand dame of the city.

A pull on the old iron lion's-head knocker had a snowy-haired fellow opening the door to them. He wore green-and-white livery as if he were born to it, took one look at Tate, and invited him inside. In effusive German, he welcomed Tate with the joy of an old friend.

He led them into the foyer. Stars twinkled in the heavens above through the glass-domed ceiling. The butler continued in effusive greeting, going to a corner of the atrium and pulling a bell to summon more servants. A maid and two burly footmen appeared in a trice, and off the two footmen disappeared out the front door. Viv assumed they were to collect luggage—of course, there was none.

Tate took her arm and explained, "The butler is William Bartel, who assures me we are to be shown to a sitting room and bedrooms immediately. He apologizes that Lord Fournier is presently detained. He has an unexpected visitor and will receive us as soon as he—"

"*Prinzessin!*" From a floor above, a man bellowed like a wounded buck. "*Halt!*"

A young woman stomped down the stone stairs as if she had bricks strapped to her shoes. She held up her head in defiance, her silken skirts swishing in fury as she descended. Her disheveled golden hair hung from a once-elaborate coiffure, and her pinched face spoke of danger and frustration.

"*Prinzessin!*" The man who chased her appeared at the landing. A tall fellow, he held a towel around his lean hips. His effort to conceal his accoutrements was fraught with the challenge of running after her. In his fury, he lapsed into English. "Damn it! Wait. We must talk!"

To which the lady whirled toward him and proclaimed, "We have, sir."

"No!" He took the last few stairs to stand before her, a foot taller and glowering. "You yelled at me."

She tsked at him as if he were a naughty child. "I will repeat softly, then, so you can hear." She smiled ruefully and poked one fingertip to his bare ribs to punctuate her words. "You. Have. Failed. I will report that."

"Report the truth, then!" He caught up to her again, towered over her, and stalked her backward to the open door. "We make progress."

She did not blanch or yield, but tipped up her pert chin, and, as her foot went back and hit the threshold, she retorted, "You've had a year. Now you are done."

After which, she nodded with apologetic violet eyes to Viv, Tate, and the startled, open-mouthed butler. Then she spun away into the night.

Their host—because that was the exasperated man Viv assumed stood before them—held one hand to his sagging towel, one to his hip. With a light flashing in his hazel eyes, he pushed back a lock of his white-blond hair and growled like a frustrated beast.

But when he turned, he gave Tate the biggest, most welcoming smile. With one arm out, he took his friend into his embrace.

"I do not usually welcome guests in the nude," he said to Viv. "Appleby, whatever in hell you are doing here, I welcome you and your lady. I leave you both to Bartel and will see you at breakfast. Forgive me." He ran back up the circular staircase.

Within minutes, she and Tate climbed the same stairs to the third floor and their suite of rooms.

"Does Lord Fournier know that lady well?" Viv asked as they walked behind Bartel.

"I will have a discussion with him over breakfast about that. But I will answer your question and tell you that I know her."

"You do?"

Bartel opened the sitting room door and bade them good evening.

"I do not know her personally," Tate said when they were alone and eager for the inviting bed. "But I was shown her portrait—a sketch, really—a few weeks ago. She has been in Paris recently, assuming three different names."

"A talented lady." Viv was surprised that someone could manage that. "I could not even do one."

Tate took her in his arms. "You, my darling, did very well with that one. This lady… I am not certain what her objective is."

"Lord Fournier knows. She means to tarnish his name."

"The footmen will bring up hot water for your bath. Enjoy that and think not of anyone's challenges. Ours are about to end."

"I want to believe that. But the coast is a long way off."

"We are safe now. The French cannot touch us. Dirk will ensure our passage north. We will be home a week from now."

⊰⊱

VIV WAS GRATEFUL Fournier had given them separate bedrooms. It was proper, after all, but she turned to Tate to explain her need to be alone.

He bent near and squeezed her hand.

"Sleep well. We both need it." Since Chateau-Thierry, they had slept in each other's arms in rough bedding and cramped quarters, but never comfortably. Their accommodations had been crude. Even if their affections were those of tender care, they had not been intimate. Nor had she wanted that, because she was still too bruised by the truth of Diane's death and Charmaine's complicity.

Viv felt oddly like a being living outside her own skin. The journey from Paris to Baden had been one in which she attempted to accept what she'd learned. That her oldest sister had betrayed Diane—them all, really—for her own gratification appalled Viv. The enormity of Charmaine's crime filled her with an incredulity that robbed her of any ability to accept what had happened and how.

"Go." Tate hugged her and left her at her door. "Tomorrow we leave."

She went to her room and waited for the maids to fill the tub in the boudoir. She anxiously awaited it, pacing the floor.

Minutes later, she dismissed the maids. Then, submerged to the roots of her hair, she allowed the water to wash away her regrets. Her regret she hadn't recognized what Charmaine had planned or manipulated. Her regret that she had not stopped Diane's abduction. Her regret that she had no idea of the depths to which Charmaine could go to aggrandize herself.

Then, at once, she went still, the waters swirling around her.

She sat straight up. The bathwater sloshed over the sides.

She had always known Charmaine was interested only in herself. But her sister was cunning. Had been her whole life. No wonder Vaillancourt had seen it.

"But I didn't." *Neither did Mama. Nor, it would seem, Diane.*

So then. For myself, I accept I was unaware or too naïve to notice Charmaine's actions. I can regret for the rest of my life that I did not recognize what she did, and I did not call her out. But the responsibility for what happened to Diane is solely Charmaine's.

She rose from the tub and grabbed two towels the maids had left for her to dry off. They had taken her clothes away to wash, but left a clean shift for her on her bed. Her damp hair hanging over her shoulders, she stood gazing at the mirror and knew what she had to do.

In her bare feet, she padded to the sitting room and entered Tate's bedroom. In the adjacent boudoir she heard him bathing in his own tub. When she heard splashes, she assumed he was climbing out. Anxiety gnawed at her, and she could not wait for him to appear.

She walked in just as he was emerging from the water. All slick skin over rippling muscles, he used a towel to dry his torso.

But at the sight of her, he paused.

"I have not been able to discuss what I learned with Vaillancourt," she managed. "Forgive me. Amid those revelations, I am lost."

He dropped the towel to the tile floor and came toward her, naked and beautiful and forgiving. Then he wrapped her against his might and, with kisses to her wet hair, held her tightly. "You look for ways to accept what happened. I have seen your search. I applaud it. But you must not apologize to me for any lapse. There is none. You are here with me, and we go onward to home and a future together."

She reached up on her toes to kiss him. In his fervent response, she knew his acceptance of her every word. "I want that new life, untarnished by the past. I want to find…" She shook her head.

He brushed tendrils of her wet hair from her cheeks. Then he swooped her up into his arms and took her to his bed.

There he slid her garment over her wet hair and lay down beside her. Curling her close, he kissed her lips then smiled at her.

"In happiness and sadness, through life's turmoil and joy, you and I will be together. True to each other."

"And in love," she said. But she could not yet declare that she was worthy to have such grace.

"Stay here with me tonight," he said, and tucked her against his warm body. "I need you beside me as much as you need me."

⤞⤝

THE NEXT MORNING, they boarded a boat owned by Lord Fournier's cousins. They were princes of the Rhine and owned small territories all along the river north. She and Tate traveled in comfort, cozy in warm cabins with good food and no threat of any arrests by French gendarmes.

They arrived in a small fishing village near Antwerp six days later. The next morning they were ferried out to a waiting ship, a Dutch merchantman accepting passengers sailing for Dover. Blown off course by a wild storm in the channel, the vessel pulled into docks south of Ipswich four days later. Tate hired a private carriage and took them twenty miles north to Cantrell Manor and the land Viv had cherished for more than a decade as her most peaceful home.

Chapter Sixteen

TWO DAYS LATER, Tate and Viv left Cantrell Manor for London. The day before, Tate had announced their betrothal to his household staff, and later he'd walked down to his tenants' cottages in the vale and done the same to them. He returned to Viv to tell her how happy they were and how they encouraged her to go visit them when she returned as the lady of the manor.

"I hope by then I may feel as though I merit their regard," she told him.

She'd grown more tormented since Tate and she had arrived at his estate. Once, she had lived here as a refugee, an immigrant, a girl without a home and only a few of her family left. Those in Tate's little cottages had befriended her, made her one of their own despite her background and her language and her vain older sister. Viv had built a life here. A good one. Filled with laughter and accomplishment. She had learned how to raise chickens and ducks. Fat ones who were good layers. She had acquired an old donkey, whom she adored as much as the dear old gentleman loved her. She would not present herself to them until she was repaired of the rift in her heart and renewed in her soul. The only way to do that was to confront Charmaine, and she had impressed on Tate her desire to go south to see her sister as soon as possible.

"They welcome you to visit them soon. Especially Fred."

She laughed.

"He gave me a loud talking-to about your whereabouts."

"I long to see him, too," she said, holding back tears. "When I am myself, it will happen."

TWO MORNINGS LATER, they climbed into Tate's traveling coach and headed south. Two of his maids had donated a few items of clothing to Viv. Save for her serviceable cloak, her clothes from the journey were nigh unto rags. As for Tate, he fared no better. But he would take items from his own dressing room in London. He also told her he would hire a modiste to attend her and create a garment for their wedding. The wedding, Tate and she assured each other, was more about what they would become to each other than any items they would wear for the occasion.

The next afternoon at dusk, Tate's coachman pulled up to his house, 44 Berkeley Square. Viv had never been here before, and the façade of the house, only three stories tall, appeared modest. How wrong she was.

The entrance hall quickly took her breath away. She stood before a double Carrara marble staircase leading straight up to the first floor, then on to a balcony accessed by stairs against the back wall. Above her head was a plastered ceiling etched in gold filigree. The family crest took center stage, glimmering in the fading light of day shining through the tall Palladian windows at the front of the house. She stood, counting the plaster cherubs who danced upon the walls of the stairs.

"I'm not sure I am equipped to become lady of this house, sir." Viv was agog at the beauty of the house and its furnishing and appointments.

Tate tipped up her chin and, in front of his butler, kissed her on the lips. "I have no doubts."

Minutes later, when they were alone in the grand salon, she sought to explain. "I am sorry to be so...contrary. I do not question my desire to marry you."

"Never question it, please. I love you, Vivienne. We will be good together."

As solace for her weary mind, his words had her walking into his arms...and never parting from him again that night. The servants, she concluded, would think whatever they wished. They would marry. In a few days, too. And she loved him.

More than that, she had not yet told him.

First she would free her mind of the past. Settling her affairs with Charmaine would do much for how she faced a vast and glorious future with a man she adored.

CHARMAINE'S LITTLE COTTAGE along the banks of the Thames was a charming brick and timber with a stone floor and three fireplaces to keep the great room warm. Viv climbed down from Tate's traveling coach, her hand in his. They had spent only two nights in London. She wanted to confront Charmaine as soon as possible, for Viv could not live with the hideous facts she had learned.

She stared hard at the cottage.

Tate nodded. He would wait for her. His handsome blue-green eyes widened with a reassuring smile, and she had to reach up on her toes to kiss his firm lips. She marveled each day that he was to be her husband. In truth, he had been meant to be her mate in temperament and heart since she was sixteen. To have him soon in the sight of God and man overwhelmed her with humility and gratitude.

She let go of his hand and left him.

She had not written to alert her sister of her visit.

At that moment, a few sharp barks alerted Viv to the advance of an overjoyed Louis. The dog ran around the far corner of the cottage like his tiny heart depended on it, and as he drew nearer, he launched himself into Viv's arms.

"Hello, pet! You missed me!" She giggled while the dog licked her throat and chin. "Take him, will you, Tate? I need to go in." She handed over the squirming animal, who proceeded to lick Tate's chin in welcome.

Viv trod onward to knock on the rough wooden door.

A maid Viv had hired last spring to assist Charmaine opened it and stepped aside with a soft welcome. The older woman was from Richmond's town center, a person who had seen life and did not flinch from the looks of Viv's sister. Mabel had previously assisted Alice, who had traveled with Viv to Paris.

"Your pelisse, miss?"

"No, thank you, Mabel. Is Alice not here?" From Norfolk, Viv had written to Alice and instructed that she was to take Louis and go to Charmaine's. Viv would meet her there.

"She went into town, miss. She's doing the shopping and returns soon."

"I shall not stay here long. So if Alice returns and I have left, please give her my regards. I am pleased to see you are well." Indeed, the woman was stout of body and of mind. Prior to working for Viv here, Mabel had nursed the ailing Duke of Banfield and his cantankerous wife on their nearby estate for many years. She was used to those who were diminished of body and spirit.

Charmaine sat in an oversized Chippendale chair, her posture erect, her arms to the rests, her gloved hands tapping the blood-red upholstery with her characteristic impatience.

For one wild moment, Viv saw her sister as the duplicate of Jocelyn Gatel's invalid mother. Confined forevermore to the chair, she tried to maintain some dignity.

She spun to Mabel. "Do please wait outside while I speak with my sister."

Charmaine leaned forward, dropped her head when she heard the door open and close, then asked, "Who's there?"

Her hearing, like her eyesight, had begun to deteriorate before Viv had left England. Now too, her hair was gone. Or, at least, from the wisps Viv saw beneath the tight black cloche on her head, Charmaine had few strands left.

Viv strode forward, her compassion rising in her chest for the thin figure before her.

Charmaine wore a clean white muslin gown in voluminous folds around her. She also wore a veil. A woven net of gray, the veil obscured details. But the fall of the net from the brim of the cloche told Viv that her sister squinted at her. "Vivienne?" Charmaine's voice cracked with strain. "Is that you?"

"Yes, Charmaine." Viv strode forward and took the straight wooden chair opposite.

"You come from France?"

"I do." Viv noted how Charmaine had stopped tapping on her armrest. "I come with news."

Beneath the murky veil, thin lips spread wide. Triumph was the portrait of Charmaine in that moment.

Viv recoiled. "I had a successful debut in Paris. I was well received."

Triumph went to joy. "No one knew?"

Viv opened her reticule, took out the two étui, and put them on the small table to her right. "I return your two étui to you."

"You prevaricate."

"I came to say goodbye."

"What? Goodbye? You just got here!"

"I will be leaving after I tell you about those whom I met in Paris."

Charmaine folded one gloved hand over the other. Satisfaction was now her demeanor. "As you should. Continue!"

"I earned rave reviews. Talleyrand and a few of his assistants. Bankers. A few British in Paris for the peace."

"Ba! The filthy British. French don't give a damn about a

peace with the British."

As well you know.

"Who else?"

Viv would not give her the satisfaction of names like Ashley or Ramsey. Certainly not Tate. "A few lovely ladies. Leaders of Society."

"*Merde.*" Charmaine had always had a foul mouth. "Women! Did you find the scullery maid? The one I told you betrayed us to the police?"

"Jocelyn Gatel?" Viv pronounced her name with a certain relish. "*Oui*, I did."

Charmaine pulled back in her chair. "That was her name?"

"It is. But then, I think you knew it. Knew her very well."

Wary now, Charmaine cocked her head to one side. "Why would I?"

"Because you paid her money."

"I did no such thing."

"Enough for her to do the task you assigned her."

"*Oui.* Keep us safe from the police," she said like the practiced liar she was.

"You mean alert the police to our family's flight from Paris."

Beneath the veil, Charmaine's mouth dropped open. "Absurd."

"You also knew the man she attempted to persuade."

Charmaine shrugged. "Some local gendarme."

"*Oui.* A gendarme. Not just any gendarme, but one who was handsome."

"*Oui.*"

"A man cunning and destined to rise in rank."

Alert as an animal being cornered, Charmaine flicked her head to one side. "What do you mean?"

Viv changed to the matter that tore at her. "You paid him two gold Louis."

Charmaine froze.

"His task was to hire a few in the mob to take one of us from the coach."

Charmaine scoffed. "You dream."

"It is, in fact, a nightmare." Viv leaned closer. "You paid him gold. I suspect you took it from Papa's vault in the library."

"This is ridiculous. How do you manufacture this?"

"Better is the question, how did you?"

"You are quite mad, Vivienne."

"Yes, very mad. Quite outraged. Angry. Wild that my own sister, my flesh and blood, paid someone to have our sister abducted."

"No."

"Yes."

"You are insane." Charmaine swept out a hand. The move was so swift, she startled in pain. "You have no proof."

"I do, Charmaine. I do. What I want to know is, why?"

The woman sat silent as stone.

"Why? Hmm? I know. Diane was too pretty for your comfort. You didn't care for anyone whom you considered a challenge."

"Hell, there was you!" Charmaine pointed at Viv. "You looked just like me. The very image."

"Yes, but I was young and so unlike you that you did not see me as a challenge. But Diane? Ah, yes. Our Diane was smart, wise to what happened in the Croix-Rouge in the tribunal."

"What could I care for that, eh?" Charmaine growled.

"I suspect she caught you at your game."

"No."

"You learned she knew about your scheme to pay the maid or the man she met and kissed in the kitchen doorway. Diane knew, and you had to have her taken away. You had to have it appear to be an act of the mob."

"No."

"The abduction happened so easily, so according to your plan, that no one suspected. Not my mother and not me." Viv caught her breath. "What you did not expect was that the man to whom you paid the two gold Louis would want greater payment."

"No. No. This is fantasy. Get out."

"Monsieur René Vaillancourt has had a stellar career in the French police. Handsome as the devil, charming as sin, he uses his intellect and his wiles ever so well. He is now deputy chief of police," Viv declared with little satisfaction. "But you knew that."

"Get out!" Charmaine pointed a shaking finger to the door.

"Oh, I will go. Believe me, I have no desire to stay longer than I need. But you will know this." Viv stood. "Vaillancourt had me followed from the time I arrived on French soil near Rouen. He wanted to learn why you were in France. Fortunately for me, he questioned if the woman he saw was Charmaine…or someone almost exactly like her. When my own desire to learn what happened to Diane brought me to Monsieur Vaillancourt's salon, he told me himself of the payment he demanded you give him for taking our sister from us."

"He lies!"

"No, Charmaine. He has no reason to do that. He believes he paid you well for your services as his spy in London. Indeed, he gloats over his success. He counts the information you sent him about British men in politics as worth every penny he gave you."

"How did he find out who you were? Did you tell him?" Charmaine was screeching.

"Oh, never fear. He was going to arrest me, but as we talked about your…career in espionage, he realized who I was. Your twin, but not. Your duplicate, but not."

"You were supposed to go to Paris, pretend to be me, and kill the maid and him!"

"Yes. I failed. Poor fool you that you thought I had that in me. Poor fool me that I went with such sorrow in my heart for what happened to Diane that I sought revenge. And then I realized I could not. It was not in me. What I did do was my own bidding. I learned what happened to Diane, and why and how."

"She died!" Charmaine said with such venom that Viv recoiled.

"She did." Viv swallowed hard on the information she would now impart. "Vaillancourt had his gendarmes take her to Carmes. She lived there for years. I know not precisely how long, but she was still there when a few of my acquaintances were also imprisoned. They tell the tale of a young woman who aided the abused, the sick, the dying. A lady who fought the guards for good food and water and decent treatment. The men marked her as one who harassed them, and they punished her for it, brutally, often. Then came one other young woman into the prison whom they intended to starve. Diane gave the girl her own porridge. For that, she was taken away and never seen again."

Viv wove, unsteady on her feet, yet drained of her anger at Charmaine. She was void of her despair at Diane's loss. She could accept, finally, that her sister was gone, that she had lived true to herself, and now it was Viv's purpose in life to give back to others love and support, just as Diane had done.

"You blamed yourself," Charmaine had the audacity to say. "You were a child, yet you always talked about how you should have run to help catch her. Like Cantrell. Like your dog. I laughed at your foolishness."

If Viv had not already come to terms with Diane's loss, she would have slapped her sister.

"You have such a sense of honor," Charmaine spat. "What does that get you, little bastard?"

"A life filled with the joy of love." Viv turned and strode to the door.

"Wait!"

Viv paused but did not turn to face her.

"Wait. I—I need food. That maid you pay. And money."

Viv opened the door wide to let in the sun—and to admire the view of the dashing man she loved standing in front of his carriage.

"You—you will return, won't you?" Charmaine cried. No thanks, no apology—only her own self-interest graced her lips.

"Never," was Viv's last word.

TATE HELPED HER into their carriage, then sat beside her. Louis had decided after Viv went into the cottage that wherever Tate and she went in that coach, he would go too. That was fine with Tate.

She sat silent, still and very pale. He took her into his arms and spoke near her ear. He'd predicated she would be undone by her confrontation with her sister. She had not told him the details of her encounters with Countess Nugent or René Vaillancourt. Viv's long hours of contemplation of those visits were fair notice that he could wait until eternity for her to reveal the details. If perchance she did not, that too was her choice. He would accept it.

In the meantime, he could do a few things to alleviate any further suffering she had.

They were well on their way back to London when he removed her hat and said, "I am burning this thing tomorrow. I hate it."

She rolled her eyes at him and gave him an actress's outraged look. "My perfect little chapeau? How dreadful!"

"Truly." He rolled his own eyes. "Black and yellow. Who wears those colors?"

"Canaries."

"Yes, well." He opened a window and threw the thing to the wind. "Not you."

"Now I am not properly dressed." She tsked.

He hugged her. "You cannot care."

Louis sat on his seat opposite and watched them as if he expected a resolution.

"What do you say, Monsieur Louis, if we go to a quiet little house where no one else is about? No butlers, no maids. Only a vicar, his wife, and his oldest son?"

Viv wrapped her fingers around the wealth of Tate's carefully tied cravat. "You know of such a place?"

"I do. The three wait for us to arrive, and then—"

"They leave?"

"They do." He nodded. "After you and I are officially, irrevocably married."

"You arranged this," she said in awe.

"I did."

"Yesterday?"

"After breakfast and my visit to obtain our marriage license, yes."

"You are a wonder, Tate Cantrell. All my life, it seems, you have been there to grace me with the necessities of life—a cottage, a bit of money, a plot of land, two chickens to start my hutch. After that it was your friendship you gave, and lately your assistance."

He traced the arch of her cheek. "And my criticism."

"Justly so, too." She glanced out the window. "I was not cut out to exact revenge—only to learn, if I could, what had happened to Diane."

"And you did that."

"Astonishing, isn't it, that the scullery maid is still alive and was willing to speak to me? More surprising still that Vaillancourt told me what he did."

Viv paused a moment, then turned to him. "Charmaine paid Jocelyn Gatel to influence Vaillancourt. He took advantage of the situation and told Gatel to get Charmaine to pay him, and he would do her bidding and kidnap Diane. He told them he wanted to learn where our father was. Whether Papa was captured because of anything Diane told them is something we will never know. But I doubt she said a word."

She took a breath. "But Vaillancourt's men caught Diane and sent her to Carmes. There, she—God love her—was her noble self and helped others. Standing up for those who could not help themselves, Diane made a reputation that the guards could not allow her to sustain. One day when another young woman was to be starved, Diane gave the girl her own food and the guards would have no more of her insubordination. They took her away and killed her."

Tate held Viv against him, her tale draining her of all movement. Long minutes later, she stirred. "But the story does not end there." She caught Tate's gaze and held it. "Vaillancourt was not satisfied with Charmaine's so-called payment. Two gold Louis, it was. Pitiful." She scoffed. "How or when, Vaillancourt did not say, but he made Charmaine serve him as an agent in London."

Tate could not say he was surprised. Scarlett Hawthorne had spoken often of those émigrés in London and Edinburgh who frequented drawing rooms where delicate political and economic news was often shared. Scarlett, as well as those in the Home Office, suspected many of espionage. "Is that why he had his men arrest you?"

"Yes. He meant to put Charmaine away, I do believe. Would he accuse her of dereliction of duty, perhaps? Or acting as a double agent?"

"Joseph Fouché puts people away on less evidence," Tate said. "But Vaillancourt did not have the chance to take you away."

"No." She kissed him with a merry grin. "He did not. You were there. You are always there for me. Oh, that I may return the honor—"

"You owe me nothing, Viv."

She cupped his cheek. "But I will give to you all that I am, for all my days and beyond. I love you, Tate Cantrell. I have for many, many years. I would have loved to marry you when I was sixteen. Would have loved to comfort you when you were treated so poorly by your father. But now I have the opportunity to give you all the love I bore for you then, and bear for you now, and want to share with you for all our lives."

He kissed her then with a fierce joy that he had never before felt.

"I love you," she whispered, and kissed him with all the caring she had held for him and had never been able to show him.

Many kisses later, Tate sat back. "So then, my darling, may I assume you like the idea of marrying me this afternoon?"

She grinned, put her hand around his nape, and sank her fingers into his silken hair. "I do. I do indeed! How do you perceive such things?"

He kissed her again. "I thought after that, we would stay in our cocoon for a few days."

"A week."

"Very well. A week."

"Or two?"

He laughed. "Two!"

"Wonderful! By then you will be very bored with just me and ready to greet your friends."

He clamped her closer. "I have a few things I wish to teach you that are far from boring."

Her eyes sparkled with interest. "Begin now, my darling. I love you, and I promise to be a good student."

Chapter Seventeen

THE THINGS TATE Cantrell taught Viv about love had as much to do with erotic delights of the flesh as they did the tenderness of the heart. They required only the intimacy of a great room in their cozy cottage with a fire blazing and baskets of bread, fresh vegetables, and a stout roast of beef delivered now and then.

Tate learned his new wife was adept at cooking in a fireplace. Viv learned that her husband was a fine hand at washing dishes—and at sweeping her up into his arms and taking her to their little bed after lunch, dinner, and sometimes in between.

As when they were young, she beat him at chess. He beat her at cards. "You really are quite awful," he told her. After that, she rose, hands on her hips, removed every stitch of clothing she wore, and led him, awestruck, to their bed.

"I think we will play cards every day, wife." He laughed.

To which she rolled over him and teased and fondled him so unmercifully, he was too breathless to make love to her again.

WITH THEIR TWO weeks gone, they reluctantly left their cottage and returned to London.

There, their life became more regular. Though for another week they did not rouse from their bedroom until well after noon, they set about creating their place in the town. They announced their wedding formally with cards to friends and neighbors. The announcement appeared in the *Times*. They called upon distant relatives of Tate's, then made their calls upon Scarlett Hawthorne in her offices in the city, and the Ashleys and Ramseys, each couple at their home.

Their visits were short, meant as courtesy calls only, and so in mid-July, Viv and Tate sent out an invitation to their first dinner party as husband and wife. Lady Ashley had given birth in May and still recovered. Lady Ramsey was great with child and was very selective about which events she attended in Society because she lacked stamina.

Viv liked Augustine, Lady Ashley, and Amber, Lady Ramsey, very much, and took recommendations from them for a modiste and a hatter. Viv had no need for new staff, except for a new cook and a lady's maid for herself. Augustine had a good suggestion for an agency to hire new servants. Amber proclaimed she was no help at all for a cook.

"I find no one who can please me," she told Viv with a smile. "I prefer to shoo them out of my kitchen and do it myself. Ram is horrified. So is my mother-in-law and my grandmother-in-law, but we eat well, don't we, darling?"

The man rolled his large, dark eyes and proclaimed, "I do not argue with my wife, especially when she wants to cook dinner!"

After dinner, Viv had a moment alone with Augustine and Amber when the men retired for brandy.

They sat on either side of Viv on a settee. Augustine took her hand. "We have heard what you faced in Paris. I am glad our Aunt Cecily was helpful to you."

Amber was more solemn, with tears in her eyes. "I want you to know that it is very difficult for me to speak of what happened in Carmes in any detail. I doubt I ever will be able to. But I want you to be very, very proud of Diane. I know nothing of how your sister died. But I do know how she lived. She was a noble girl, joyous and bright. Irrepressible with her *joie de vivre*. She lifted everyone's spirits and demanded fair treatment and humane consideration for all of us. She suffered for that. The guards and the concierge could not allow her to win. They tried to beat it out of her and failed. Time after time, they could not discourage her, and so she was one day taken away for her demand that one young woman receive her own daily bread."

Viv could not control the sobs that shook her. All three women sat together and cried.

"I thank you both for this," she said at last. "I am proud of Diane. She was the best of all."

"You," said Augustine, "were brave to face Paris and learn what happened to her."

"I had to. I felt guilty for many years that I had not gotten out of the carriage and chased after her."

"You could not have done that," Amber said. "Face it. Tate could not do that. I doubt anyone could do it. René Vaillancourt knew what he was about. Few can defeat him."

"Ramsey did," Augustine said with a smile.

"And Ashley," Amber said around her grin.

"And Tate," Viv added. Her own husband had bested the beast of Paris.

"Enjoy what you have earned," Augustine assured her.

"Forgive yourself for failure," said Amber. "It is a gift we give ourselves recognizing our humanity."

The weight of Viv's remorse fell from her shoulders. To hear about Diane from this woman made her heart return to its normal beat.

Viv was done with the past. She had served Diane as only she could, and now she had a good life to lead and an honorable man to love.

Minutes later, the two couples left, and Viv could not wait to get her husband alone.

No sooner was the front door closed than she seized his hand

and led him up the stairs at a run. In their suite, she spun, shut the door, and put her arms tightly about his waist.

"I love you, Tate Cantrell."

He dropped kisses to each corner of her mouth. "I will not tire of the words."

"And I promise to be a merrier wife."

"I love you as you are, whatever you feel. Come to me, I am yours. Lean on me, I am yours. Laugh and love with me—"

"I am yours."

ON THE FIRST of September, Tate and Viv left London for Cantrell Manor in Norfolk. He wanted to get back to his estate and into the old business of working with his tenants. At Heidelberg as a student, he had studied chemistry, and in Germany and France on his journeys, he had studied farming methods. He wished to put what he knew to good use.

Viv had longed to return to Norfolk, to the estate she loved, the tenants who were her friends—and her animals too. She told Tate she planned to finish her book on housekeeping. Young women had to learn efficiencies to find satisfactions in their daily lives. One day she hoped to publish it.

Meanwhile, she rode out often with Tate on horseback to supervise the taming of dykes and the raising of barns. She asked him to have a new plot of land plowed for her near the great house. She had herbs and fresh vegetables to grow. She had brought Fred up to the stables near the main house so that he and she could "talk" every morning. It was a good thing, too. Days after Fred took up his new quarters in the stalls with six horses for company, a fire broke out in the back. The old fellow could be heard for miles around, alerting those in the house to bring their fire buckets. He saved his friends with his diligence. Viv rewarded him with even more hugs for his service and his bravery.

One afternoon, her former suitor George Farland came to pay his respects to the new Countess of Appleby. He stood in the formal parlor, twirling his hat in hand. A handsome fellow with windswept, fair features, he was a swashbuckling hulk of a man. All the young girls in the manor, servants and tenants alike, pined to be favored by the tall blond who resembled the Vikings who had once raided this land.

"Hello, my lady," he bade her with a small bow of deference.

She took his big hands and led him to the settee. "Never bow to me again, George."

"Oh, ma'am, 'tis my duty."

"No. I am Viv to you always. We were friends. I hope we still are."

"Aye. Course we are. I am honored you received me."

"I always will, George."

He took a quick gaze at the room, then frowned at her. "I had to come, Viv. You are the lady of the manor now, but I came to see you." He examined her then as he always had before. An astute man who saw people's emotions in their faces and in their stances, he read her as if she were the pages of a new book. "I have to know. All this? Is it...?"

"Yes?"

"Are you happy?"

"Very much so."

"You married him for...?"

"Love, George. I married him because I love him."

"I see." He winced, then delved into her eyes. "And he loves you?"

"He does."

"He should," he said like a man who would scold another if he treated a woman badly.

She grinned. "Thank you, George. I want you to be happy. To find a young lady who loves you for the fine gentleman you are."

"You are kind, Viv. A real lady. I wish you many happy days."

SHE STOOD BY the window and watched George mount his very fine black stallion.

Behind her, her husband wrapped his arms around her waist and dropped kisses to her temple. "Is he well?"

"He will be."

"What will that take?" Tate turned her in his arms and smoothed the backs of his fingers over the arch of her cheek.

"When he continues to see you are good to me—and that I love you with all my heart." She reached up on her toes and brushed her lips across his.

Tate pressed her flush to his virile form. Clearly, he was not thinking of George at the moment. "Hmmm. Shall we find him a nice lass to cuddle up with at night?"

"A few smart girls have that plan already in force." She wiggled out of his embrace, tossed her head at him, and headed toward the hall. There she stopped and faced him. "At the moment, I have my own plans in mind."

He sauntered forward, chuckling. "Tending to your garden?"

"Actually," she said, and cocked a brow at him, "I thought that was your job."

He swung her up in his arms and headed up the stairs.

After all, they both knew from regular practice that some afternoons were best spent in bed.

THE CHALLENGES CONTINUE...

About the Author

Cerise DeLand loves to write about dashing heroes and the sassy women they adore. Whether she's penning historical romances or contemporaries, she has received praise for her poetic elegance and accuracy of detail.

An award-winning author of more than 50 novels, she's been published since 1991 by Pocket Books, St. Martin's Press, Kensington and independent presses. Her books have been monthly selections of the Doubleday Book Club and the Mystery Guild. Plus she's won nominations and awards for Best Historical of the Year, Best Regency and scores of rave reviews from *Romantic Times, Affair de Coeur, Publisher's Weekly* and more.

To research, she's dived into the oldest texts and dustiest library shelves. She's also traveled abroad, trusty notebook and pen in hand, to visit the chateaux and country homes she loves to people with her own imaginary characters.

And at home every day? She loves to cook, hates to dust, goes swimming at least once a week and tries (desperately) to grow vegetables in her arid backyard in south Texas!